The Madcap Masquerade

Nadine Miller

A SIGNET BOOK

SIGNET
Published by the Penguin Group
Penguin Putnam Inc., 375 Hudson Street,
New York, New York 10014, U.S.A.
Penguin Books Ltd, 27 Wrights Lane,
London W8 5TZ, England
Penguin Books Australia Ltd,
Ringwood, Victoria, Australia
Penguin Books Canada Ltd, 10 Alcorn Avenue,
Toronto, Ontario, Canada M4V 3B2
Penguin Books (N.Z.) Ltd, 182-190 Wairau Road,
Auckland 10, New Zealand

Penguin Books Ltd, Registered Offices:
Harmondsworth, Middlesex, England

First published by Signet, an imprint of Dutton NAL,
a member of Penguin Putnam Inc.

First Printing, August, 1998
10 9 8 7 6 5 4 3 2 1

THEO NOTED THE LOOK
ON MISS BARRINGTON'S FACE. . . .

"Have you ever been kissed, Miss Barrington?" he asked, turning her to face him.

"No," she answered, and for some reason he couldn't begin to explain, he believed her.

A glint of something akin to fear lingered in the depths of her eyes, but she raised her little pointed chin in a surprising show of defiance that he couldn't help but admire. Her nerves might be taut as a wound-up top, but she didn't resort to tears as most gently reared women he knew would have done when faced with submitting to the demands of a man they distrusted as much as she obviously distrusted him. He had half a mind to call off the blasted experiment. He was not accustomed to having to work so hard to convince a woman to share a simple kiss.

Cupping her face with his two hands, he stared deep into her belligerent emerald eyes and felt a shock of awareness ripple through him. Foolishly, he'd let their unfortunate beginning convince him she was an insignificant, mousy kind of woman. He was starting to see now she was anything but. . . .

SIGNET REGENCY ROMANCE
Coming in September 1998

April Kihlstrom
Miss Tibbles' Folly

Anne Barbour
Lady Hilary's Halloween

Nancy Butler
Keeper of the Swans

To Linda Levine, my "other daughter,"
whose unfailing love and support
mean more than I could ever express.

Chapter One

Lily St. Germaine was dead—struck down in the street by a coach and four while departing a fashionable West End gambling establishment after a night of heavy losses at the faro table.

There were those who pronounced it a fitting end for one of London's most notorious courtesans. Certainly her long-suffering family, which had disowned her some twenty-two years previously, felt nothing but relief at her passing. Lily had been the only blot on the long, distinguished history of the St. Germaines, and took wicked delight in rubbing their noses in it by using her maiden name rather than that of her estranged husband. One and all, they echoed the sentiments of Edward St. Germaine, the Marquess of Eversham and patriarch of the clan, when he said, "God willing, the silly jade will soon be forgotten now that she's finally turned up her toes."

It was left to Lily's daughter, Maeve Barrington, to follow the simple casket to its lonely resting place and to weep heartfelt tears as it was lowered into the ground. For though Lily had been an unconventional parent, she had, in her own haphazard way, been an affectionate one, and Maeve had dearly loved her outrageous mother.

It was also left to Maeve to face the hoard of shopkeepers, modistes, wine merchants, and gambling hell owners who converged on Lily's small house on the outskirts of London, demanding payment of her mountain of debts. "How could my mother have been so irresponsible?" Maeve asked Bridget Higgins, Lily's longtime housekeeper and confidante, as they shared a cup of tea in the kitchen while the creditors pounded on the front door.

Bridget smiled reminiscently. "Lily was Lily, my dear. There's no use asking why she did what she did, for there was never another like her."

"I shall sell her jewelry, of course, after I have it appraised at Rundell and Bridge." Maeve sighed. "Though I doubt even a collection as magnificent as hers will garner enough to pay all she owed."

Bridget took a sip of her steaming tea. "Don't waste your money on appraisal fees. I can tell you now that with the exception of the pearls the Marquess of Sandford gave her, the pieces are all paste."

"Paste?" Maeve stared at her mother's plump, blue-eyed housekeeper in horror. "Surely, you're mistaken."

Bridget tucked a stray strand of gray hair behind her ear. "Have you forgotten that the marquess was Lily's last wealthy protector and that he died more than three years ago?"

Maeve shook her head. "Of course not. I remember how surprised she was that he'd willed her this house after such a brief . . . arrangement."

"But he left her no money, and she was already up to her eyebrows in debt. When she failed to attract another protector, she was forced to sell all the pretty baubles her various patrons had given her to keep up appearances. There is no one more vulnerable than an aging courtesan. If the word had gotten out she was sailing the River Tick, the wolves would have been yapping at her door."

"Instead, they're yapping at mine," Maeve said grimly. "But, of course, Lily would not have considered that." She studied the soft, matronly features of the woman who faced her across the kitchen table. "And what of you, Bridget? After all your years of faithful service, she should have provided an adequate pension for you to enjoy in your old age. Instead, you are left with nothing but the clothes on your back. Where will you go? What will you do?"

"Don't worry about me, dear child. I have a married sister in Yorkshire who will take me in," Bridget said in her usual placid manner. "And as for Lily's many creditors, you'll just have to charm them into waiting for their money and pray they'll eventually give it up as a hopeless cause. It's what Lily would have done."

Maeve couldn't help but smile at Bridget's ridiculous suggestion. "I doubt I could carry it off. In case you've failed to notice, I'm not a blonde incomparable like my mother. I can neither hypnotize irate tradesmen with my beauty, nor twist them around my little finger as she did."

Maeve had lived too long in Lily's shadow to have any illusions about herself. She knew full well she was a plain woman—small of stature, with a thin, sharp-chinned face and a mass of fine mouse brown hair that always seemed to be escaping from the chignon at her nape. Since her large emerald green eyes were the only feature she'd inherited from her mother, she assumed she could attribute the rest of her unremarkable appearance to the man whose name she bore.

She knew nothing about her father except the little Lily had divulged one cold winter's evening when they'd shared a bottle of fine old claret. "Harry Barrington was a boorish country squire who seduced me when I was but sixteen," Lily had confided. "He married me when he found I was breeding, but went his own way once he knew the baby was a girl."

That telling bit of information, plus the fact that he had never contributed a farthing toward her support, had given Maeve a profound contempt for the man who'd sired her. In truth, she had little use for any man. A lifetime of watching her beautiful mother sell herself, body and soul, to one wealthy patron after another had fostered a deep resentment toward all males.

Lily had found life as a courtesan exciting; Maeve considered it a degradation of the human spirit. Now at the ripe old age of two and twenty, she was a sharp-tongued spinster whose bible was Mary Wollstonecraft's radical treatise, *The Vindication of the Rights of Women.*

"I had hoped to keep this house, but I see now I shall be forced to sell it to pay the most pressing of Lily's debts," she said more to herself than to Bridget.

"But why?" Bridget's forehead wrinkled in a puzzled frown. "I doubt the authorities will throw you into debtors' prison for failing to pay another person's debts, even if that person is your mother. And I know you too well to believe you care what a gaggle of greedy shopkeepers and gambling hell owners think of you."

"The reason is simple. I cannot afford to have anyone prying into my affairs—which some enterprising merchant will be certain to do if he thinks I intend to cheat him. Have you forgotten that my ability to provide for myself depends on my keeping the secret of my identity from my employer? How long do you think I'd remain a political cartoonist for the *London Times* if it became known that Marcus Browne was in reality a woman?"

Bridget's eyes widened. "Oh dear, I'd quite forgotten about your 'secret.' To be honest, I can never equate you with those wickedly humorous drawings that have all London buzzing."

She sighed. "Of course, you are absolutely right. It will never do to have the Bow Street Runners investigate you at the behest of some angry creditor. But surely there must be some way to come up with the money other than selling this house. It is the only real security you have."

"If there is, I cannot think of it." Maeve had had years of experience watching Lily make the best of a dicey situation. That experience stood her in good stead now. "First, I shall stall the creditors by telling them I'll settle their accounts once I receive payment for the house," she said matter-of-factly. "Then I'll put it on the market as soon as we can clean out Lily's personal effects and sell off her furs and ball gowns and the best of the paintings. Some nobleman is certain to see it as the perfect hideaway for his mistress—which, after all, is the use for which it was originally designed."

Bridget, too, had learned to be a realist during the years she'd served Lily. "An excellent plan," she agreed after but a moment's hesitation. "I'll leave you to deal with the creditors, while I begin the task of removing Lily's gowns from her armoire."

As it turned out, convincing the creditors to wait for their money was much easier than Maeve had anticipated. To a man, they grumbled loudly, then agreed to give her time to sell her mother's house and possessions before pushing for a settlement.

Sorting through those possessions was not so easy. Maeve had known the task would be a heartbreaking one; she had just not realized how heartbreaking. Each gown and bonnet and pair of slippers evoked memories of Lily wearing them; each painting and knickknack recalled the look of pleasure on Lily's expressive face when she acquired it. In mutual misery, Bridget and she tearfully set about eliminating from the charming little house all traces of the flamboyant woman they had both loved.

As if even the weather conspired against them, on the third day of their thankless task, London was beset with one of the fierce spring storms for which it was famous. Without warning, the noon sky darkened to where Maeve had to light a candle; a moment later, rain pelted the window of the bedchamber in which they worked and rat-a-tatted on the roof above.

Maeve was in the process of constructing the wooden crates for the paintings she was planning to send to the auctioneer, while Bridget counted the bed linens, when over the noise of the storm they heard pounding on the front door.

"Another creditor, no doubt." Bridget sniffed. "The fool must be either excessively greedy or excessively desperate for his money to come out in weather like this."

Reluctantly, Maeve put down her hammer. "I'll answer the door and give him the same story I've given the others. Like it or not, he'll have to accept it."

Lighting another candle, she made her way down the narrow winding staircase to the street floor and opened the door. To her surprise, the rain-soaked man on her doorstep was not garbed in the traditional dark merchant's clothing with which she'd become so familiar in the past few days. Instead, his narrow shoulders were draped in an elegant green cape trimmed in gold braid. A gust of wind blew the cape open, and Maeve could see he was wearing an equally elegant green-and-gold footman's livery, which perfectly matched the colors of the carriage waiting at the curb.

"I have a note for Miss Maeve Barrington from Lady Hermione Brathwaite," the young footman said, raking her flyaway hair and drab brown gown with insolent eyes.

Maeve recognized the name. Lady Hermione was Lily's first cousin once removed and the only member of her family who had kept in contact with her since her fall from grace. Maeve had met the lady on a number of occasions and remembered her as a pretty blonde with a soft voice and a quick smile, who bore a strong family resemblance to Lily.

"I am Maeve Barrington," she said, holding out her hand for the note. "If Lady Hermione requires an answer, you may wait inside out of the rain while I write it."

Though he looked a bit dubious, the footman stepped through her doorway, produced a square of folded paper from his pocket, and handed it to her.

The note consisted of one brief sentence scrawled across the paper in a childish-looking handwriting:

> I must see you immediately on a matter most urgent.
>   Hermione Brathwaite

Puzzled, Maeve stared at the cryptic note. She couldn't imagine what urgent matter she might have in common with one of the *ton*'s most popular hostesses. But out of gratitude for Lady Hermione's loyalty to Lily, she felt obliged to honor her request.

"If you please, miss, her ladyship said I was to bring you to her with all haste, and she'll have my hide if I fail to do so." The young footman's disapproving tone of voice implied he considered his employer's choice of companions somewhat suspect, and Maeve could scarcely blame him. She had been hammering and sawing since dawn, and a fine film of sawdust had settled on her hair and skin and on the faded old gown she'd chosen to wear while she worked.

The thought popped into her head that the ever-fastidious Lily would think it a great joke that her daughter looked so disreputable, even a footman took her in disgust—until she remembered she would never again share a laugh with her charming, irrepressible mother.

A wave of stark, black grief engulfed her. Reeling beneath its impact, she choked out, "Wait here while I get my bonnet and pelisse," before the sob rising in her throat rendered her incapable of speech. Then, leaving the wide-eyed footman to stare after her, she bolted up the stairs to tell Bridget where she was going.

*   *   *

Lady Hermione's town house was a graceful three-story mansion on one of the most fashionable streets of Mayfair, and Maeve's knock was answered by an elderly butler who was even more elegantly turned out than the young footman. "Miss Barrington, I presume," he said with a barely concealed contempt, which made Maeve all too aware that even her best bonnet and pelisse were sadly drab and out of date.

Lily had been the peacock of the family. Since Maeve had long ago accepted she could never hope to be anything but the "little brown sparrow" Lily had laughingly dubbed her, she'd devoted all her energy to her drawings and her music and worried little about her appearance. She wished now that she'd given a bit more thought to how she looked before presenting herself to a lady of fashion like Lady Hermione.

The stiff-necked butler led her to a small salon on the first floor and instructed her to wait while he informed his mistress of her arrival. Maeve seated herself on a green velvet loveseat and let her gaze wander around the lovely room. From the subtle greens and blues of the Axminster carpet and heavy damask draperies to the creamy silk wallpaper and delicate crystal chandelier, Lady Hermione's salon was a masterpiece of understated elegance. Maeve cringed, aware of how out of place she must look in such an exquisite setting.

She had risen to her feet with the vague notion of quitting the scene before she could further embarrass herself, when the door of the salon burst open and Lady Hermione sailed through.

"My dear child, how lovely to see you again. I apologize for summoning you here on such short notice, but I have a houseguest who is most anxious to meet you, and since he plans to leave London within the next few hours . . ." She favored Maeve with a nervous smile. "Well, you can see what a quandary I was in."

Maeve glanced up as a heavyset man, with iron gray hair and the mottled complexion of a fellow who enjoyed his liquor, entered the room. Lady Hermione smiled. "Ah, here he is now."

Puzzled, Maeve stared at the stranger, wondering who he was and why he would have expressed a desire to meet her, of all people. She watched Lady Hermione's anxious gaze dart first to her, then to the stranger, and a horrible thought struck her. It was through this social butterfly cousin of hers that Lily had met her last protector. Did the woman think to perform the same service for Lily's daughter?

Maeve stiffened her spine and raised her chin, prepared to set both Lady Hermione and her houseguest straight, but the fellow found his voice before she could utter her first word. "Bloody hell," he said, studying her features with pale, somewhat bleary blue eyes. "As alike as two hairs on a dog. Ye're right, Hermione, she'll suit me right as a puddle suits a duck."

"Now wait just a minute," Maeve protested. "If you think I have any intention of taking up my mother's profession—"

"Oh la! Nothing of the sort, though I can understand your confusion," Lady Hermione interjected in her soft, breathless voice. "You must forgive Harry his rag manners." She cast a look of warning at her portly houseguest. "He never was one to observe the social niceties."

Her nervous smile once more in place, Lady Hermione declared brightly, "Before we go any further with this, I think I should introduce you two. Maeve, my dear, this impatient gentleman is Squire Harold Barrington, your father."

"My father?" Maeve stared blankly at the man whose face she had imagined a thousand times, but whom she had never hoped to meet.

"Aye," the squire said, "and father of yer sister, Meg, as well."

Maeve's heart skipped a beat. "You must be mistaken, sir. I have no sister."

The squire gave her a toothy grin. "So ye was given to believe, for 'twas how Lily wanted it, but—"

Lady Hermione laid a restraining hand on the squire's arm. "Let me tell her, Harry. Tact is most definitely not your long suit."

She gestured toward the loveseat Maeve had just recently vacated. "Please sit down, my dear. You too, Harry. This is a story that should have been told years ago. Now that I finally have the opportunity to tell it, I intend to do so properly."

She paused, drew a deep breath, and began. "Twenty-two years ago, on April 1, 1792, Lily St. Germaine Barrington gave birth to identical twin girls, whom she named Maeve and Margaret. I know, because I assisted the midwife with the birthing."

Maeve closed her eyes and gripped the arm of the loveseat for support as the shock of Lady Hermione's disclosure sent the room reeling around her in sickening circles. In a matter of minutes, this woman, whom she scarcely knew, had turned her life completely upside down. She could have dealt with meeting the man who was her father; she felt nothing but contempt for him. But a twin sister was something else entirely. The idea that she was no longer the solitary individual she had always considered herself to be, but one of a pair of identical twins, boggled her mind. At long last she understood why she sometimes had the disquieting feeling that a part of her was missing.

"Are you all right, my dear? You're pale as a ghost." Lady Hermione leaned forward and covered Maeve's hand with one of her own.

Maeve shook her off, unable to bear her touch. "I'm fine," she said coldly. "Finish your story, my lady. I want to know what part my mother played in this miserable business."

Lady Hermione's hazel eyes filled with tears. "Do not judge Lily too harshly. She was terribly unhappy in the marriage, which had been forced upon her by her unexpected pregnancy."

"That made two of us," the squire grumbled.

Lady Hermione ignored him. "But she was prepared to make the best of it rather than lose her child, which she most assuredly would have done if she'd left her husband. As you well know, a married woman has no rights under British law."

"With good reason, if ye ask me." The squire's florid face turned a shade redder. "Never met a woman yet with anything but nonsense in her brain box."

"Oh, do be quiet and let me finish, Harry," Lady Hermione snapped. Turning a pleading look on Maeve, she continued, "Try to put yourself in Lily's place. She was desperate. The birth of twins seemed a God-given solution to her problem. She could have both her freedom and her child.

"I admit I was horrified when she first proposed to Harry that they each take one of you and go their separate ways. But once I thought about it, I could see the merit in the idea. Harry was no happier with her than she was with him."

"Amen to that," the squire muttered.

"So, I take it you immediately agreed when my mother made her infamous proposal," Maeve said, addressing her father for the first time.

"Not right off, I didn't. If ye want to know the truth, it struck me as a demmed odd thing to do. But then everything about Lily was a bit odd, if ye ask me."

"But you did eventually agree."

"I did," the squire admitted. "No point arguing with Lily. She always got her way in the end." He shrugged. "And the way she put it—two halves of a whole divided evenly—made a certain sense. At least that way, nobody got the short end of the stick."

"Nobody except my twin and me." A terrible anger gripped Maeve when she thought of how cruelly Meg and she had been used by both their beautiful, care-for-nothing mother and this buffoon who'd sired them. "Did it never occur to either of you that this wonderful solution to your problems deprived us of the joy of growing up together as we were meant to," she asked with undisguised bitterness.

She watched the squire squirm as he considered the truth of her accusation and decided to sink the knife a little deeper. "Tell me, sir, why did you bother to seek me out now, when you cared so little you could cut me out of your life with no regret when I was a babe?" she asked.

"Don't take that snippy tone of voice to me, miss. I had me reasons for looking ye up."

"Dare I ask what they might have been?"

"Women, that's what. Silly, pestiferous creatures, every one of them, and yer sister, Meg, the silliest of them all. Scared of her own shadow, she is, which I can see right off you ain't. For more years than I care to count, I've put up with her whining and whimpering every time I reminded her of her duty to me and to the name of Barrington—and I've never yet raised a hand to her. But, by God, this latest bumblebroth is more than any man should be asked to bear. So, ye can see why I'm pleased as punch ye look enough like her so's not a soul could tell ye apart."

Maeve scowled. "I see no such thing, sir. Please be more explicit."

Lady Hermione raised a silencing hand. "Let me explain it, Harry. You're just muddling it up."

Her expression solemn, she turned to Maeve. "The gist of it is the squire recently negotiated a most advantageous marriage for Meg with the Earl of Lynley. It is the ideal arrangement since the earl's estate marches beside Harry's and the heir the marriage produces will one day own it all.

"Harry brought Meg to London and asked me to oversee the purchase of her bride clothes—a grueling task at best and an absolute nightmare in the brief time he allotted us." Lady Hermione hesitated. "As Harry intimated, Meg is terribly shy and reclusive. Between the shopping trip to London and her apprehension over the upcoming betrothal ball that the Earl of Lynley is planning—"

"Which is but two days away," the squire interjected.

Lady Hermione gave him a look that quickly silenced him. "The strain was too much for her, poor thing. Taking her maid with her, she ran away to Harry's sister in the Scottish Highlands. She'll come back, of course, once she's rested up and gathered her wits, but in the meantime—"

"What will the earl and his high-in-the-instep mama think when his bride-to-be buggers out on the blasted ball?" the squire grumbled. "They'll think she's a dimwit, that's what, and the earl will start looking around for another heiress to pull his fat out of the fire."

Maeve turned a baleful eye on her father. "Are you saying that earl is marrying my sister only for the money she brings to the union?"

"Why else would a grand fellow with a fancy title agree to marry a mousy little nobody like Meg?" the squire asked sourly.

"Harry is right," Lady Hermione agreed. "I know the earl personally. There's not a handsomer, nor more charming man in all of England. Meg is the luckiest of women. Which is why it is so important that nothing disrupt Harry's plans for her."

She smiled. "And that's where you come in, my dear. Since I knew how closely you resembled your sister, having seen you both in recent years, I suggested you could stand in for her at the ball—and until such time as she sees fit to return to England. Once he saw you, Harry instantly agreed. No one will be the wiser, and an otherwise sticky situation will be avoided."

Maeve bolted from her chair. "You must both be mad," she exclaimed.

"On the contrary, my dear, it is another heaven-sent solution to an unfortunate problem. Lily would be the first to applaud my idea. For all her extravagances, she was basically a practical woman—as I feel certain you must be also. Your father is a very wealthy man. He will make it worth your while if you do him this favor, and I happen to know Lily's untimely death left you strapped for money. Think how handy a few hundred pounds would be right now."

Maeve studied the faces of the two schemers and felt nothing but disgust. Still, Lady Hermione had given her something to think about. On the one hand, she abhorred the thought of falling in with her father's plans. On the other, she could see that doing so could work to her advantage, as well as place her in the best possible position to protect her twin.

If Meg was truly as timid as they claimed, she would need protection from them and from the Earl of Lynley, whom Maeve felt certain was far from being the paragon Lady Hermione had described. For no woman, no matter how shy, would hie herself to the wilds of Scotland simply to avoid appearing at a ball. It was obvious poor Meg was fleeing from the dreadful earl.

Maeve's heart pounded wildly at the very idea that she had a twin sister who desperately needed her help. She had never before been needed by anyone—certainly not by Lily, who had been a force unto herself.

At the thought of Lily and the heartless plan she had conceived two and twenty years ago, Maeve felt a wave of pain surge through her. She clenched her fists, determined to outscheme the schemers who once again were trying to manipulate hers and her twin's lives to suit their own purposes.

She had one advantage. Living with Lily had sharpened her instinct for survival, and that instinct told her the squire was more desperate than he cared to admit to bring about this marriage between Meg and the earl. There was more involved here than acquiring a title for his daughter, or even combining the two estates. She had no idea what that might be, but she sensed it gave her the leverage she needed to drive a hard bargain.

"I will masquerade as my twin at the ball and for a fortnight afterward, but only if you agree to my terms," she said finally.

The squire and Lady Hermione exchanged a look of surprise. "And just what are yer terms?" the squire asked.

Maeve drew a deep breath, exhaled, and calmly declared, "I want Lily's outstanding debts paid in full."

Lady Hermione gasped. "But that is unconscionable. Rumor has it she owed more than ten thousand pounds at her death."

"True, and the figure mounts daily," Maeve said. "As her only known daughter, I am being hounded by her creditors—a situation I find unconscionable. But, nevertheless, I shall not be unreasonable. I'll settle for exactly ten thousand pounds—no more, no less."

Actually, Lily's debts amounted to but a little over six thousand pounds, but Maeve felt no compunction about nicking her father for the balance. He owed her for all the years he'd failed to contribute to her support when she was a child.

Between what was left after she paid off Lily's debts and her snug, little house, she'd have the security she'd always longed for. If all went well, she might even be able to offer her twin an alternative to marrying a man she obviously feared.

"Ten thousand pounds! Ye're yer mother's daughter all right, ye greedy little witch," the squire grumbled.

"And you, sir, are free to accept my terms or reject them and explain Meg's absence at her betrothal ball to the earl, if you can. The choice is yours."

"I am bitterly disappointed in you, young lady," Lady Hermione declared in a coldly disapproving tone of voice. "What you demand is out-and-out robbery, and no man in his right mind would agree to it."

A scowl darkened the squire's beefy face. "Now just a minute, Hermione. I haven't said I would—but I haven't said I wouldn't either. I'm thinking on it."

"You can't be serious. Surely you're not considering meeting her demands."

But Maeve could see her father was already close to agree-

ing to her outrageous terms—terms she would demand be in the
form of a written and signed contract.

Slowly and precisely, she removed her worn gloves, finger
by finger. She intended to write that contract herself, just as she
intended to orchestrate every turn her life took from this minute
forward. Painful and disillusioning as this past hour had been,
it had taught her one very valuable lesson. She could trust no
one except herself—and maybe, just maybe, the twin sister who
was the other half of that self.

Theodore Hampton, the eighth Earl of Lynley, rose from the
bed of his mistress shortly before dawn and gathered up the
shirt and breeches he'd so hurriedly tossed to the floor some six
hours earlier. He dressed quickly, placed a farewell kiss on the
forehead of the woman with whom he'd spent a vigorous and
satisfying night, and silently slipped from Sophie Whitcomb's
small, neat house before her neighbors wakened to the new day.

He doubted there was a soul in the village who was not aware
of his relationship with the voluptuous widow. Still, it would be
the height of bad taste to be caught exiting his mistress's domi-
cile the day before the ball at which he was scheduled to announce his betrothal to his neighbor's daughter.

Mounting his horse, which he'd tethered behind the house,
he set off for his nearby estate just as the first flush of rosy light
painted the eastern sky. A picture of the mousy little creature
his precarious financial position had forced him to agree to
marry flashed through his mind, and something akin to panic
gripped him.

In all the years Meg Barrington had been his neighbor, he
had exchanged fewer than a dozen words with her. Furthermore, when he'd tried to kiss her hand the day he'd offered for
her, she'd cringed in horror and fled from his presence.

"Meg is a wee bit shy," her gargoyle of a father had explained when he'd signed the marriage contract. But how was
a man supposed to build a marriage, much less produce an heir,
with a woman as timid as that?

Not for the first time, he cursed his father for his incompe-
tent management of Ravenswood, an estate that had once been
one of the richest and most productive in all of Kent. The illus-

trious house of Hampton had fallen low, indeed, to be forced to align itself with a loose screw like Squire Barrington and his attics-to-let daughter.

In due time, he arrived at the Ravenswood stables, dismounted, and handed his favorite stallion over to his head groom, who was well acquainted with his employer's nocturnal habits. For a long moment, the earl stood watching the pale morning sun caress the mellow stone walls of the ancient manor house that was now his to maintain as seven generations of Hamptons before him had.

"Whatever it takes to save Ravenswood from the auction block, I will do," he vowed to himself as he strode toward the rear door that allowed him private entrance to his suite of rooms on the third floor. Grimly, he reminded himself that he'd survived horrors during his five years on the Spanish Peninsula that were far worse than any miserable marriage might produce.

And there were compensations. Sophie, for instance. Good sport that she was, Alderman Whitcomb's generous-hearted widow had accepted his need to marry the Barrington heiress without a whimper—even assured him that as far as she was concerned, their "arrangement" need not be altered. After all, he would have more of the ready to see to her needs as well as those of Ravenswood.

Then there was the London season, where he'd cut such a swath before purchasing his colors, despite the fact that, with his jet black hair and dark eyes, he looked more like an Italian or Spaniard than an English aristocrat. It would be good to put his work at Ravenswood, and his witless countess, behind him for a brief period each spring. He could visit his club, see his friends, look over the latest crop of opera dancers—partake of all the pleasures available to a titled man of means.

By the time he'd climbed three flights of stairs and arrived at his chambers, his gloomy mood had brightened considerably. Now all that stood between him and his peace of mind was the niggling thought that if and when he did manage to get his skitterish wife with child, he had no guarantee the resulting offspring wouldn't take after her loony side of the family.

Chapter Two

The ride from London to Kent seemed interminable to Maeve, particularly the last hour when a sudden squall drove the squire to relinquish his saddle horse for one of the stained velvet squabs inside his antiquated travel carriage. She had thoroughly despised him before ever meeting him, and so far he had not improved with acquaintance. Furthermore, he had obviously been imbibing freely from the flask of brandy she had seen him slip into his saddlebag just before they left London. Still, she made a halfhearted attempt to initiate a conversation.

"I am curious about my sister," she said. "Tell me about her if you please, sir."

"There's nothing much to tell. She's just a plain as dirt kind of woman, same as ye. Only where ye're cheeky and sharp-tongued, she's so shy she fair turns herself inside out just trying to say a simple word or two."

"How interesting." Maeve didn't care much for her father's description of herself, accurate though it might be, and she suspected her twin's social ineptitude stemmed from a lifetime of living under the clod's tyrannical thumb. "Won't our glaring differences present a problem when it comes to convincing Meg's friends I am she?" she asked sourly.

"She don't have any friends, far as I can see, except maybe the local vicar, and he strikes me as something of a dimwit. Why just last month the fool preached a sermon against the hunt, of all things. Made out it was some kind of sin against nature instead of the fine, gentlemanly sport everyone knows it to be."

Maeve felt it prudent to keep mum about her violent opposition to the ghastly pastime with which a large segment of England's richest inhabitants were obsessed.

"Just keep yer eyes looking at the floor and yer mouth shut, same as Meg does," the squire continued, "and there's no one will twig ye ain't who ye're pretending to be—least of all the earl. Only time he's seen Meg in the past ten years is when he made his marriage offer, and what'd the silly twit do then? Run from the room, bawling like a babe with a bellyache, that's what. So, quit yer fretting. There's no reason whatsoever why anything should go wrong."

Maeve could think of any number of reasons why such a crazy scheme might blow up in their faces, but before she could voice them, the squire dismissed the subject and launched into a discourse on his pack of hunting hounds. In glowing words, he extolled their fine bloodlines, their uncanny ability to sniff out the poor fox that was their victim, and the fine litter of pups he expected his prize bitch to whelp shortly after he returned home. It was all too obvious his interest lay with his hounds, not with his daughter.

Maeve soon came to the conclusion that she had been lucky to have been the twin Lily took as her "half of the whole." With all her faults, her beautiful, self-centered mother had once in a while managed to show a little affection for her plain offspring.

She found herself wondering if Meg's shyness stemmed from a feeling of unworthiness because she felt no one cared about her. If so, finding a twin sister to love and support her might be the very thing she needed to make her blossom as she should.

At long last the carriage passed through the massive iron gates of the squire's estate, just as the first shades of night darkened the rain-soaked landscape. With the luggage coach trailing behind them, they slowly traversed the muddy lane that led to Barrington Hall—a huge, three-story stone structure with a recessed entry and at least eight tall chimneys protruding from its high, gabled roof.

Maeve stepped from the carriage into a driving rain and stood for a moment surveying what, except for a quirk of fate, might have been her home for the past twenty-two years. It was not an inviting sight. Ugly patches of moss clung to the gray stone walls of the ancient manor house; the square, mullioned windows looked dark and dirty and forbidding; and a rivulet of rain water spilled from a clogged drain in the eave directly above the front door.

"Damn and blast, meant to have that drain cleaned out after the last rain. Plain forgot it once the sky cleared," the squire mumbled, stepping through the miniature waterfall to bang on the door with an iron knocker in the shape of a dog's head. He knocked again, tried the knob, then gave the door a sharp kick with the toe of his boot when no one answered. "Hallo in there. Open up if ye know what's good for ye," he bellowed at the top of his lungs.

Finally, the door creaked open, revealing a woman whose plump, pink cheeks were framed with vivid, henna-colored sausage curls. Cook or housekeeper, Maeve surmised, since the woman's barrel-shaped body was covered by a voluminous apron that might once have been white, but was now as gray and stained as the stone of the ancient manor house.

"Hold your water, Squire. It's a fair piece from the kitchen to this door, and these hell-bred hounds of yourn don't make it no easier," the woman snarled, tripping over a pair of ancient fox-hounds that chose that moment to wriggle past her and leap on the squire in a frenzy of devotion.

"Down, lads. Down. I've me fancy town clothes on," he ordered, pushing them aside to step through the doorway. Crooking his finger, he beckoned Maeve to follow him, and a moment later she found herself in a huge, high-ceilinged entry hall that reeked of stale tobacco smoke and damp dog.

"Where's the demmed snooty-nosed butler I hired on me last trip to London?" the squire demanded, hunkering down to rub behind the ear of first one dog, then the other. "With the prodigious wage I pay him, ye'd think he could stir his lazy bones to answer the door in weather like this."

He looked around him with obvious frustration. "And where's the footman? There's trunks of bride clothes to be carried up to Meg's bedchamber."

"Don't you remember, you crazy old fool, you sacked Mr. Fogarty the day afore you left for Lunnon—and the footman with him—'cause you got it into your head they was helping themselves to that pricey brandy you bought off some Frog smuggler."

"Demmed if I didn't! And good riddance, too, if ye ask me," the squire muttered, intent on petting his dogs. To Maeve's surprise, he seemed completely oblivious to the fact that he'd just been called a fool by a servant.

"I'll not argue with you there," the housekeeper said with an indignant sniff. "But I'm all the house staff what's left in this pile of stone, save the half-wit pot boy, and you'll soon see the last of me, less you get me some help."

"Stop yer grouching. I'll hire a couple of village girls in the morning," the squire grumbled. "A fine welcome home this is after the hellish fortnight I just been through."

Sticking his head out the door, he shouted to his rain-drenched coachman, "Fetch a couple of grooms to come unload the luggage—and mind ye give them wet nags a good rubdown afore ye bed them down for the night."

He turned to Maeve. "In case ye're wondering, this mouthy old woman is me housekeeper, Mrs. Emma Pinkert," he said, turning beet red when he realized his slip of the tongue. "An almond to a parrot ye've forgot her, with being away so long," he added lamely.

Mrs. Pinkert's bright blue eyes grew round as teacups. "Lord luv us, you've slipped a cog for sure. Miss Meg's not going to forget me in a fortnight, when I've been here nearly five years. She may be shy, but she's not stupid like some I could name."

She glanced out the open door. "And where's Betty?" She threw up her hands. "Don't tell me you've sacked Miss Meg's abigail, too! Whatever were you thinking of? Betty was the only one her own age the poor little mite ever talked to."

"I didn't sack the chit," the squire blustered. "I . . . I give her a couple weeks holiday to visit her sick mother in . . . in Shropshire."

"Shropshire? I never heard tell Betty was from Shropshire."

The squire scowled. "Well she was, and that's a fact. Now leave off your blooming nagging, and put me dinner on the table. Me belly's so empty, it's all but collapsed against me backbone."

He gave Maeve a toothy grin. "It's glad I am to be back here in Kent, where we keep decent country hours. Me stomach got all out of kilter staying at Hermione's place. Never once sat down to dinner before eight or nine o'clock the whole time I was there. 'Fashionable' she called it. More like 'numskullery' if ye ask me."

He paused. "But I expect before ye come to table ye'll be wanting to wash off some of yer road dirt and use the chamber pot in that pretty bedchamber of yourn what's the first door to the left of the stairs on the second floor."

Cheeks flaming, Maeve excused herself and fled up the nearby staircase before her less than subtle father gave the entire game away. The last thing she heard before she entered the chamber to which he'd directed her was a loud, smacking noise like a hand striking buttocks and the squire's gravelly voice inquiring, "So Emma, ye old tart, did ye miss me whilst I was gone up to London town?"

Maeve woke to bright sunshine streaming through her window her first morning at Barrington Hall. An omen, she hoped, that this madcap masquerade of hers would end happily for both Meg and herself.

She stretched lazily and took her first good look at the room that belonged to her twin; she'd been too preoccupied to see much of it the night before. All pink and white with a delicate Hepplewhite dressing table and chair and a ruffled canopy over the bed, it was a bit too fussy and frilly for Maeve's taste. Still, it was a pretty, feminine room, and she found it a pleasant relief from the rustic masculinity of the rest of the manor house. Furthermore, it was blessedly free of the odor of dog—something that appeared to be an integral part of every other room in Barrington Hall.

She ran her fingers over the linen sheet that stretched beneath her and the pillow on which she'd laid her weary head the night before, and felt a strange bonding with the woman whose bed she inhabited and whose identity she had temporarily assumed.

If her first evening at the Hall was any example of life with the lusty squire and his housekeeper cum cook cum mistress, Maeve could understand why her sister had turned into a shy recluse. There was no middle ground with such people. To keep

one's sanity, one would either have to join in their vulgar rib-
aldry or retreat into a shell of silence, as Meg had.

Dinner had been a hearty affair—and a democratic one. Mrs.
Pinkert's idea of serving a meal to her employer was to plunk a
huge platter of mutton, potatoes, and vegetables in the middle
of the table, then sit down and help herself before the squire
could nab the choicest morsels for himself.

There was no conversation during dinner, indeed no sound at
all, except that of the hounds chomping on the bones that both
the squire and Mrs. Pinkert tossed them once they'd sucked
them clean of flesh and marrow. The hour was reserved for serious eating and drinking. Only after the squire had finished off
his last bite of mutton, sat back, and given a tremendous belch,
did he turn sociable. It transpired that he had returned from
London with a collection of lewd jokes, the like of which would
have curled the hair of the most decadent Corinthian and, as
Mrs. Pinkert happily remarked, she dearly loved a good joke.

Maeve was no stranger to such humor. Lily and her admirers
had often entertained themselves with the suggestive kind of
stories that were taboo in the proper salons of Mayfair. But
while Lily had had an earthy sense of humor, she'd favored a
clever turn of phrase, a subtle use of the double entendre. There
was nothing subtle about the squire's humor. The more he
drank, the raunchier his stories grew—and the raunchier his
stories grew, the louder Mrs. Pinkert laughed.

Maeve had to chuckle in spite of herself. One could search
the world over and never find two more thoroughly unlovely
specimens of humanity than Squire Barrington and Mrs.
Pinkert. Yet the two of them were so delighted with each other,
they'd apparently forgotten all about her. Quietly excusing herself, she slipped from her chair and sought her bedchamber.

It was much too early to retire, but by the time she'd un-
packed the three trunks holding her twin's bride clothes and
hung the collection of exquisite gowns in the armoire, she was
too tired to stay awake a moment longer.

She was awakened from a deep sleep sometime in the middle of the night by the familiar sound of creaking bedsprings.
Just for a moment, she imagined herself a child again, alone in
her trundle bed, while Lily "entertained" one of her gentlemen

friends in the adjoining chamber. Then she remembered where
she was, and what had precipitated her coming there, and wept
bitter tears, more for the death of her illusions than for the death
of a mother she realized she had never really known at all.

But now it was a new day. The sun was shining, and nothing
looked as bleak as it had in the dark of night. She could even
admit to seeing a modicum of humor in her situation. It was out
of the pan, into the fire, where parents were concerned. For if
ever there was a more outrageous parent than Lily, it surely had
to be the squire. With her usual optimism, Maeve decided there
was something to be said for being stripped of everything one
held dear. Whatever the future, it had to be an improvement
over the moment at hand.

She rose, washed her face and hands, and dressed in a styl-
ish blue bombazine walking dress, sturdy half boots and a chip
straw bonnet that Lady Hermione had purchased for Meg. The
particular shade of blue turned her green eyes a muddy, nonde-
script color, but other than that, it was a vast improvement over
the drab brown or gray gowns she usually wore. Wrapping her
own warm shawl about her shoulders, she slipped silently from
the manor house to explore her father's estate before the other
occupants of the house awakened.

She was in the habit of walking the streets surrounding Lily's
small house early each morning, but she had never before
walked in the country. She found herself wondering how one
kept from getting lost without the usual city landmarks to find
one's bearings. She would, she decided, simply keep the eight
tall chimneys of Barrington Hall in sight at all times as her
guide.

With that in mind, she set off at a brisk pace, past the stables
and down the driveway she'd ridden up the day before. Turning left at the gate, she followed the road until, after an hour of
steady walking, it dwindled into a country lane just wide
enough for one carriage. An orchard in full, glorious bloom
bordered the lane on her right, a meadow dotted with grazing
sheep on her left. Swept up by the sheer beauty of the landscape, she plowed on, though the lane was still muddy from the
heavy rains of the previous evening.

A mile or so farther, she stopped to catch her breath and get her bearings. She breathed deeply, amazed at the crystalline purity of air free from the smoke and dirt of the capital—and even more amazed at the silence, broken only by the faint chirping of a flock of birds nesting in the hedgerows bordering the lane.

The city was never silent. She wondered if she could ever accustom herself to the quiet of the country. Her urban ears automatically listened for the rattle of carriage wheels over cobblestones, the voices of street vendors hawking their wares.

Then all at once the stillness was broken by the sound of voices—strong male voices raised in a bawdy country song. The sound appeared to be coming from beyond a small hill to her right. Curious, she wriggled through a break in the hedgerow and waded through the dew-damp grass to the stand of beeches at the top of the hill.

"Spring planting," she said to herself, studying the activity in the valley below. She wondered if the men involved were her father's tenant farmers or if she had walked so far she had crossed over into the Earl of Lynley's estate.

A confirmed city dweller, she had never actually witnessed the planting of crops, but she had read about it, and the scene before her was just as she had envisioned it. A dozen or more men, with huge canvas sacks of seeds strapped to their left shoulders, walked beside shallow, neatly spaced trenches, spreading seed as they went. Behind each man, a young boy with a hoe covered the trench with the dark, rich loam piled alongside it and tamped it firmly in place. Men and boys alike, they sang as they worked, and every dip of a hand into a sack, every sweep of a hoe across the soil was as rhythmic and precise as the movements of dancers executing the steps of a minuet.

The sun was higher in the sky now, and its rays warmer. Maeve removed her shawl and seated herself on a fallen log to watch the age-old springtime ritual that had probably been carried out in this very valley for centuries. The farm laborers ranged in age from very young to very old, but one and all, they looked to be strong and healthy and well fed. If they were, in fact, the squire's tenants, he was a much more conscientious landowner than she would have credited him.

One fellow in particular caught her eye. A head taller than

the other men, he had a dark, foreign look about him that set him apart from the rest. As she watched, he reached the end of a row, dropped his sack, and proceeded to strip off his shirt, leaving him bare to the waist.

Maeve gasped. Despite her unconventional upbringing, she had never actually seen one of Lily's patrons in such a state of undress. Her knowledge of the male body was limited to Lord Elgin's famous sculptures at the British Museum. But cold, hard marble, no matter how explicit, had not prepared her for the sight of powerful muscles rippling beneath sweat-sheened skin the color of fine bronze. The incredible masculine beauty of the tall, black-haired farmworker literally took her breath away.

As if suddenly sensing her presence, he turned his head in her direction and raked her with eyes that, even from a distance, she could see were as inky black as his hair. She fully expected him to snatch up his shirt and quickly cover his nakedness. He did no such thing; instead his perusal of her grew even bolder.

In vain, she tried to tear her gaze from him. For a long, heart-stopping moment he held her spellbound with a brazen stare that sent tremors of awareness ricocheting through the most feminine parts of her body—until the satisfied male smile curving his full, sensuous mouth shocked her back to reality.

The nerve of the cheeky fellow! A total stranger, and an ordinary farmhand to boot, ogling her with the same proprietary look she'd seen on the faces of the men who had bought and paid for Lily's services. Gathering her shawl about her, she rose from her log and made as dignified an exit from the grove of trees as the humiliating circumstances afforded.

Far to her left, the chimneys of Barrington Hall, while still in sight, now looked more like a row of toothpicks than the imposing appendages she'd spied when first alighting from the squire's carriage. She wondered what had possessed her to walk so far, when she'd known full well she would have to walk just as far on the return trip. Resigned to her fate, she scrambled down the hill to the lane and hastened back to the manor house as fast as her legs would carry her.

Hot and tired, she stopped just inside the gate to catch her breath and put her thoughts in order before continuing to the house. What in the world had happened to her back on that hill? Try as she might, she could not ignore the unsettling tremors she'd experienced—tremors that still echoed deep inside her.

But why? She had been around men all her life—handsome, urbane, sophisticated men. Not a one of them had ever evoked a reaction in her such as she'd experienced watching the dark-haired farmhand strip to the waist. She shuddered, wondering if she'd inherited more of her mother's alley-cat tendencies than she'd realized.

With a toss of her head, she instantly dismissed the idea as utter nonsense and marched resolutely toward the manor house. She was simply out of her element here in the country; the city was her natural venue. She had no doubt whatsoever that once she returned to familiar surroundings, she would be her normal, disciplined self.

In the meantime, she would have to make very certain she never again wandered into territory where she might encounter such a disturbing sight.

In an unusually thoughtful mood, the Earl of Lynley mounted his horse and rode slowly home from his day of working in the fields with his tenant farmers. It was something he'd done every spring he'd been in Kent since he was old enough to take his place as a hoe-boy. But the experience had somehow failed to satisfy him today.

To begin with, the last person he'd expected to find walking alone so far from home was the oh-so-proper Miss Meg Barrington. Nor would he have expected her to sit herself down on a log to watch him and his men at spring planting. She was country born and bred; she had to know men who worked the fields shed their shirts when the sun grew too hot. Yet, from her gaping mouth and crimson cheeks when he'd shed his, one would think he had taken her completely by surprise.

And she had been different somehow from the timid mouse who had run in terror from him a mere fortnight ago. The Miss Barrington of this morning had displayed none of the lowered eyelids and trembling limbs that had repelled him at their last meeting. There had been a certain boldness in her gaze when it locked with his, a self-assurance that had sparked his interest in a way her former timidity never could.

He had delighted in it at the moment, but now that he thought more about it, he found it strangely troubling. The squire had sent word two weeks before that he was taking her to London to buy bride clothes. What could have happened during that fortnight in the city to have changed her?

Instantly, a dozen things came to mind. He knew all too well what brought sparkle to a woman's eyes and roses to her cheeks. He'd accomplished the miracle himself more times than he could remember.

She'd undoubtedly met some man while in London. Most likely one of those powder-and-paint dandies who prowled the salons of Mayfair, looking for just such an innocent country goose as Meg Barrington. He gritted his teeth at the thought of another man touching the woman who was to be his bride. Never mind that he was marrying her against his will or that he, himself, was far from chaste. There were rules about such things. If he must marry a plain-faced frump, then, by God, he would at least demand that she be one who was pure and untouched.

But how could he tell before his betrothal was announced and it was too late to call the whole thing off?

"Kiss her," he advised himself out loud. He had often boasted that with his vast experience, he could instantly tell all there was to know about a woman by the way she kissed. He would apply that test tonight at the ball. He would take Miss Barrington aside and kiss her before the squire could make his announcement and if she failed the test. . . .

He smiled to himself. There would be time enough to worry about that when the time came.

After a hearty tea shared with the squire and Mrs. Pinkert, Maeve retired to her chamber to ready herself for the ball at which she was to make her debut impersonating her twin. With the exception of the one disturbing incident with the farmhand, her first full day at Barrington Hall had gone surprisingly well.

She'd toured the vast house in the morning before the squire and Mrs. Pinkert rose from their beds, and in the early afternoon she'd begun work on the third in a series of cartoons she'd been commissioned to do on the unpopular Prince Regent and the crowd of sycophants who surrounded him. She had even, during her long hours of solitude, managed to come to grips with her disturbing reaction to the handsome farmhand. It had taken some doing, but she'd finally chalked it up to hunger. She was, she suddenly remembered, never at her best before breakfast.

True to his word, the squire had ridden into the village shortly before noon and hired two of the local innkeeper's buxom daughters—the oldest to serve as a housemaid under Mrs. Pinkert, the younger one, Lucy, to act as abigail to Maeve.

Lucy was a treasure. She confessed she had always aspired to be a lady's maid in some grand house in London and had made a point of studying the gowns and jewelry and hair styles of the ladies of quality who stopped at her father's inn. As a result, she had an eye for color and style that was remarkable in a country innkeeper's daughter, and she could also read and write.

She quickly passed over the pink and blue and white gowns hanging in Meg's armoire and chose a vivid green silk with a shockingly low neckline and tiny puffed sleeves that perched provocatively below Maeve's shoulders. "I rather think Lady Hermione meant this one for the honeymoon—not the betrothal ball," Maeve protested. "As I understand it, unmarried ladies are not supposed to wear bright colors."

"Pooh," said Lucy with a wave of her plump white hand. "Maybe that's true in London. But who around here would know it, miss, except the earl's mother, and she never approves of anything."

Maeve offered no further objections. In truth, she rather liked the way the green dress enhanced her eyes, and when Lucy suggested she snip a few tendrils of hair and let them curl about her face to soften the look of her severe hairdo, Maeve could find no objection to that idea either.

"La, miss, you do look nice," Lucy declared once she finished her work. Maeve took a critical look at herself in the cheval glass and decided that Lucy was right. While she could not, by any stretch of imagination, be termed a beauty, Lucy's clever ministrations had turned her into a far more attractive woman than she had ever before been.

Lucy rolled her pretty blue eyes heavenward. "How I envy you, miss, going to a ball at Ravenswood. Maybe you'll be lucky enough to have the Earl of Lynley ask you for a dance."

"I wouldn't be the least bit surprised," Maeve said dryly.

"He's the grandest, most handsome man I've ever seen in all my born days," Lucy rhapsodized as she straightened up the dressing table and returned the walking dress Maeve had just stepped out of to the armoire. "I remember the day last winter when he rode home from the wars after the old earl died. Stopped at the inn, he did, and looking more like a prince in his fine uniform than Prinny himself. My sisters and me fair swooned away at the sight of him." She pressed a hand to her heart. "My mam would whip me for sure if she heard me say it, but I can't help wishing I was the Widow Whitcomb."

"Why in heaven's name would you wish to be a widow?" Maeve asked, failing to see how the odd statement fit into Lucy's impassioned dissertation on the earl.

"Took her as his mistress his first week home, the earl did, and you should see the fine presents he brings her whenever he goes to London. And her a bit long of tooth and nothing much to look at, less you're looking at her bosom."

Which the earl apparently did, Maeve surmised. So, her vulgar boor of a father had forced her twin into a betrothal with a man who not only admitted to marrying her solely for her inheritance, but was a known rake who openly flaunted his mistress as well. No wonder poor Meg had fled to Scotland.

By the time she'd ridden the short distance to Ravenswood and listened to her father's ideas on how she could ingratiate herself—and therefore Meg—in the eyes of a high flyer like the earl, Maeve had taken the fellow in such violent dislike, she wanted nothing more than to abandon the mad scheme she'd become involved in and return to her safe, peaceful life in London.

She pressed her fingers to her aching temples. But unfortunately, with Lily's debts hanging over her head, her own future security, as well as her ability to save her twin from the earl's evil clutches, depended on the ten thousand pounds she would earn for masquerading as Meg for the next fortnight.

Grimly, she placed her hand on her father's arm, entered the massive carved doors of the imposing Elizabethan mansion, and climbed the broad staircase to the ballroom.

"Remember to keep yer eyes looking at the floor and yer mouth shut like Meg would've done," the squire whispered in between boisterous greetings to his fellow squires who, with their wives, had turned out en masse for the earl's ball.

At long last he stopped before what appeared, from Maeve's limited view, to be a greeting line. At least all the toes were side by side and pointing in her direction. "Well now, yer lordship, ain't this a grand party ye're having and ain't I happy to be invited," the squire bellowed, clasping an elegantly gloved hand that extended from a black satin sleeve edged with a frill of exquisite silver lace. Maeve raised her eyes a fraction, then blinked, awed by the magnificent diamond gleaming from the snowy folds of an intricately tied cravat. For a man reported to be in dun territory, the earl certainly managed to project an appearance of great wealth.

"The pleasure is mine, sir," a rich, melodic voice answered. "Doubly so since your lovely daughter has accompanied you."

"Yes, well, she don't often look as good as she does tonight in that green thing me friend Hermione bought her, but she'll do, if ye like 'em kind of skinny and shy like."

"Which I believe, by my recent offer, I have already demonstrated I do," the melodic voice declared.

"Hear that, Meg? Didn't I tell ye things would be right as rain?" The squire gave Maeve a hearty slap on the back that nearly sent her sprawling at their host's feet. "Enjoy yerself, daughter. I think I'll join me hunting cronies in the card room. We've next month's hunt to plan, and now's as good a time as any."

"But you can't just leave me on my own," Maeve cried, snatching at his sleeve. But to no avail. He was already beyond her reach.

The elegant gloved hand reached out to clasp Maeve's and raise it to what she could see through her lashes was a wide, expressive mouth. "Don't be alarmed, Miss Barrington," the voice purred. "I shall see you are provided with an escort."

She could stand it no longer. She had to see for herself the face of this velvet-tongued rake who struck terror in the heart of her twin sister. Lifting her head, she found herself staring into a pair of all too familiar bold black eyes. "You!" she gasped without thinking.

"I'm delighted to see you, too, Miss Barrington, and so soon after our last, somewhat unusual meeting," the Earl of Lynley said in a pleasant, conversational tone of voice. But to Maeve's way of thinking, he looked very much like a great black panther viewing the victim it had just selected as its next kill.

Chapter Three

Maeve snatched her hand from the earl's. Even through her gloves, and his, she could feel the heat of his fingers. The same knowing smile that had infuriated her that morning crossed his arrogant face, and the realization that he understood exactly what effect his touch had on her caused an embarrassing flush to creep up her neck and across her cheeks.

She felt gripped by a strange combination of loathing and fascination for this elegant, perfumed dandy in whose black eyes she glimpsed a spark of laughter. Nothing about him hinted of a man who liked to work his fields as a common laborer. Yet he obviously did, and the combination of the two personas presented a tantalizing puzzle to someone who was a student of human nature. She found herself wondering how she would draw him if she ever decided to put him in one of her cartoons.

"I look forward to dancing with you later, Miss Barrington." The sound of the earl's voice snapped Maeve back into reality, making her realize she must stop her woolgathering about the enigmatic fellow. She was supposed to be playing the part of her twin—and Meg had run from him in terror.

Lowering her gaze as she imagined Meg would have done, she stammered something to the effect that she, too, looked forward to dancing with him. Then, with a sigh of relief, she moved on to the tall woman standing beside him in the receiving line, whom she felt certain must be his mother.

The Dowager Countess was apparently still in mourning for her late husband. Austere, but elegant, in a high-necked, long-sleeved, black silk gown, she had the same look of supreme arrogance as her son. Maeve decided it must be a family trait. But where the earl was as dark as one of Satan's fallen angels, the dowager was a perfect fair-skinned, golden-haired English aristocrat, whose beauty had dimmed but little with the advent of middle age.

Raising a jewel-encrusted lorgnette to her cold blue eyes, the dowager perused Maeve with the look of intense disapproval Lucy had predicted. "What an amazingly colorful gown, Miss Barrington," she said in a voice as chilly as the Thames during a winter freeze. "I cannot remember ever having seen an unmarried woman wear that particular shade of green."

Maeve's hackles instantly rose, but she managed to reply demurely, "Thank you, my lady. I like it, too." To her surprise, she heard the earl give a snort of what sounded very much like laughter.

Two spots of angry color flared in the dowager's pale cheeks, but she dismissed Maeve without further comment and turned her attention to the next guest in line.

Maeve immediately regretted her cheekiness. Even the countess's acid comments were preferable to being cut adrift in a sea of strangers who expected her to know them on sight. Her father had obviously forgotten his promise to stay close beside her and whisper the name of anyone Meg should recognize. She should have known better than to rely on the wily old dodger.

Her only hope was to find the card room he'd mentioned and latch onto him for the balance of the evening. She cursed her small stature. Even on tiptoe, she couldn't see over the heads of the many guests ringing the open dance floor.

"May I be of service, Margaret?" The voice belonged to a slender man of average height with kind gray eyes and an unruly thatch of light brown hair. Maeve vaguely remembered that her father had acknowledged him rather curtly when they'd passed him on the staircase leading to the ballroom.

"The crowd," she murmured. "I can't find my father."

"Will I do as a substitute? Theo seemed to think I would." He offered her his arm. "Why don't we seek a quiet spot where we can sit out the first set? You know what a sorry dancer I am, and Theo won't come looking to partner you until the second set because the countess will expect him to lead her out in the opening country dance."

"Of course she will," Maeve said, deducing the mysterious Theo must be the earl. But who was her kind rescuer?

She fanned herself briskly. "In answer to your suggestion, sir, I can think of nothing I'd rather do than find a quiet spot, preferably out on the terrace, where I can get a breath of fresh air."

"Would that be wise, my dear? The terrace, I mean. I may be your vicar, but I am also a man. You could start tongues wagging if you are seen leaving the ballroom on the arm of one man shortly before your engagement to another is announced."

"Let them wag," Maeve said. Now that she knew who her escort was, she felt amazingly secure.

She linked her arm with that of the vicar and smiled up at him. "My father once remarked that you were my only true friend. He was right, you know. The earl be hanged. I prefer your company to that of any other person in Kent—and I prefer seeking a breath of fresh air on the terrace to sweltering in this crowded ballroom."

"Margaret!" The name sounded halfway between a reprimand and a prayer on the lips of the young vicar. "I shall escort you to the terrace for the fresh air you desire, but I shall do my best to forget I heard you say what you just said about preferring my company. I must. Theo has been like a brother to me since we were both in leading strings, and I owe him too much to ever betray him by the slightest hint of impropriety where his intended wife is concerned." His earnest face twisted in pain, and it occurred to Maeve that he showed every sign of being hopelessly in love with her shy sister.

She wondered if Meg knew it; she wondered if she returned his love. She wondered if Meg's feelings for the vicar had played a part in her decision to flee to Scotland.

Well, well, so the plot thickens, she thought as she and the vicar wound their way around the perimeter of the crowd and stepped through the French windows onto the broad stone terrace.

Together, they strolled back and forth across the long, torch-lighted terrace in companionable silence. The vicar was the first to speak. "You seem different tonight, Margaret, as if your two weeks in London changed you somehow."

"It's this green gown," Maeve said, instantly alert to the puzzled look in the eyes of this man who was Meg's close friend. He, of all people, would be the most apt to recognize she was not who she pretended to be.

As if drawn by a magnet, the vicar's gaze dropped to her revealing neckline. "No, it is not the gown. Though I confess it is not what I would have expected you to wear." A thoughtful frown furrowed his brow. "It is more a matter of personality. You seem less timid, less withdrawn—less of everything I have come to expect of my shy little friend."

Maeve laughed softly. "And something tells me you prefer the old Meg."

"I was not implying criticism, Margaret. You will need a bit more spirit to survive—I mean to enjoy—marriage with Theo. He is a very exuberant fellow." He stared straight ahead into the shadows beyond the low stone wall bordering the terrace. "It is just that I . . . that is . . ." He turned his head to regard her with agonized eyes. "Dear little friend, I cannot believe the key to your happiness lies in trying to be someone you are not. What you have always been is more than any man on earth deserves."

Maeve ached for the earnest young vicar. She could see he had found his ideal woman in her shy sister, only to lose her to his noble benefactor—a man whose "exuberance" he feared would crush her gentle spirit. She longed to confide in him, but dared not, for Meg's sake as well as her own. She felt tears of pity spring to her eyes and instinctively tightened her hold on his arm.

"Thank you for standing in for me with Miss Barrington, Richard." The earl stepped out from behind a large potted plant as they approached the entrance to the ballroom.

Maeve and the vicar stopped dead in their tracks, startled by the sudden appearance of the man who had been uppermost in both their minds. "My pleasure, Theo," the vicar said gravely.

The earl's cold, obsidian eyes studied first Maeve's face, then the vicar's. "I hate to interrupt what is obviously a very serious and very personal discussion, but the usual collection of local antidotes is waiting breathlessly for you to make your choice of partners for the second country dance, Richard. It is to be the Roger de Coverly, if I am not mistaken."

"Luckily one I can manage without too much difficulty," the vicar said, quickly withdrawing his arm from Maeve's grasp. He executed a rather stiff bow. "Adieu then, Margaret. I have enjoyed our quiet interlude."

"As have I, Richard," Maeve replied, inexplicably angered by the earl's intense scrutiny. "It may well be the highlight of my evening."

Head held high, she stepped forward to enter the ballroom, but the earl restrained her with a hand on her arm. "I, too, would like a quiet interlude with you, Miss Barrington." His proprietary tone of voice made Maeve wonder if he was aware of the special friendship that existed between her sister and the kindly vicar. If she didn't know the nature of his relationship with Meg, she'd swear the disagreeable fellow was jealous.

"It is time we became better acquainted," he continued. "We can dance the next set, which I understand is a waltz." He raised an eyebrow. "You do waltz?"

"I have never waltzed in public, my lord—only with my dance instructor." Actually, it had been Lily's dance instructor who had passed his time teaching Maeve the waltz, as well as a number of country dances, while he waited for the proverbially late Lily to appear for her lessons. Maeve smiled to herself. Wouldn't the high and mighty earl be shocked if he knew her dance instructor's clientele had consisted of London's highest priced Cyprians?

"Tears for your vicar; smiles for your dance instructor. I had feared I would be bored with a country squire's daughter, but I find your emotional mood swings quite fascinating, Miss Barrington," the earl declared with the same insufferable arrogance with which he'd dismissed Richard. Maeve clenched her teeth as he caught her hand, tucked it into the crook of his arm and proceeded to lead her across the terrace and down the shallow stone steps into the moonlit garden.

"Where are you taking me, my lord?" she protested.

"Somewhere where we can be alone, away from prying eyes."

"But why?"

"As I told you, I think we should become better acquainted, and what better way to do so than to share a kiss?"

"A kiss?" Maeve sputtered, unable to believe her ears.

"Exactly. And since I find an audience distracting, I think the Greek temple in the center of the garden will do nicely as the setting for our first taste of future intimacies."

"How dare you assume you can take such liberties with me without my permission, you arrogant boor," Maeve declared, struggling to withdraw her hand from his arm.

To no avail. The earl only tightened his hold. "I was under the impression you had given your permission, Miss Barrington, or so I was informed by your father. We are engaged, are we not?"

"Oh, that!" Maeve was an expert on the rules governing the "arrangements" between a courtesan and her protectors, but she knew nothing about engagements. None of Lily's friends were the marrying kind. For all she knew, the earl was within his rights to expect a kiss from his betrothed. In the interest of maintaining her masquerade, she would simply have to grit her teeth and survive the ordeal.

"Very well, if you feel you must, I suppose one kiss will be all right," she agreed in a solemn tone of voice.

Theo noted the look on Miss Barrington's face. It was the same one he'd seen on the faces of raw recruits before their first taste of battle—part terror, part impatience to get it over and done with. Had he been wrong to suppose she'd had more experience with men than her father had led him to believe?

He drew her into the shadowy temple. "Have you ever been kissed, Miss Barrington?" he asked, turning her to face him.

"No," she answered, and for some reason he couldn't begin to explain, he believed her.

A glint of something akin to fear lingered in the depths of her eyes, but she raised her little pointed chin in a surprising show of defiance that he couldn't help but admire. Her nerves might be taut as a wound-up top, but she didn't resort to tears as most gently reared women he knew would have done when faced with submitting to the demands of a man they distrusted as much as she obviously distrusted him. He had half a mind to call off the blasted experiment. He was not accustomed to having to work so hard to convince a woman to share a simple kiss; he was not certain the reward would justify the effort.

Don't be a fool, he chided himself. *Start as you mean to go on. If she's this squeamish about a kiss, imagine the trouble you could have consummating the marriage. Best you learn where you stand now, rather than after the vows are spoken.*

Cupping her face with his two hands, he stared deep into her belligerent emerald eyes and felt a shock of awareness ripple through him. Foolishly, he'd let their unfortunate beginning convince him she was an insignificant, mousy kind of woman. He was starting to see now she was anything but. In truth, she was a small green-eyed cat who would either purr with contentment or scratch a man's eyes out if he rubbed her wrong.

Then why, he wondered, had she cringed from his touch the one and only time he'd called at Barrington Hall? And why had she turned into a hysterical watering pot when he'd offered for her?

A sudden thought struck him that just might explain the bewildering situation. It had to have been her time of the month. He'd known perfectly sane women to turn into certified Bedlamites when the flux was upon them.

That settled, he returned to the problem at hand. "It is only a kiss, Miss Barrington," he said, treating her to the smile that had unlocked half the bedroom doors in Mayfair the last time he'd been on the prowl in London. Her grave expression didn't change one iota.

"I have no intention of ravishing you," he continued in his most seductive voice. "Certainly not in my own garden with a houseful of guests but a few hundred feet away."

She inclined her head in a sad little nod. "I know. I am being very silly. But one's first kiss is an important milestone. I had always hoped . . ."

A flush of heat suffused the cheeks framed beneath his fingertips, and he knew, as surely as if she had completed her sentence, that she had hoped she would share her first kiss with a man for whom she cared deeply.

The bitterness he usually managed to keep buried inside rose up to choke him. Didn't the foolish woman know that only the poor and the untitled could afford maudlin sentimentality? The daughters of wealthy squires and the sons of noble spendthrifts were expected to substitute duty to family and fortune for such plebeian longings.

Angry that her naiveté had reminded him of the empty state of his own heart, he yanked her to him and claimed her mouth in a savage, punishing kiss. But to his surprise, her lips were warm and moist and surprisingly responsive despite his inexcusable behavior.

An unexpected tenderness swept over him when he recognized the innocence in her instinctive reaction to his cruel assault on her senses. He felt his lips gentle to match hers and his heart pound with the same frenetic staccato he could feel pulsing in the soft breast crushed against his chest.

With a groan, he dragged his mouth from hers before his mounting desire swept every sane thought from his head. Stepping back, he held her at arm's length. Her eyes looked glazed, her lips softly swollen. He inhaled deeply and felt his own chest heave as if he'd run a long distance. *Good God!* The last time he'd had such a reaction to a mere kiss, he'd been sixteen and as wet behind the ears as a newborn lamb.

"Well, Miss Barrington, now you've been kissed," he said because he could think of nothing else to say.

Her lips parted in a tremulous smile. "Yes, my lord, I certainly have been, and I must say it was a remarkable experience." She hesitated. "Is kissing always so—I'm not sure how to describe it—so emotional?"

"No, not always," he said, and left it at that. He found himself strangely loath to discuss the amazing intensity of feeling this small, rather plain woman engendered in him. Even now, just looking at her triggered a tender protectiveness he could not remember ever having felt for any other being.

Their brief moment of passion had left her endearingly untidy. A lock of wispy brown hair had worked loose from her chignon. He tucked it behind her ear. One small, puffed sleeve dangled an inch or two lower than the sleeve on her other shoulder. He straightened it up, then retrieved the fan she'd dropped to the floor of the temple and placed it in her hand.

All the while, she stood statue-still and silent, her green cat eyes following his every move, her impassive face giving no hint of what thoughts filled her head. It occurred to him that what he had originally seen as her painful shyness was actually a quiet reserve that gave her an intriguing air of mystery. He felt strangely elated; the last thing he had expected was to find himself fascinated by the woman whom fate had forced him to make his wife.

Behind him the musicians played the first chords of the waltz he had promised to dance with her. Since kissing her again was unthinkable at the moment, the next best thing was to take her in his arms and waltz her around a dance floor.

"Our set, I believe, Miss Barrington," he said, and grasping her hand, hurried her back to the manor house and onto the dance floor before the momentary delirium he was suffering caused him to do something unforgivably foolish.

Maeve soon discovered that waltzing with the Earl of Lynley was nothing like waltzing with Lily's dance instructor. The earl moved with a sinuous grace all his own, which struck her as not unlike that of the great black feline she had first likened him to. She had always been conscious of having to think about following Monsieur Daudet's lead; she felt as if she and the earl and the music had merged into one fluid being that revolved in wondrous, breathtaking circles with no conscious effort on her part.

As if reading her mind, the earl executed a complicated maneuver to miss colliding with another couple, then swung them through two rapid revolutions toward an open space in the center of the floor. "You dance like a dream, Miss Barrington," he said with obvious delight. "You should recommend that dancing master of yours to the ladies of the *ton* when next you go to London. I can think of at least a dozen of the heavy-footed little dears who might profit from his instruction."

Maeve felt a flush heat her cheeks. "Thank you for the compliment, but I suspect my competence on the dance floor at the moment is due more to my talented partner than my teacher," she said, chuckling to herself at the idea of the fashionable impure sharing their dance instructor with the prim and proper ladies who patronized Almack's.

The earl raised an eyebrow. "Are you by any chance flirting with me, Miss Barrington?"

Maeve shook her head. "I don't believe so, my lord. At least I was not aware of it if I was."

The earl's hearty peal of laughter seemed to fill every inch of the vast ballroom. "You are a delight, Miss Barrington," he exclaimed. "I can never remember being cut down to size with such expertise."

Maeve's cheeks grew even warmer. She was dimly aware that all eyes were upon them—that the ladies on the sidelines were gossiping behind their fans and the gentlemen were raising speculative eyebrows as she and the earl spun past them. She didn't care. This was her first real waltz at her first ball, and she intended to savor it with the same delight she'd savored her first kiss.

Never mind that she was dancing in another woman's shoes and had kissed another woman's betrothed; never mind that the arms that held her and the lips that had enthralled her belonged to a rake and fortune hunter. Once she'd collected her promised fee from her father, she would be perfectly content to return to London and never see the handsome earl again. But somewhere in the middle of his amazing kiss it had occurred to her that this evening which she'd dreaded was turning out to be one she would remember with pleasure all the rest of her life.

Raising her head, she smiled happily at the man who had unknowingly provided her with such delightful memories—memories a plain, bookish kind of woman like her could never normally hope to collect.

He smiled back. "You look positively radiant, Miss Barrington. Dare I ask the reason?"

"I am enjoying myself," Maeve said simply.

A look of astonishment crossed his handsome face. "By George, come to think of it, I am too, Miss Barrington. More than I have in a long, long, time."

"I must speak with you, Theo. In private. Immediately." His mother's glacial tone of voice made it plain she was exceedingly annoyed. This did not surprise Theo in the least. He could never remember when she was not annoyed about something. The question was, what had raised her ire at this particular moment?

He moved away from the pillar against which he'd been leaning since his waltz with Meg Barrington had ended. He'd reluctantly turned her over to Richard Forsythe as his partner in a quadrille, and had spent the last fifteen minutes watching the two of them stumble their way through the figures to the amusement of the three other couples. Apparently the quadrille had not been in the repertoire of Miss Barrington's talented dance instructor.

"Can't it wait until the ball is over, Mother?" he asked. "I have a hundred guests relying on me to entertain them."

The countess sniffed. "If you ask me, you have entertained them sufficiently for one night," she hissed behind her fan. "What in the world were you thinking of to disappear with that hussy for a good half hour, then bring her back looking as if she'd been mauled by a bear?"

Theo was tempted to admit he had taken his betrothed out in the garden to kiss her. He resisted it. Such an admission would be sure to set his mother off on one of her endless tirades about the disgusting similarities between male humans and the lower species of animals.

"Then, as if that wasn't enough, you had to make a further spectacle of yourself waltzing her about the floor in that indecent fashion," the dowager continued, apparently unfazed by his silence. "Have you no thought for our good name?"

Theo glanced about him to make sure no one was within hearing distance before he answered. "In case you've forgotten, that 'hussy' is the woman I am pledged to marry," he said patiently. "It is only natural I should wish to make an effort to become better acquainted with her." Not for the first time, he found himself wondering how a woman with such a horror of anything hinting at physical attraction between a man and a woman had managed to give his father a son.

"Precisely what I need to speak to you about. I think you should postpone the announcement of your betrothal."

Theo made a monumental effort to control his temper. "You can't be serious. That announcement is the sole reason I've gone to the expense of giving this infernal ball—an expense I could ill afford at the moment, as you well know." His mother was always difficult, but all things considered, this latest peccadillo of hers was beyond enough.

"Hear me out, Theo. It occurs to me that we may have made a serious mistake in our choice of your future countess."

"*We* have done nothing of the sort, Mother. If it's Miss Barrington's green gown that's bothering you, it is not all that scandalous. Granted the neckline is a bit low for a country ball, but I rather like the way the color compliments her eyes." Eyes which at that moment Theo could see were laughing into Richard Forsythe's as he led her from the floor at the end of the rollicking country dance. He frowned. Odd, he'd never before realized what a handsome fellow Richard was, for a vicar.

The countess gave another derogatory sniff. "The dress is but one example of how the dreadful girl deceived us. She is not at all the diffident little creature she pretended to be."

"Indeed, she is not," Theo readily agreed. "Personally, I find her combination of innocence and independent spirit quite fascinating. I can happily state I am not looking forward to my marriage with the same dread I felt yesterday."

The countess's nostrils flared with anger. "Your flippant manner does you no credit, Theo. As your mother—and the mistress of Ravenswood—I demand you show the respect due me."

Ravenswood. So that was what this was all about. His mother had apparently decided Meg Barrington posed a threat to her position as mistress of the historic manor house. He had wondered at her willingness to accept the squire's shy, reclusive daughter as the future Countess of Lynley, despite her less than auspicious bloodlines. Now he understood her reasoning. A self-deprecating female such as Miss Barrington had appeared to be would be only too happy to leave control of the vast manor house in the dowager's hands.

But as it turned out, his bride-to-be was not so timid as she'd first seemed. The vibrant young woman who had arrived at her betrothal ball in a shockingly inappropriate dress might very well demand her mother-in-law be removed to the dower house, as was customary.

He couldn't help but feel a little sympathy for his mother. What she had lacked in warmth, she had more than made up for in her dedication to Ravenswood in the four-and-thirty years she had been mistress of the Hampton family's principal estate. The thought of relinquishing her position to a younger woman must be devastating to her.

On the other hand, for his own part, he found the idea of sharing Ravenswood with an enchanting little green-eyed cat much more appealing than his original plan of sharing it with a mousy frump and his demanding mother.

"Don't worry. We'll work something out to everyone's satisfaction," he said in the patient tone of voice he always used with his mother. He even halfway believed what he promised her. This evening he'd been dreading had gone so swimmingly up to now, he'd begun to think the same phenomenal luck that had seen him through many a close scrape on the Peninsula was once again his. With luck like that, how could a man go wrong?

"Now if you'll excuse me, Mother," he said with a conspiratorial smile he felt certain would placate her, "I believe it is time I made the announcement that will start all that lovely Barrington money flowing into Ravenswood's depleted coffers."

With a perfunctory bow, he whirled around, headed for the musicians' platform, where he planned to make his speech, and came face-to-face with his mistress, Sophie Whitcomb.

Chapter Four

Theo swallowed the anger that threatened to choke him. What in God's name was his mistress thinking of to show her face at his engagement party? And decked out in an outrageous purple ball gown, the like of which he'd seen on the strumpets parading their wares outside Drury Lane. It was the last thing he would have expected of a practical, no-nonsense person like Sophie.

All too aware that an expectant hush had fallen on the crowded ballroom, he pasted a welcoming smile on his face and lifted her outstretched hand to his lips. "How pleasant to see you, Mrs. Whitcomb," he ground out between gritted teeth.

"I'm happy to see you too, my lord." Sentimental tears puddled in Sophie's huge brown eyes. "I can't tell you how pleased, and surprised, I was to receive your gracious invitation."

Invitation! Theo stared at her, mouth agape. He'd left the compiling of the guest list to his efficient man-of-affairs with instructions that cards should be directed to everyone of consequence within a twenty-mile radius. He groaned. Now that he thought of it, the widow of a county alderman would be one of those favored individuals.

Why hadn't he thought to check that list before the invitations were delivered? More to the point, why hadn't Sophie had the sense to decline an invitation that was obviously issued by mistake? Damn the woman! This embarrassing bumblebroth was all her fault.

With sinking heart, he saw the squire approaching—a smile on his florid face, his daughter on his arm. There was naught for it but to pretend nothing was amiss and make the proper introductions. Theo cleared his throat. "Miss Barrington—Squire, may I present Mrs. Sophie Whitcomb, the widow of our late alderman."

The squire turned a baleful eye on Sophie. "Already met the silly chit a hundred times in the village, ye looby," he grumbled. "This ain't London, ye know."

Miss Barrington was a bit more gracious. Her smile was sweetness itself. "I don't believe I've had the pleasure, Mrs. Whitcomb, since I rarely visit the village." Her remarkable cat eyes narrowed. "However, I've heard so much about you, I feel as if I know you very well."

Theo held his breath as Sophie made a sound halfway between a nervous giggle and a hiccup. "Don't believe all you hear, Miss Barrington. People around here are given to exaggeration."

"As are people everywhere," Miss Barrington agreed with a sage nod of her head. "You must come for tea at Barrington Hall some day soon, Mrs. Whitcomb. I am certain we would find much of interest to chat about."

The roses in Sophie's cheeks instantly paled to a sickly white, and Theo felt the color drain from his own face as well, until it occurred to him that Miss Barrington must not know who Sophie was. No proper young lady would invite her betrothed's mistress, or indeed any man's mistress, to drink tea with her.

The squire, on the other hand, turned an angry purple that rivaled Sophie's outlandish dress. "Invite the jade to tea? In a pig's eye," he muttered, and seizing his daughter by the arm, headed for the pre-arranged spot near the musicians' platform where the engagement announcement was to be made.

Theo watched Miss Barrington's rigid, emerald-clad figure disappear into the crowd ringing the dance floor and found himself struck by a sobering thought. The two most colorfully—and inappropriately—gowned females in the entire room were his current mistress and his future wife. He wondered if that said something about his taste in women.

"I'll speak to you later, Sophie," he said grimly. "I have other business I must attend to right now."

"Oh! Well, if you must." Her plump, white fingers clutched

at his sleeve. "I was hoping to have one dance with you, Theo. I should like it ever so much." The roses bloomed again in her cheeks. "We've done just about everything else together, but we've never danced."

The idea was so preposterous, Theo couldn't bring himself to dignify it with an answer. He simply turned his back on his soon-to-be ex-mistress and walked away. He could feel her puzzled gaze follow him as he collected his mother and wound his way through the crowd to where the squire and Miss Barrington waited. Determinedly, he shrugged off his brief twinge of guilt at the thought of her apparent bewilderment. If Sophie chose to be dense, she would simply have to live with the consequences.

Maeve had always had a quick temper, but she couldn't remember ever having felt a rage equal to that which consumed her at the moment. To begin with, she'd been treated to a lecture from her father, of all people, on the impropriety of inviting a "loose woman" to drink tea at Barrington Hall.

"I felt certain the earl's mistress and Mrs. Pinkert would have much in common," she'd explained sourly.

The squire's eyes fairly bulged from his head. "Emma Pinkert may be no better'n she should be, but she knows her place and keeps it," he said indignantly. "Which is more'n I can say for that trollop Lynley takes his pleasure with. But not to worry. Mark my word, daughter, the widow'll be last week's news once ye slip the leg shackles on him. I ain't blind, ye know. I seen the way he looked at ye when the two of ye were dancing."

"But *I* am not marrying the Earl of Lynley. Have you forgotten it is my shy, retiring twin whom you're planning to sacrifice for the sake of this monstrous scheme of yours? How will a gentle creature, such as you've described Meg to be, cope with a husband who has no more respect for her than to invite his mistress to his engagement ball?"

The squire's silence was an answer in itself, which left Maeve to wonder why her sister, or indeed any woman in her right mind, would consider marrying a man like the Earl of Lynley. She had met some conceited fools in her day; Lily had favored men of that ilk. But the arrogant, full-of-himself earl made the gaggle of titled rakes who had clustered around her mother look like innocent schoolboys.

She watched him give an imperious wave of his hand, alerting his waiting servants to circulate among his guests with glasses of champagne to toast his engagement. How charming!

"The cat'll soon be out of the bag now," the squire said smugly, as a sound like the buzzing of a hive of bees spread through the assembly of curious guests. His words were somewhat slurred, and Maeve realized he was in his cups, as were his three cronies, who converged on him, demanding to know what was going on.

"Bounced me bran-faced daughter off to a blooming belted earl, that's what," he gloated, too pleased with himself to keep the secret a moment longer. This privileged communication instantly inspired his hunting companions to make earthy conjectures on what the wedding night of said daughter and a rakehell like Lynley might entail. By the time the earl and his mother arrived to take their places beside her and her father in front of the raised musicians' platform, Maeve was red of face and spitting mad.

And she soon realized her torture had just begun.

The earl's speech was a masterpiece of sham and fabrication. If she didn't know better, she would think, from the glowing words he used to describe his bride-to-be, that after a lifetime of searching he had finally found the one woman who would make him the perfect wife, the perfect mother of his children, and the perfect countess. He did not, of course, mention that her huge dowry was the perfect solution to the financial problems with which he was reportedly beset.

It was all so false. Particularly since the Widow Whitcomb had moved to within a few feet of where he stood and stared at him with soulful brown eyes the entire time he delivered his tongue-in-cheek address.

Mrs. Whitcomb brushed a tear from her cheek, and all at once Maeve was struck with an eerie premonition of disaster. There was an air of pathetic vulnerability about the widow that brought back painful memories of a friend of Lily's—a pretty dimwit who had made the fatal mistake of falling in love with her protector.

A shiver crawled Maeve's spine as she recalled the cold January morning when Lily and she were called upon to identify the girl's body, found floating facedown in the Thames shortly after the titled rake gave her her congé. Maeve shivered again and silently prayed Mrs. Whitcomb's was a stronger, more resilient nature.

She found herself wondering why a high-stickler like the dowager countess would permit her son's mistress to be invited to Ravenswood for any occasion, much less one as important as his engagement ball. It had to have been the earl himself who made up the guest list, which meant he was an even more insensitive lout than she had imagined.

Things were certainly done differently in the country than they were in London society. The same admirers who'd fawned over Lily at the Cyprians' Balls and entertained her in their private boxes at the theater had cut her dead if they met her in Hyde Park with their "proper" ladies on their arms.

But, Maeve reminded herself, who was she to judge anyone on a lack of propriety? At least Lynley didn't represent himself to be someone he was not. In her own way, she was even more despicable than he—a hired impostor who had demanded an obscene amount of money for a sordid piece of work. The only innocent in this whole miserable fiasco was her sister, and Maeve made herself a solemn vow that no matter what it cost her, she would save Meg from the unhappy fate the squire and the earl had planned for her.

With that in mind, she managed a somewhat strained smile when the earl concluded his artful piece of claptrap and raised her fingers to his lips. Luckily, she was not called upon to converse with the handsome hypocrite or with her gloating father. She was instantly deluged with well-wishers, most of whom made it all too clear they were utterly amazed that the Earl of Lynley would consider marrying a plain-faced commoner like Meg Barrington. Furthermore, from the venomous looks the dowager cast in her direction, it was plain she agreed with them.

Maeve survived the hour or so of backhanded congratulations with stoic indifference, but once the crowd around her thinned, she decided she'd had enough.

"I'm tired and I want to go home," she said to her father.

The squire looked at her as if she'd just sprouted an extra head. "Ye're daft. The party's just getting interesting, and I've no intention of leaving."

"You may live to regret that decision, sir," Maeve said, aware the earl could hear every word of their conversation. "If I have to listen to one more person tell me how fortunate I am to have won the admiration of the Earl of Lynley, I swear I shall scream. Are these people all as idiotic as they appear, or is it a deep, dark secret that he must marry an heiress to save his precious Ravenswood?"

The squire's face contorted with rage. "Demme it, girl, keep a civil tongue in yer head. I'll not have ye mucking up me plans."

"I can understand your fatigue, Miss Barrington; I, too, am tired of standing in one spot." The smile the earl turned on Maeve was the same amicable one he had worn for the past hour, but the look in his eyes was murderous. "I hear the musicians tuning up for another waltz. Shall we dance?"

"No, thank you, my lord. I do not feel the least inclined toward dancing."

"To be perfectly truthful, neither do I, Miss Barrington. But for the sake of propriety, we must keep up appearances." Without further ago, he grasped Maeve's elbow in a viselike grip and propelled her through the crowd of watching guests and onto the dance floor.

"Propriety!" Maeve gasped. "How can you have the gall to mention the word? Or are you so ignorant of social custom you consider it appropriate to invite your mistress to the ball at which you announce your engagement?"

Theo swallowed hard. He could see he'd made a serious error in judgment where his intended was concerned. She was neither so naive nor so reticent to speak her mind as he'd been led to believe. There was no point in trying to lie his way out of this one. She had him dead to rights.

"If you are referring to Mrs. Whitcomb, it was all a mistake and none of my doing," he explained with the same careful patience be normally reserved for his mother when she was being her most difficult. "My man-of-affairs sent a card to everyone of note in the vicinity, which, of course, included the widow of our late alderman.

"I am devastated to think her presence caused you a moment of pain and embarrassment, dear lady," he purred in the dulcet tones that had inspired many an incomparable of the *ton* to offer herself to him body and soul.

"Don't be an ass!" Miss Barrington frowned. "Why would you think her presence would disturb *me*, my lord? I do not care in the least how you conduct your personal affairs; ours is purely a business arrangement negotiated between you and my father.

"When I questioned your lack of consideration for a woman's sensitivities, I was thinking of Mrs. Whitcomb. One has only to look into those pathetic bovine eyes of hers to recognize the foolish creature believes herself in love with you. Think of the pain you caused her, prattling on about how happy you were to marry another woman, when most likely you'd warmed *her* bed but twenty-four hours earlier."

For the first time in his life, Theo found himself utterly speechless. He didn't have to pretend shock at his betrothed's bizarre reaction to the unusual situation they found themselves in; he was jolted to the core by her unconventional attitude.

"Miss Barrington!" he exclaimed, when he finally found his voice. "This is not a conversation I would expect to be having with my future wife."

"And why not, my lord? I believe in speaking the truth as I see it."

Theo felt consumed with anger at the injustice of her accusation and the insult it implied. "I have already explained it was not my fault she was invited to this ball," he said coldly. "Furthermore, for your information, there has never been a question of love between Sophie Whitcomb and me. We are friends, nothing more, as we have been since we played together as children."

Miss Barrington's eyes fairly blazed. "Which telling statement only proves you are even more callous than I had judged you to be. For no right-thinking man would subject a 'friend' to the kind of scorn Mrs. Whitcomb must suffer at the hands of the so-called proper folk of the village—to say nothing of the position she will be in once you tire of her and withdraw your patronage."

She raked him with a look of such loathing, it was all Theo could do to keep from cringing. "You, of course, will simply have enhanced your reputation as a charming rogue when you end the sordid affair. Men are never called to account for their actions in such matters."

Theo stared at her—stunned. Nothing in his background had prepared him to defend his treatment of his mistress to the woman he was pledged to marry—a woman who, by rights, should not even be aware of the existence of the demimonde.

The balance of the waltz was accomplished in uneasy silence. Like it or not, Miss Barrington had forced him to take a good look at what he had done to Sophie when he'd made her his mistress—something he had never before considered. The picture was not a pretty one. Nor did it help that he could see the object of his betrothed's concern standing alone in a far corner of the ballroom—a plump, purple pariah, shunned by the "proper folk" of the village.

The set finally came to an end, and with Miss Barrington on his arm, he exited the dance floor. She was the first to break their long silence. "Well, that's that then, my lord. I believe I have fulfilled my duty as far as this evening is concerned. If any of your guests should remark on my absence, you have my permission to tell them I retired with a headache."

She pressed her slender, tapered fingers to her left temple, as if to prove her headache did, indeed, exist. "Since my father refuses to escort me home, I would appreciate the loan of one of your carriages."

Theo dropped her arm and executed a courtly bow. "Your servant, ma'am," he said, and hailing a nearby footman, sent him to the stable to request a carriage be brought around.

A full moon greeted him when he escorted Miss Barrington to her waiting conveyance. A "lovers' moon" he'd often heard it called. The irony of the term as applied to him at the moment brought a bitter smile to his lips.

"Good night, my lord. It has been a most informative

evening," Miss Barrington said, and maneuvering the single step into his carriage without aid, settled herself on the seat facing forward. With a final curt nod in his direction, she tapped on the roof of the cab with her fan to signal the coachman she was ready to be driven home.

Long after the carriage had disappeared down the drive, Theo stood alone at the foot of the steps leading to the entrance to Ravenswood. "A most informative evening" his betrothed had called it shortly after she'd castigated him for his lack of concern for his mistress's feelings and informed him that he was of no more consequence to her than the beetle she'd squashed beneath her heel in her rush to quit his presence.

And what had he done when the prickly little porcupine loosed her quills at him? Defended himself with all the brilliance and sophistication of a ten-year-old caught with his fingers in the jam jar, that's what. But in all fairness, she had taken him unawares; proper young ladies did not normally concern themselves with the fate of their "fallen sisters." He found himself wondering if, God forbid, he had allied himself with one of those radical Methodist ladies who devoted their energies to bringing sinners back into the fold.

Whatever her reasoning might be, he couldn't remember ever having spent a more unusual or a more frustrating evening than the one just past, thanks to the puzzling woman he had chosen as his future wife. Until a few hours ago he had believed that, despite his precarious financial position, he was conferring a unique honor on the plain little nobody by offering her his name and the ancient title that went with it. Now he was not so certain.

Difficult as it was to comprehend, he was beginning to think this commonplace daughter of a humble country squire was not the least bit taken with the idea of becoming the next Countess of Lynley. Oddly enough, he found this more challenging than infuriating.

It was imperative that he secure the Barrington money for Ravenswood; since the heiress was apparently not interested in his title, he would simply have to educate her concerning the other advantages that marriage to him offered.

He smiled to himself. If the one kiss they had shared so far was any example, he would thoroughly enjoy his role of teacher.

The morning after the ball dawned gray and chilly—more like autumn than spring. With Maeve's first glance out her chamber window, she decided the likelihood of rain was much too strong to risk a walk. Instead, she stretched beneath the covers, put her hands behind her head, and gave serious thought to the disaster she'd made of Meg's betrothal ball.

What had the squire instructed her to do to ensure everyone would think she was Meg? "Keep your eyes down and your mouth shut." Ten minutes into the wretched ball, she'd raised her eyes and looked at the earl, and nothing had gone right from that moment on.

But how could she have been so foolish as to expect she could successfully impersonate a woman whose personality was the exact opposite of her own?

She rolled onto her side, propped her head on her elbow, and surveyed her twin's tasteful bedchamber. Her gaze lighted on the shelf holding Meg's collection of beautifully preserved, exquisitely dressed dolls. The only doll she'd ever owned had ended up in the dustbin, headless and sans one arm.

A tambour frame holding an intricately embroidered runner stood in one corner, an easel supporting a partially completed watercolor in another. She'd never sewn a stitch nor painted a picture. The room was filled with the accoutrements one would expect a proper lady to collect. By some miracle, despite her vulgar surroundings, Meg had apparently emerged that lady.

Maeve knew for a fact there was not a ladylike bone in *her* body. She was a courtesan's brat by birth and a bluestocking by nature, neither of which qualified her for any role but that of a sharp-tongued hoyden—a role she'd played to the hilt last evening.

There would surely be repercussions; even a pockets-to-let rake like the Earl of Lynley would have to be desperate to take such a woman to wife. Well, so be it. She may have put a crimp in the squire's plans—and probably her own—but chances were she'd solved Meg's problem.

Her stomach rumbled, reminding her she had been too keyed

up to eat much dinner and had left the ball before supper was served. She doubted Mrs. Pinkert would be in the kitchen at this hour; neither she nor the squire appeared to be early risers. There was nothing for it but to cook her own breakfast—something she was accustomed to doing since she was an early riser and neither Lily nor Bridget ever rose before noon.

She washed her face and hands, dressed in a pretty yellow muslin morning dress from Meg's hoard of bride clothes, and found her way to the kitchen without encountering a soul. Apparently the two new maids were the same kind of slug-a-beds as the rest of the household.

Slicing three thick slices of bacon from a slab she found in the larder, she proceeded to cook herself a meal of bacon, toast, and coddled eggs. She had just taken her first bite of the hearty repast when a sleepy Mrs. Pinkert opened the kitchen door.

"Lord luv us, Miss Meg, what are you doing in my kitchen?" she demanded. She stared at the heaping plate in front of Maeve, and her bleary eyes widened. "When did you learn to cook? And bacon of all things? Last time I made the mistake of serving you hog meat, you come near to casting up your accounts at the very sight of it."

"I . . . I acquired a taste for it while in London," Maeve stammered.

Mrs. Pinkert poured herself a cup of the tea Maeve had just set to steep and sat down at the table. "There's something don't smell right here—hasn't since you and the squire come through the door Friday evening."

She studied Maeve with a jaundiced eye. "I didn't come down in the last rain, you know. It's enough to expect me to believe Miss Meg could change her way of eating and take up cooking in the past fortnight. I ain't such a gapeseed I'll swallow some tomfoolery about how she managed to change the color of her eyes as well."

Maeve swallowed hard. "Her eyes?"

"Miss Meg's is a soft, grayish kind of color with but a hint of green—not green as grass like what's staring at me out of your face, Miss Whoever-You-Are. Though that ain't hard to guess, seeing as how my mam was housekeeper here when the squire's wife birthed her twins and the squire and her divided them up between them like they was a litter of his prize pups."

Maeve slumped in her chair. "You know then that I'm Maeve, the other twin," she said. She searched the housekeeper's face, wary of what the woman would do with the damning knowledge, but relieved it was no longer necessary to maintain her masquerade for someone as sharp-eyed as Mrs. Pinkert.

"I know you ain't who you're pretending to be. What I don't know is what's happened to Miss Meg since I saw her off in the squire's travel coach two weeks ago Friday. I'll not pretend we're great friends. She's too fine a lady to take up with the likes of me; her prim and proper governess seen to that, till the squire run the old witch off first year I was here. But Miss Meg's always kind and polite, and if any harm's come to her 'cause of the squire's conniving, I'll pull that old buzzard's tail feathers and stuff 'em down his blooming throat."

Maeve couldn't help but smile at the picture Mrs. Pinkert's threat conjured up. Furthermore, it was comforting to see she had Meg's welfare in mind; her twin was sorely in need of champions. "According to the squire and Lady Hermione, Meg is in Scotland, visiting her aunt," she explained.

"Run away from the marriage the squire forced her into, did she? Good for her. Didn't think she had it in her."

Maeve nodded. "That's what it looked like to me. Though Lady Hermione tried to gloss it over by claiming Meg was so shy she couldn't face the betrothal ball."

"Well, she is that all right. But I'm guessing it's mostly the earl himself she's scared of."

"I can't say I blame her there," Maeve said between bites of toast. "He is utterly despicable."

"If that means he's as handsome a rogue as walks the face of God's green earth—and that he's too much man for a timid soul like Miss Meg, I say amen to that. Still, the lad has a good heart, and he's a fair landlord, as any as works his land will tell you."

Mrs. Pinkert raised her cup and took a noisy slurp of tea. "So, missy, are you planning to stand in for Miss Meg at the altar? From what I've seen of you so far, you look to suit the bridegroom a mite better than she does."

For some reason she couldn't begin to explain, Maeve felt a flush of heat stain her cheeks. "Good heavens, no!" she exclaimed, staring at the rotund housekeeper in horror. "I have no intention of marrying any man, and if I had, it most certainly would not be the Earl of Lynley."

"That taken with him, are you? Well, no wonder. He's a charmer all right." Mrs. Pinkert poured herself another cup of tea. "But beware that she-devil mother of his. You'll clash with her for sure if you show the least bit of spirit."

"I have already clashed with her," Maeve said, ignoring the housekeeper's ridiculous comment about her being "taken" with the earl. "But I doubt I'll have an occasion to see the dowager again. I promised the squire I'd impersonate my twin at her engagement ball and possibly a fortnight after, at which time he assures me she will return from Scotland."

"He does, does he? And how is he going to arrange that? He can't go after her. Lady Tansy MacDougal, his mother's sister, won't let him get within a mile of that great pile of stone of hers in the Highlands. She hates the sight of him."

Maeve felt the first twinges of a headache creep into her left temple. "What are you saying?" she demanded.

"I'm saying Miss Meg just might decide to stay away now that she's finally made the break—which leaves you, as his other daughter, to pull the squire's fat out of the fire. Or didn't he tell you why he's so anxious for this wedding to come off?"

"Only that it would unite the two estates and give his grandson a title."

Mrs. Pinkert nodded, sending wisps of stringy gray hair swirling Medusa-like around her plump white face. "There's that too, but mostly he's desperate for a grandchild—male or female—and he figures a lusty young fellow like the earl is certain to give him one."

"I suppose every man wants a grandchild," Maeve said absentmindedly, still grappling with the idea that her twin might not be planning to return to Barrington Hall.

"But not every man has all he owns tied up in a land grant what his great grandfather snabbled from the king in exchange for letting his wife warm the monarch's bed—a grant what says if any generation of Barringtons don't produce legitimate offspring by the age of twenty-five, the land and all that's on it goes back to the crown."

"Good heavens! Does Meg know this?"

"Aye, she knows." Mrs. Pinkert looked grim. "For haven't I heard the squire tell her a hundred times and more it's her duty to save Barrington Hall for all those what comes after her." Mrs. Pinkert wrinkled her nose. "I'm that fond of the randy old goat, as you may have noticed, but there's things he does where Miss Meg's concerned that don't sit well with me."

Rising from the table, Mrs. Pinkert proceeded to cut herself a thick slab of bread and spread it with the bacon grease Maeve had poured from the skillet before cooking her eggs. She plopped back down in her chair, took a healthy bite, and regarded Maeve solemnly. "My point is, missy, you'd be smart to pin squire down and find out what kind of flimflam he's up to here—for your sake as well as Miss Meg's."

Maeve studied the older woman's face with anxious eyes. "Why do you say that?"

"Think on it," Mrs. Pinkert said between chews. "If knowing what she did about that land grant, Miss Meg still couldn't bring herself to show up at her betrothal ball, it don't seem too likely she's planning on coming back for her wedding."

Chapter Five

Maeve spent the balance of the morning in a state of nervous agitation, touring the house accompanied by Mrs. Pinkert and the two old hounds who'd met her at the door when she'd arrived at Barrington Hall. She had no real interest in her father's manor house, but it helped pass the time until he put in an appearance. She fully intended to confront him with the new knowledge she'd acquired regarding the marriage he'd arranged between Meg and the earl; she just had to determine how to do so without getting Mrs. Pinkert in trouble.

Most of the rooms in the rambling manor house had been closed off and the furniture draped with holland covers. The few rooms the squire used were furnished with massive chairs and couches, all upholstered in a faded brownish-colored damask depicting one hunting scene or another.

The same smell of stale tobacco smoke and dog that had assailed Maeve's nostrils when she'd stepped into the entryway two days earlier still permeated every room in the lived-in portion of the house, with the exception of one room. Unlocking a door on the second floor, Mrs. Pinkert led Maeve into what she called "Miss Meg's music room." The sparsely furnished salon was sparkling clean, free of odor, and like Meg's bedchamber, amazingly bright and cheerful, considering the dark ambience of the rest of the manor house.

It was the first rewarding moment Maeve had experienced in an otherwise grimly frustrating morning, for sitting in the very center of the room was a pianoforte. "Miss Meg locks herself in here by the hour," Mrs. Pinkert confided. "Sometimes I stand out in the hall, listening to the pretty tunes she plays."

Maeve beamed at the genial housekeeper. "At last I find

something my sister and I have in common." Seating herself on the bench, she ran her fingers over the keys, and grinned happily. "For I, too, love music and studied a number of years with a friend of my mother's, who claimed he was once Louis XVI's court musician. If you don't mind, I'd just as soon end my tour here. I haven't had a chance to play since I left London, and my fingers are itching to try out this pianoforte."

She glanced up at Mrs. Pinkert. "However, I do need to speak to the squire as soon as possible. Would you please be kind enough to send one of the maids to tell me when he leaves his bedchamber."

"He ain't sleeping in his bed. He's curled up in the kennel with his pack of hounds, like he always does when he's four sheets to the wind. I sometimes think there's more hound blood than human in the man's veins."

"But how can that be when the hounds are lying here at my feet?"

"These two old duffers?" Mrs. Pinkert gave the largest of the dogs a nudge with the toe of her house slipper. "They're too old to run with the pack, and if you're wondering why they're living in the house, it's 'cause squire thought t'would be too hard on their old bones to spend the winter in an unheated kennel. Of course, that was two years ago, and he's gotten so used to having them sleep on his bed every night, I doubt he'll ever send them back to their proper quarters."

"Very well," Maeve said patiently. "Please let me know when he comes in from the kennel."

"I'll do that, Miss Maeve. But since there's three bottles of brandy missing from the liquor cabinet, I wouldn't count on seeing him much before Tuesday if I was you—and he'll be mean as a snake for a couple of days after that. Best you wait till next Friday to speak your piece."

"Damn and blast," Maeve muttered under her breath, but in the next moment she realized it might not be a bad idea to put off her talk with the squire for a few days. By then he might have forgotten how angry he was when she left the ball early.

Furthermore, now that she'd discovered Meg's pianoforte, she'd be content to bide her time until he emerged from his drunken stupor. Between that and the work she must accomplish on her cartoons to have them ready to submit to the *Times* when she returned to London, she would have plenty to keep her busy until Friday.

Half an hour later, lost in the joy of being reunited with the instrument she loved, she finished playing the last few bars of one of Mr. Bach's beautifully precise fugues. Then without a moment's break, she let her fingers drift into a lilting fragment from one of Mr. Beethoven's symphonies, only to look up and find Mrs. Pinkert standing in the doorway.

"You've a visitor, Miss Maeve—or rather Miss Meg has."

"A visitor?" Maeve's heart skipped a beat. Surely, the earl wouldn't be calling on her. They hadn't exactly parted on the best of terms.

"It's the vicar, which ain't surprising. He's always here once or twice a week. Him and Miss Meg is thick as inkle weavers. I put him in the small salon off the entryway."

Maeve's fingers crashed onto the keys. "Oh dear, what shall I do? If he's spent that much time with Meg, he's bound to notice my eyes. In fact, he looked at them rather oddly last night, but he apparently thought they reflected the green of my gown."

Mrs. Pinkert threw up her hands. "Lord luv us, you're right. If there's anyone besides me what knows the true color of Miss Meg's eyes, it's her friend the vicar." She shrugged her plump shoulders. "Well you can't turn him away; Miss Meg would never do that. Just don't look at him straight on."

Mrs. Pinkert's advice seemed sound enough, but as Maeve soon discovered, it was not all that easy to implement. She'd barely stepped through the doorway of the salon when Richard Forsythe rushed forward and clasped both her hands in his. "My dear, Theo told me why you left the ball so early, and then when you weren't in church this morning, I knew you must be seriously ill."

Maeve cursed her own stupidity. She should have known that, unlike herself, Meg attended church faithfully.

"These dreadful headaches of yours seem to be happening more frequently of late," Richard continued. "Have you thought to discuss them with Dr. Mabley?"

"No, I haven't," Maeve murmured, suddenly struck by what

seemed a perfect way to keep the vicar from noticing the color of her eyes. "The light," she moaned, collapsing onto a well-worn sofa. "Would you please close the drapes." She could never remember having had a headache herself, but Lily had suffered from them, and the first thing she'd done when she felt one coming on was lie down in a darkened room with cold compresses on her forehead.

The vicar instantly rushed to do her bidding. Drawing the heavy velvet drapes across the window, he immersed the room in gloomy twilight. "I cannot bear to see you suffer like this," he said, seating himself beside her. "Is there anything I can do to help alleviate your agony?"

Maeve raised her head. "Talk to me," she said weakly. "It will help take my mind off the pain." With the light in the room only that which shone through the unlined drapes and the open door, she felt safe from his scrutiny.

"What would you like to talk about, my dear?"

Maeve thought for a moment. "Tell me what you know about Sophie Whitcomb."

"S-Sophie Whitcomb?" The vicar sounded as if there were something caught in his throat he could not quite swallow. "Perhaps you should first tell me what *you* know about Mrs. Whitcomb."

"I know she's the widow of the local alderman and that she grew up with the earl—probably with you, too, since I remember your mentioning that you and he had been close friends since childhood. Oh, and of course, that she's currently the earl's mistress."

The vicar made another strangled sound. "How . . . how could you know so much of the local gossip? You never venture into the village or anywhere else outside Barrington Hall except to attend church on Sundays, and I've never seen you speak to a soul then."

"My new maid told me a little about Mrs. Whitcomb; the earl supplied the rest shortly after he introduced her to me."

"Theo introduced you? Surely, you cannot mean it." The vicar pulled a handkerchief from his pocket and mopped his brow. "I knew, of course, that Sophie was at the ball. Which was surprising enough. But I never dreamed Theo would . . ."

His voice rose to a strangled squeak. "I mean, the earl is usually such a gentleman."

Maeve shrugged. "To give the devil his due, I don't think he had any intention of introducing us until his hand was forced. Furthermore, he claimed Mrs. Whitcomb's invitation was mistakenly issued by his man-of-affairs. At least that's what he said when I told him what I thought of his inviting his mistress to his betrothal ball."

"Margaret! You didn't! Whatever has come over you lately? I scarcely recognize my shy little friend." The vicar covered her hand with his. "My dear, that was simply not the thing to do. I know you have had little opportunity to learn how one should go on in proper society, so you can be forgiven small mistakes. But this was not a small mistake. No true lady would ever acknowledge the existence of a man's mistress, much less discuss such a vulgar creature with him."

"Vulgar creature?"

"Exactly. Such women are all unspeakably vulgar, my dear, and Sophie more so than most. No one could understand why Alderman Whitcomb would consider marrying the trollop when it was common knowledge she had consorted with virtually every young lad in the district by the time she was eighteen."

Including you, no doubt. Maeve's jaw tightened, but before she could tell the vicar what she thought of his "local gossip," she was interrupted by voices in the entryway. One, she knew was Mrs. Pinkert's; the other was a deep rumble, too low to recognize.

A moment later, a tall, masculine figure filled the doorway. "What the devil! Are you sure this is the right salon, madam? The drapes are drawn."

"Theo!" The vicar dropped Maeve's hand and shot to his feet.

"Richard? Is that you?" The earl blinked. "What's going on here? Why, may I ask, are you sitting in the dark?"

"Margaret . . . Miss Barrington has a headache." The vicar cleared his throat; the sound ricocheted around the darkened room like a stray bullet. "I pulled the drapes because the light was hurting her eyes."

"The devil you say!" The earl stepped through the doorway and peered about him, his eyes apparently adjusting to the darkened room. A moment later, Maeve felt the heat of his scorching gaze light on her.

"Good morning, my lord," she said in a voice that quivered slightly. She had somehow faced him squarely the previous evening despite the monstrous deception she was carrying out; now, when she'd done nothing wrong, she hung her head like a naughty child caught in the midst of a shameful bit of mischief.

"Good morning, Miss Barrington." Icicles dripped from every word.

"Please come in and take a chair, my lord. There's one directly to the right of you, in case you've failed to notice it." Maeve took a deep breath. Lord he was handsome—magnificent in his rage. And rage it most surely was. Did he think he was being betrayed by his longtime friend and his bride-to-be?

The earl seated himself in the chair she had indicated. "Are you troubled with these severe headaches often, Miss Barrington?" he asked in the same chilling tone of voice.

"No," Maeve said.

"Yes," the vicar said simultaneously. "I wish you would persuade her to speak to Dr. Mabley about them, Theo. I've tried, but to no avail."

The earl nodded gravely. "I shall insist upon it once we are married." His tone of voice left no doubt that he intended to exercise the same control over his wife as he did his tenant farmers and the sheep that grazed his pastures. Maeve clenched her fists, but managed to remain silent. Only two more weeks, she reminded herself; then she could put the autocratic earl out of her mind as she might a bad dream once the night was over.

Theo's eyes had actually adjusted to the dim light more quickly than he'd let on—quickly enough to see that Richard had been holding hands with Miss Barrington. A damned odd thing for a vicar to be doing, in his opinion. A fiercely possessive rage welled up inside him. Was Richard so naive he was unaware that he had put the future Countess of Lynley in a compromising position?

"You appear to be amazingly well versed concerning Miss Barrington's health, Richard," he remarked coldly.

"I am Margaret's vicar, Theo."

"Indeed. Do you feel the same personal concern for all your parishioners, or is Miss Barrington unique?"

Once again, Richard cleared his throat self-consciously. "I try to be available for any in the parish who need me. As a matter of fact, I must take my leave of you now, since Annie Jennings is near her time and I promised to drop in on her."

Richard made a quick bow. "Good afternoon, then, Margaret. Theo." His voice sounded unnaturally thin, and Theo felt his conscience prick him. He pitied his poor friend if he'd lost his heart to the intriguing squire's daughter, but it changed nothing.

There were bigger things at stake here than the longings of one human heart, and the die was cast. Miss Barrington and her fortune were destined to save Ravenswood and the honor of a family name far older and more noble than that of the pathetic German prince who was currently the titular head of England's government—and save it they would, no matter who got hurt in the process.

Rising from his chair, he crossed to the sofa and sat down next to Miss Barrington. Even in the dim light, he could see the startled look in her eyes. She didn't move, at least not perceptibly, but he felt her withdraw behind an invisible barrier that shut him out as effectively as if she had slammed a door in his face.

"Did you have a specific purpose in mind for this visit, my lord, or are you merely fulfilling your social obligation to your betrothed?" she asked with quiet dignity.

"As I told you last evening, I think we need to become better acquainted."

Her eyes widened perceptibly. "Are you saying you came here to kiss me again?"

Theo sucked in his breath. He had never met a woman as forthright in her manner of speaking as Miss Barrington. He hadn't yet decided if he was more charmed or unnerved by the experience.

"Not expressly," he said, making a valiant effort to keep from laughing. "But now that I think on it, I must admit the idea has merit, and what could be a more appropriate setting than this darkened room?"

"As to that"—she rose quickly—"I find my headache much improved. I believe I shall open the drapes."

"Not so fast." Theo stood up, caught hold of her upper arms, and turned her to face him. "My kiss first, if you please, Miss Barrington." Drawing her slight form to him, he bent his head to claim her lips in what he was determined would be a kiss as gentle and tender as their first kiss had been fierce and punishing.

But as if mesmerized by that other kiss, her lips parted invitingly the instant his touched them, and before he was fully aware of what he was doing, he found himself once again plundering her soft, vulnerable mouth with a passion that left him feeling as if he'd been struck by a bolt of lightning.

"Dammit, that's twice I've attacked my betrothed with all the finesse of a sailor home from a year at sea," he muttered to himself as he ended the kiss. Releasing her abruptly, he stepped back before she became aware of the reaction her touch was having on his traitorous body.

"Now, with your permission, I shall open the drapes," he said, quickly crossing to the window while he gathered his wits.

What was there about this particular woman that made him lose his legendary control when the reigning beauties of London and Paris had failed to do so? She could not by any stretch of imagination be called a beautiful woman, or even a handsome one. Nor did she have a figure that would make a man look twice if he passed her on a London street.

Yet, somehow, the look of wonder in her emerald eyes reminded him that a lifetime ago, before the hellish carnage of the Peninsula, he, too, had looked on the world with wonder. And somehow the innocent sensuality of her eager response to his kisses made him feel as if all the other women he had known had been but a gaggle of lifeless, unfeeling dolls.

A flick of his wrist and sunlight flooded the small room, illuminating the object of his momentary insanity. "My goodness," she exclaimed, dropping back onto the sofa as if her legs had been knocked out from under her. "I wouldn't have thought it possible, but this kiss was even more . . . emotional than the first one."

She stared up at him, her small, heart-shaped face a picture of amazement. "Do they grow progressively more intense, my lord? For if they do, I wonder how any woman can be expected to survive her engagement with her senses intact—and I shall not even let myself think about the marriage bed."

Theo sat down beside her. He realized his own legs felt a bit shaky. He smiled. "I take it, then, you are not averse to my kisses."

"Good heavens, no! Quite the opposite, my lord. They are the nicest thing about you—although you do waltz superbly as well."

"Thank you, Meg. But be honest, I sense there is something about me you distrust; possibly even dislike. I would very much like to know what that something is."

So now she was "Meg" not "Miss Barrington." Without so much as a by-your-leave, the supercilious fellow had dropped the formal form of address. She felt a shiver crawl her spine; she very much wished he hadn't. The diminutive of the name she'd temporarily assumed sounded frighteningly intimate when spoken by lips that had just moments before sent her senses reeling.

Still, she doubted it would do her much good to quibble over such a minor impropriety. "Very well, *Theo*," she said, following his lead, "if it's the truth you want, then the truth you shall have. To begin with, I find your monstrous arrogance a bit disconcerting."

"Do you, indeed? How interesting." He stretched his left arm along the back of the sofa behind her and sent an odd tingling sensation coursing through her neck and shoulders. "It is a trait I learned at my mother's knee. She assured me it was as essential a part of being the Earl of Lynley as administering my estates and taking my seat in the House of Lords. I fear, little commoner, that you may have to learn to live with my 'monstrous arrogance.' Old habits die hard at the advanced age of two and thirty. Though if anyone can put me in my place, it will surely be the sharp-tongued lady who is about to become my wife."

But that union will never come about. Oddly enough, that thought failed to afford Maeve the comfort she'd expected. She felt tortured with guilt over her part in the deception perpetrated on her sister's intended bridegroom. But more than that, she suspected she might have found taking the toplofty earl down a peg to be the most exciting challenge she'd ever faced.

"Surely, my arrogance is not the only thing you hold against me, Meg. I can think of any number of my sins that might give you pause for thought."

Maeve heard the note of derisive laughter in Theo's voice. Apparently the conceited fellow had such a good opinion of himself he found it impossible to take her criticism seriously.

"You're right." She smiled sweetly. "Enumerating the sins of a known rake would be like counting the fleas on a dog—an endless task. But since you are so insistent, I shall mention the one with which I'm most familiar—namely, your deplorable treatment of poor Mrs. Whitcomb."

"Ah yes, Sophie." Theo sobered instantly. "I have given serious thought to our rather bizarre conversation last evening, and I fear there may be some truth in what you said about her suffering the censure of the so-called 'proper ladies' of the village because of her close friendship with me."

He paused and drew a deep breath. He had never understood why his papist friends derived such comfort from confessing their sins. He found the experience damned embarrassing. He was not accustomed to airing his feelings out loud to his closest male friends, much less a woman he scarcely knew.

But sometime in the middle of a sleepless night, he had come to the realization that there had been more truth than fiction in the extravagant prose with which he'd announced his engagement. It was beginning to look as if fate may indeed have provided him with the kind of woman he had unknowingly waited for all his life.

He had always had an uncanny instinct where women were concerned, and both that instinct and his equally astute common sense told him he could trust Meg Barrington implicitly. For how could a woman so openly honest and outspoken have a deceitful bone in her body?

The more he thought about it, the more convinced he was

that the two of them had every chance of creating one of those rare marriages built on respect . . . and passion, such as his friend the Duke of Montford enjoyed with his commoner wife, Emily. Furthermore, the feisty little cat had already proved she was more than a match for his impossible mother, which boded well for his future peace of mind.

If renouncing his mistress and indulging in a little verbal soul-searching was the price he must pay to convince her that he was prime husband material, then so be it.

Gritting his teeth, he prepared to make the speech he'd carefully rehearsed on the ride from Ravenswood. "I have not yet determined how, but I must find a way to give Sophie back her respectability, now that the nature of our friendship is altered by my pending marriage," he said and was gratified to see a look of approval on his future bride's face.

"Sophie is not terribly bright," he continued, "but she is a generous, warm-hearted woman who has seen me through a difficult period. She should not be made to suffer for my lack of discretion."

A generous, warm-hearted woman. The earl's description of Sophie Whitcomb was a far cry from the vicar's harsh condemnation of what he considered a "fallen woman." Maeve studied the handsome features of the man who had just made such an amazingly humane observation, and found nothing in them to suggest he was being the least bit facetious. This was a new, compassionate side of the earl—one she found even more disquieting than his undisputed charm.

He turned his head and surveyed her expectantly, apparently waiting for her to applaud his surprising about-face. She couldn't bring herself to utter a word, though she was aware it could not have been easy for such a proud man to humble himself as he had. The very idea that her condemnation of him had caused him to go to such lengths to ensure the success of a marriage she knew would never take place left her feeling sick with guilt. She, of all people, should have been the last one to hurl stones at another sinner.

"I shall take your silence as agreement then, Miss Barrington," he said in a chilling tone of voice that told her how deeply she had offended him with her apparent indifference to what he must have considered an earthshaking decision.

Agreement to what, she wondered, but was afraid to ask. For gone was the kindly man of but a moment ago, and in his place the arrogant aristocrat who had first greeted her when she'd arrived at Meg's engagement ball.

"Very well then, since that is settled, I shall take my leave of you," he said, rising to his feet and heading for the door.

"What is settled?"

He turned back with obvious impatience. "Have you listened to nothing I've said? I have agreed to sever any connections that might endanger the success of our upcoming marriage, and I shall expect you to do the same."

Startled, Maeve heard herself protest, "You cannot be serious. I have no such connections."

"Maybe not in the true sense of the word, but you are dangling Richard Forsythe like a puppet on a string." The earl's eyes glittered dangerously, and a certain inflection in his voice told her he was indeed deadly serious. "Cut him loose. He is a good man and deserves better than to waste his time pining for a woman he can never have—and he can never have you."

He reached for his gloves and high-crown beaver, which he'd earlier deposited on a small table just inside the door of the salon. "The idea might not appeal to you, but the fact remains you are mine, Meg Barrington."

His beautifully defined lips curved in a smile, but his eyes remained cold, hard chips of gleaming onyx. "And you would do well to remember that I never share what is mine."

Chapter Six

Maeve watched out the window as Theo mounted his horse and rode off down the long, tree-lined driveway. She found herself wishing desperately she could have told the high-and-mighty Earl of Lynley that the woman about whom he had suddenly become so possessive was an impostor. Even worse, that both she and his bride-to-be, whom she impersonated, were the daughters of a high-priced London whore and a drunken country squire who slept in the kennel with his hounds.

She smiled to herself, imagining the look of horror on his handsome face when he realized that to get his hands on the Barrington money, he would have to merge such tainted blood with the blue blood flowing through his aristocratic veins. She felt certain the squire had never touched on that interesting fact when he negotiated the marriage settlement.

In truth, if there hadn't been so much at stake for everyone concerned in this bizarre betrothal, it might almost be considered comical. Certainly, it had all the elements of a Drury Lane farce.

With a heartfelt sigh, she resigned herself to two more weeks of participating in the madness, and retired to the music room to take out her frustration on the keyboard of the pianoforte. By rights, she should be working on her drawings; they were, after all, where her future lay. But her nerves were much too jangled from Theo's visit to allow her to concentrate.

She didn't have to concentrate when she played her music. She had worked so long and so diligently on mastering the intricate compositions she loved, her fingers simply glided over the keys—effortlessly re-creating what she had previously stored in the depths of her mind and soul.

"There's a note come for you from Ravenswood, miss." The maid, Lucy, hovered in the doorway, her eyes bright with excitement. "It must be from the earl, and after he's already called on you and brought such pretty flowers, too." She sighed. "It's so romantical."

"If the note is indeed from him, he must have ridden *ventre a terre* all the way to Ravenswood and scribbled it before he took time to remove his hat and gloves," Maeve said dryly, perusing the square of rich vellum embossed with the earl's crest.

Her head snapped up as she suddenly realized what Lucy had said. "Flowers? What flowers are you talking about?"

"Why the red roses he asked Mrs. Pinkert to put in a vase. Must be more'n a dozen of them. Prettiest things you've ever seen, with stems so long Mrs. Pinkert near tore her hair out trying to find a vase as fit them."

A look of puzzlement crossed Lucy's bright young face. "It's too early in the year for roses to be blooming. I can't imagine how he come by them." She snapped her fingers. "Faith, I do so know. They must be from the Ravenswood sol . . . sol . . . you know, that glass house the old earl had built out behind the kitchen wing."

"The solarium," Maeve said, her pulse quickening. Theo's roses were the first flowers she had ever received, and in spite of her antipathy toward him, she couldn't help but be touched by the gesture. She wished she'd known in time to thank him. Whatever their differences, she owed him that much.

With misgivings, she returned her attention to the note and instantly determined the spidery handwriting could not be Theo's. She noted the cramped signature, and her misgivings increased tenfold. Why would the dowager countess be sending her a note? The woman had gone out of her way the previous evening to show her disapproval of her son's choice of a wife.

The minuscule script was not easy to read, but Maeve finally deduced it was an invitation to dinner at Ravenswood on Tuesday evening, and was directed to both Meg and the squire. A barely decipherable postscript added the information that the countess's brother, Viscount Tinsdale, and his distinguished traveling companion were arriving from London on Monday and would be anxious to meet the earl's betrothed.

A rather odd way of wording it, Maeve decided. She knew very well who Viscount Tinsdale was. He'd figured prominently in her first two cartoons lambasting the crowd of shallow dandies who clung to the Regent's coattails. She'd submitted them to the *Times* just before leaving London, and they should be published within the next few days. She shuddered to think what her reception at Ravenswood would be if the viscount or his sister suspected she was the notorious Marcus Browne, whose inflammatory cartoons had London holding its breath to see who would be ridiculed next.

But who could this "distinguished traveling companion" of the viscount's be, and why had the dowager chosen to be so secretive about his identity? Surely, it couldn't be the Regent himself. It was a well-known fact that Prinny never traveled without his entire entourage. Still, the fellow must be a very prominent member of the *ton*. Maeve had a feeling in her bones the dowager was counting on his providing such a glaring contrast to the boorish commoners with whom Theo had allied himself, that he would instantly realize he should look to a more suitable heiress to repair his dwindled fortune.

She felt her hackles rise at the implied insult to her twin. Furthermore, if the countess was planning on persuading her precious son to break his engagement, she had a shock in store for her. That was a privilege Maeve had already determined belonged exclusively to her sister, Meg.

She looked up to find Lucy still eyeing her with obvious curiosity. "It appears my father and I are invited to take dinner at Ravenswood on Tuesday evening," Maeve explained. "I shall want to make a good impression, and I'll need your help in choosing the proper gown—one with which I can wear my pearls."

Lucy's eyes sparkled. "La, miss, not to worry. It's the sort of thing I'm best at. Choosing a gown will be no problem. You've ever so many pretty ones in your bride clothes."

She cocked her head and studied Maeve thoughtfully. "And I'll do something grand with your hair. Another snip or two, maybe a few curl papers, and I'll have you looking as bang up-to-the-mark as the most fashionable lady in London. Didn't I turn you out fine as sixpence for the ball last night?"

"That you did." Maeve smiled, thinking of the sensation she'd created in her daring green gown. "Now, where did you put my roses? I'd like to see them."

"Why, in the little salon, where you and the earl was just sitting, miss. It seemed the proper place to show them off, what with you having so many callers and all."

"Good thinking," Maeve agreed, and sweeping past the giggling maid, proceeded down the stairs to the small salon. She stopped just inside the door and felt her breath catch in her throat. The roses were everything Lucy had claimed, and more. A mass of perfect ruby buds, their spicy sweet fragrance filled every corner of the room and drifted into the entryway beyond. She touched a velvet petal with her fingertip, so moved by their beauty, she felt tears spring to her eyes.

An image of Theo's handsome, saturnine face swam in her tear-blurred vision—her first kiss, her first waltz, now her first flowers. Like it or not, the Earl of Lynley had already carved himself a special place in her memory—and her requisite fortnight posing as her twin had just barely begun.

Theo was in a foul mood.

The business of terminating his affair with Sophie had not gone at all as he'd planned. She'd wept all over him. She'd ranted and raved and pleaded with him to continue seeing her after he was married. When he'd flatly refused, she'd shrieked like a banshee and torn her hair and threatened to kill herself. She'd even threatened to go to his betrothed and describe in detail the interesting ways he'd entertained her on the cold winter nights when he'd warmed himself in her bed.

In short, she had acted in an alarmingly emotional and shockingly un-British manner, which had given him a complete disgust of her. He'd spent the better part of the night trying to reason with her. To no avail. She was as hysterical when he left her as she'd been nearly twelve hours earlier when he'd first announced his intention to be faithful to his marriage vows.

Hell and damnation! How had a rational, well-intentioned fellow like him managed to land in such a bumblebroth? And how could an innocent country recluse like Meg Barrington have so accurately predicted the way a trollop like Sophie Whitcomb would react when he gave her her congé?

He was still pondering these baffling questions when he turned his horse over to a waiting groom and strode into the entryway of Ravenwood to find his mother waiting for him.

She raised her lorgnette and perused him as she might a particularly offensive piece of refuse found floating in the Thames. "Really, Theo, must you insult me by returning from one of your nights of debauchery, looking and smelling as if you had been lolling about in a brothel? Remove yourself to your chambers this instant, and I shall order the footman to prepare you a bath."

Theo took a deep breath and reminded himself the woman was his mother, and as such deserved his respect no matter how aggravating she might be. "I am perfectly capable of ordering my own bath, madam," he declared somewhat more curtly than he intended.

"Then please do so immediately. Our houseguests should be arriving momentarily."

"Guests?" Theo scowled. "I do not recall inviting anyone to Ravenwood."

"At my request, my brother, the viscount, is honoring us with a short visit and bringing with him his friend, the Duke of Kent."

Theo swore softly under his breath. He thoroughly disliked his uncle. There was something about the overdressed dandy that made his skin crawl. He had never met the Duke of Kent, but if the rumors about him were true, he stood second only to the evil Duke of Cumberland as the most hated of the Regent's brothers.

What had possessed his mother to invite two such unpleasant fellows as houseguests? And without consulting him. The woman was taking entirely too much upon herself. All the more reason he should install his bride as mistress of Ravenswood as soon as possible. Then he could move his mother to the dower house, where, like it or not, she belonged.

Wearily, he mounted the stairs to his bedchamber. Perhaps because of all that had happened in the past few days—perhaps because he was simply too tired to delude himself any longer, he faced a truth he had never before allowed himself to acknowledge. He disliked his mother even more than he disliked his uncle.

It was not an easy truth to face. For what kind of man would despise the woman who had given him life—even if that woman had given him none of the warmth or tenderness he'd craved so desperately as a child?

Not for the first time, he found himself wondering if the driving need he often felt as an adult to lose himself in a woman's arms stemmed from his loveless childhood. Not for the first time, he vowed that no child of his would ever suffer the loneliness of knowing he was nothing more to his parents than the means of perpetuating their noble name.

Perhaps, as much as her fortune, what drew him to Meg Barrington was his sense that she would take great pleasure in motherhood. He could see she thought him anything but the ideal man to father her children. He felt certain he could change her opinion on that. But if, God forbid, he could not, he would learn to live with it.

Far more important was the knowledge that with her as their mother, he was ensuring his children the kind of maternal love and tenderness he had never known. He had never been more serious in his life than when he'd told her she belonged to him and to him alone.

The gown Lucy selected for the dinner party at Ravenswood was as daring in its own way as the green ball gown, despite its color being more acceptable for an unmarried woman. A white Belgian lace overdress covered the deep rose silk chemise, but the off-the-shoulder neckline was, to Maeve's way of thinking, shockingly low, and the lace point hemline allowed a glimpse of ankle she was not quite sure was proper.

"La, miss, you're much too modest," Lucy declared when Maeve voiced her doubts. "Just let me finish weaving a few of the earl's rosebuds into your hair, and you'll look so pretty he'll change his mind about waiting till fall for your wedding."

Luckily for her peace of mind, Maeve could recognize a butter boat when it was dumped on her, so she ignored Lucy's blithe prophesy. The worst thing that could possibly happen would be to move the tentative wedding date up a month or two.

The squire had declined the dowager's dinner invitation shortly after he'd staggered into Mrs. Pinkert's kitchen late Tuesday morning, covered with bits of straw and smelling like something extricated from a dung heap.

"Make me excuses to the old besom," he'd said when Maeve told him of the dowager's invitation. "Just 'cause I agreed to give the earl me daughter to breed his sons and a fortune to bail him out of the River Tick don't mean I'm willing to spend me evenings doing the pretty with his mother. Demmed woman's got a disposition sour enough to curdle milk twixt the udder and the bucket."

He took a hearty swallow of the black coffee Mrs. Pinkert poured him. "Mark my word, daughter, ye'd best make certain that one's moved to the dower house afore ye say yer vows. Give her a chance to get her toes dug in, and ye'll have her breathing down yer neck till the day she sticks her spoon in the wall."

"Sage advice, sir, but you're giving it to the wrong daughter. I am Maeve, not Meg."

"What? Eh, so ye are. Can't keep ye two straight in me mind."

"Nonsense, sir. You may be many things, but a fool is not one of them. You have us completely straight in your mind. It's this scheme of yours that's beginning to look like a corkscrew." Maeve stared into her father's bloodshot eyes. "I've been waiting three days to talk to you about that very thing."

"Not now, daughter. Can't ye see I'm not well? We'll talk once I've got me health back," the squire declared shortly after he'd swallowed a mammoth bite of the slab of fried ham Mrs. Pinkert put before him.

Maeve registered the "didn't I tell you so" rise of Mrs. Pinkert's eyebrow, but she could see that with the squire in his present frame of mind, she'd be wasting her time questioning him as to his intentions. She would, she decided, wait until he was in a more receptive mood to have their little talk.

Now, more than eight hours later, rolling along the rainswept country road to Ravenswood, she wished she'd demanded the answers she wanted from the wicked old reprobate. But he'd smelled so ripe, she'd had all she could do to keep her breakfast down, much less have a serious discussion with him.

She glanced over at Lucy, whom she'd brought with her because, as Mrs. Pinkert had reminded her, "Miss Meg was a proper lady who'd never leave home without a maid by her side."

Lucy's eyes rivaled the brightness of the evening star, which Maeve could see out the carriage window. "I've an understanding of sorts with Ben Flynn, the earl's fourth-in-line footman," the young maid confessed with a blush, "but I've never seen him in his fine livery, for the dowager makes the Ravenswood servants wear their ordinary clothes when they take their once-a-month free day."

She sighed. "Ben's almost as handsome as the earl. I can't wait to see him, and won't he be surprised to see me! He don't even know I've a position of my own now."

Moments later, Maeve stepped from the carriage, and with Lucy trailing her, ascended the shallow flight of stairs into Ravenswood. Out of the corner of her eye she caught a glimpse of a red-faced, red-haired footman standing with four others dressed in the same elegant blue and gold livery. Ben Flynn, she assumed, though considering Lucy's glowing description, she found him something of a disappointment. He was nowhere near as handsome as Theo. She sighed. But then, who was? In spite of herself, she felt a shiver of excitement just thinking about seeing the arrogant man who at their last meeting had declared she belonged to him and always would.

A stiff-necked butler, who bore a strong resemblance to the one employed by Lady Hermione, met her at the door. Quickly dispatching Lucy to the servants' quarters, he escorted Maeve to where the guests had gathered in the drawing room while waiting to go in to dinner.

"Miss Margaret Barrington," he announced and stepped aside to let her enter the doorway. A quick look around told her there were thirty or more people gathered in small groups about the elegant room. One minute they were all talking at once; the next there was dead silence as all eyes turned to her.

Here and there Maeve recognized faces she'd seen at the

ball, but no one to whom she'd actually spoken. She wondered how many of these strangers would expect Meg to address them by name; how many would expect her to inquire about their children or their elderly relatives. A sick kind of panic started at her toes and worked its way upward through her rigid body.

Her heart thudded against her rib cage with such force her bosom nearly popped out of her daring neckline, and glancing downward, she found, to her horror, that her trembling knees had started the narrow skirt of her gown rippling like the surface of a pond in a windstorm.

Stop it! she ordered herself. *This is exactly how the dowager was hoping you'd act.* With every last ounce of courage she possessed, she raised her head and found Richard Forsythe hurrying toward her from one corner of the room, Theo from another. Richard reached her first. "Margaret, my dear, why didn't you tell me Theo had invited you to this dinner? I would have escorted you."

"Hell and damnation, Richard, give me credit for *some* brains." Sparks of anger glittered in Theo's black eyes. "If I'd known she was coming, I'd have escorted her myself."

Maeve felt her cheeks flame. "You didn't expect me?"

Theo smiled. "No, dear lady, I didn't. But how pleasant to see you again." Clasping her hand in his, he raised it to his lips.

"Oh dear, I'm afraid this awkward moment is all my fault." The dowager glided toward them, an elegant black bird of prey whose talons were barely sheathed. "With all I had to do to prepare for this evening, I completely forgot to tell Theo I'd invited you and your father."

Her pale brows drew together in a frown. "But where is the squire? I've told the duke so much about him, His Grace is most anxious to meet him."

"My father became ill at the last minute. He sends his sincere regrets," Maeve said. So, the dowager's houseguest was a duke, no less. How disappointing for her that one of the two clowns she'd counted on for entertainment had failed to appear.

The countess shrugged her elegant black-clad shoulders. "Ah, well, I suppose such social infractions must be expected when one is dealing with the lower classes. A man of title would have risen from his deathbed rather than throw his hostess's seating arrangement into chaos."

"Think of it this way, Mother," Theo said grimly. "In two, possibly three more months Meg will be mistress of Ravenswood, and such problems as seating arrangements will be hers to solve. While you, my lady, can retire to the peace and solitude of the dower house for your remaining days."

Turning his back on his mother, he clasped Maeve's hand in his and placed it atop his arm. "Now, my dear, allow me to introduce you to our guest of honor." So saying, he led her across the room to the group of men from which he'd detached himself but moments before.

Maeve felt the dowager's angry blue eyes boring holes into her back. Theo's cruel set-down had drained every last drop of color from the woman's face, leaving Maeve with the impression that until that moment she had believed she would remain the mistress of Ravenswood even after her son's marriage. No wonder she had approved of a timid little mouse as her daughter-in-law.

Maeve glanced over her shoulder. The dowager still stood in the same spot, her chalk-white face twisted into an ugly mask of rage. Richard hovered beside her, looking utterly miserable and unprepared to handle the embarrassing situation in which he found himself.

Only a handful of the guests had actually witnessed the imbroglio between the earl and his mother, but Maeve could hear the telltale whispers spreading from group to group around her. All things considered, she wasn't certain if she felt more grateful or guilty over Theo's staunch defense of her.

She clutched at his arm, and his taut muscles rippled beneath her fingers. "My lord . . . Theo, she is your mother," she managed in a hoarse whisper.

"And you are the woman I have chosen as my wife. She will treat you with the respect due you or answer to me." Theo's black eyes still snapped with anger. "I promise you, you will never again be subjected to one of her clever maneuvers to embarrass you or your father."

A powerful wave of guilt swept through Maeve. She didn't want Theo to care about her bruised feelings; she didn't want him to champion her against his mother. She was the worst kind of fraud and the last person in the world to deserve his loyalty.

"I don't want to cause trouble between you and your mother," she protested, gripping his arm with numb fingers.

"Don't worry about it." A note of sadness crept into Theo's voice. "The trouble was there long before you came on the scene."

He came to a sudden halt, and instantly his somber demeanor changed to that of the genial, smiling host. "May I present my uncle, the Viscount Tinsdale," he said, indicating the elegant dandy who had stepped directly in front of them. "My betrothed, Miss Margaret Barrington, my lord."

"Charmed," the viscount said and raised her fingers to his lips, but his cold blue eyes, so like his sister's, swept her with a look of utter contempt.

She felt Theo stiffen beside her, but with obvious effort, he held his temper. "And this, my dear, is our guest of honor, the Duke of Kent," he said, moving on to the portly, balding man standing a few feet beyond the viscount.

Maeve's heart skipped a beat. She had met this petty tyrant, the fourth son of Mad King George, on two different occasions. She prayed her change of hairdo and wardrobe would render her unrecognizable to him.

Lily and he had had a brief affair shortly after he'd been recalled from Gibraltar in disgrace when the troops under his command had threatened to mutiny over his harsh discipline and endless obsession with petty detail. But the liaison was doomed from the onset. Lily led too harum-scarum a life to suit a man as meticulous and precise as the duke, and he was too tightfisted for a spendthrift like her. He soon returned to the arms of his longtime mistress, Madame St. Laurent.

"I am honored, Your Grace," Maeve said once Theo had completed his introductions. Smiling warmly, she dipped into the graceful court curtsy Lily had insisted she perfect.

The duke raised his quizzing glass and surveyed her with obvious curiosity. "Why do I have the feeling we've met before, Miss Barrington?"

"I have a very ordinary face, Your Grace."

"Nonsense. No woman with such eyes could be called ordinary." He raised an eyebrow. "Ah, yes, that's it. Your eyes. They remind me of those of someone I once knew. Oddly enough, I just recently learned of her death." He returned his quizzing glass to the waistcoat pocket from which he'd drawn it. "Extraordinary. Most extraordinary."

Maeve breathed a sigh of relief for her unremarkable face and for the duke's snobbery, which could never equate the daughter of one of the demimonde with an earl's betrothed.

Dinner at Ravenswood was a lengthy affair, beginning with a delicate turtle soup, progressing through a fish course of turbot and lobster, a fowl course consisting of both goose and turkey, sweetbreads, eggs in aspic, roasted lamb, pork and beef, five different vegetables each with its own rich sauce, two ices, three custards, and a macédoine of fruit—with sherry, Madeira, and champagne served throughout.

Maeve nibbled at the plethora of food the footmen served her, took a sip of champagne, and did her best to pretend she was enjoying herself. She was seated too far from the head of the table to hear the conversation between the earl and his guest of honor, and too far from the foot to hear the angry confidence she could see the dowager was sharing with her brother.

In short, she was in that nebulous area reserved for the guests of least consequence known as "below the salt"—another public insult to the future Countess of Lynley at the hands of the dowager. Maeve found herself momentarily wishing she truly was the future countess. She would dearly love to pay the spiteful old woman back with some of her own.

But right at the moment she felt sadly out of place. Neither the gentleman on her left nor the one on her right appeared the least bit interested in conversation. She felt certain the dowager had chosen her future daughter-in-law's dinner companions with infinite care. Which left Maeve to sit in silence, bored to flinders and straining to hear what was said around her.

Most of it was simply idle chitchat, but to her surprise, she heard the name "Marcus Browne" come up in a conversation directly across the table from her. The speaker was a rather haughty fellow who had earlier been introduced as "the Duke of Kent's amanuensis." Maeve instantly perked up her ears. It was always fascinating to hear what the *ton* thought of her work.

"The fellow goes too far," the duke's secretary declared. "If the publishers of the *Times* were the responsible citizens they purport to be, they would ban his licentious cartoons. Why, he has actually dared to attack the very foundation of our society, the Royal Family. If one were to take his series of drawings depicting the royal dukes seriously, one might come to the conclusion they were naught but a collection of mindless buffoons."

His dinner companion gave a grunt of agreement. "Shocking business, that. Though I must admit I was at a loss to understand the drawing of the Duke of Kent. That word the cartoonist wrote above it was most puzzling."

"That 'word' had everyone in London rushing to the library to hunt it up in Dr. Johnson's dictionary—myself included," the secretary said. "It and the blasted cartoon it captioned was all anyone in London could talk about for months on end."

"But what did it mean?" his companion asked.

"It was listed as one of the longest words in the English language, but the meaning was simply 'the estimation of something as valueless.' "

"Aha! Now I understand. Egad, the fellow really is clever."

"Clever?" The secretary stared down his long, narrow nose at the fool uttering such blasphemy. "The cartoon was clearly a vicious attempt to exacerbate the minor misunderstanding between His Grace and the Prince Regent."

Maeve chuckled to herself. It was a well-known fact that Prinny and his brother, the Duke of Kent, cordially hated each other and constantly disagreed both privately and publicly.

She had drawn the fussy duke bent over a model of Prinny's incredibly expensive and controversial Brighton Pavilion, examining it through a magnifying glass. Across the top of the cartoon she had printed the word "Floccinaucinihilipilification."

The cartoon had launched her career. She'd had letters of congratulation from such luminaries of the world of political cartooning as James Gillray, Thomas Rowlandson, and the young genius George Cruikshank, whose cartoons appeared in both *The Satirist* and *Town Talk*—all of whom had assumed, of course, that she was a man.

As if by magic, her self-confidence returned—along with her appetite. Food that had tasted like so much sawdust but moments before now tempted her palate. Tucking in with gusto, she glanced down the long stretch of table to find Theo watching her with anxious eyes. She cast him such a brilliant smile, he blinked.

For a long, breathtaking moment their gazes locked in a shockingly intimate communion. Then Theo returned her smile with one of his own, and it was her turn to blink and duck her head.

An odd kind of ache gripped her heart that had nothing to do with the guilt she felt over posing as his betrothed. For the first time, she found herself sincerely regretting that nothing could ever come of this tenuous friendship she sensed was beginning to blossom between them.

The Earl of Lynley was really not such a bad sort of fellow after all—for a rake and fortune hunter.

Chapter Seven

With the long, tedious dinner drawing to a close, Maeve found herself dreading the time when the ladies would withdraw to let the gentlemen enjoy their brandy and cigars. She felt certain the dowager would retaliate for Theo's defection, and she had a horror of public scenes.

"You will find us in the music room, gentlemen, when you are ready to join us," the countess announced finally. As if on cue, every lady at the table rose and exited the dining room in the wake of the elegant black-clad hostess. In hushed silence, the little procession wound its way through the labyrinthine halls of the manor house to a large room on the second floor containing a magnificent pianoforte and an equally magnificent harp. Dozens of straight-back Hepplewhite chairs sat in neat rows facing the two instruments, awaiting the audience for whatever musical entertainment was planned for the evening.

Maeve hesitated momentarily as she walked past the pianoforte, her fingers itching to try the keys, but common sense dictated she remain as inconspicuous as possible. Seating herself in one of the chairs in the last row, she waited somewhat anxiously to see what the countess would do. To her surprise, and relief, she was left entirely alone. The other female guests all appeared to be in league with their hostess, and it was obvious the word had gotten around that the earl's mother did not approve of her son's choice of a bride.

It was all Maeve could do to keep an exultant smile off her face. If the dowager's idea of giving her a set-down was to arrange a cut direct from this collection of country frumps, the lady was sadly off the mark. She had simply saved Maeve the trouble of conversing with a lot of silly women with whom she had absolutely nothing in common.

In an amazingly short time, the men, led by Theo, came trooping through the door and seated themselves among the women. Richard claimed the chair on Maeve's right, Theo the one on her left. Grim-faced and tight-lipped, the two of them looked for all the world like two bulldogs determined to guard the same bone.

"Your mother was absolutely livid over that little scene before dinner," Richard said in a hoarse whisper over Maeve's head. "Knowing her as I do, I can't believe she'll simply let it go by, and I don't want Margaret hurt."

"Speaking as her vicar, I assume," Theo said coldly.

"Naturally." Richard cleared his throat. "Seriously, Theo, what do you think your mother will do?"

Theo glanced around him as if to ascertain there was no one within hearing distance. "God only knows. I may be her son, but I have never pretended to understand the woman."

"She has an odd look on her face," Maeve interjected. "Rather like a tabby who's cornered a mouse and intends to play with it a bit before dealing the death blow."

Two sets of eyes, wide with surprise, turned on her; two sets of lips proclaimed, "Exactly!"

Maeve smiled. "Well, at least you two have finally agreed on something."

She watched the dowager move to stand by the pianoforte and raise her hand for silence. "This dinner was such a spur-of-the-moment affair, I scarcely had time to issue proper invitations, much less prepare for the evening's entertainment." She surveyed her guests with a chilly smile. "Therefore, upon the advice of my son, the earl, I shall turn the balance of the evening over to the future Countess of Lynley."

She turned her basilisk stare directly on Maeve. "Would you be kind enough to honor us with a few musical selections, Miss Barrington?"

Richard Forsythe instantly leapt to his feet. "Miss Barrington is not accustomed to playing in public, my lady."

The dowager's smile chilled another degree or two. "So I have been told. But we shall not be a critical audience." She glanced around the room as if looking for confirmation of her statement, and immediately an affirmative murmur spread through the seated guests.

"Do something, Theo," Richard whispered. "This latest quirk of your mother's is beyond cruel. Margaret will die of humiliation if she is forced to perform for an audience—particularly when it includes a member of the Royal Family."

Maeve rose to stand beside the vicar. "Thank you for your concern, Richard, but I really don't mind that much." Then remembering she was supposed to be her shy, reclusive sister, she dropped her head and stared at the floor. "Of course, I shall be utterly terrified, but I feel relatively certain I shall live through it."

Richard groaned. "Help her, Theo. She doesn't know what she's saying."

Theo stood up and clasped Maeve's hand in his. "You do not have to do this, Meg. No one will think the less of you if you refuse. Least of all me. I would rather face Napoleon and his entire army singlehandedly than perform in public, and I have more than a speaking acquaintance with the pianoforte."

Maeve smiled into his face, surprised by the genuine look of concern she saw there. It occurred to her there was much more to this haughty aristocrat than appeared on the surface. Against her better judgment, she found herself beginning to like him—something she would never have thought possible when they'd first met.

"I really don't mind performing in public," she reiterated. "I can think of a number of pieces I've practiced sufficiently to play by memory."

Richard groaned again. "Be sensible, Margaret. Can't you see you're setting yourself up for ridicule?"

Theo scowled at his longtime friend. "Stubble it, Richard. If Meg isn't worried about her performance, why should you be?" He offered his arm. "Permit me to escort you to the pianoforte, dear lady," he said gallantly.

Richard ceased his protesting and sank onto his chair. "Very well, Margaret, if I cannot dissuade you from allowing the dowager to turn you into a laughingstock, I shall do the only thing left to me. I shall pray for you."

Puzzled, Maeve gave him a reassuring pat on the shoulder and promised him once more that everything would be all right. It occurred to her that her twin must be even more shy than she'd been led to believe if Richard was this concerned over something as simple as playing a couple of musical selections for people who probably couldn't tell the difference between B-sharp and A-flat.

She settled herself at the pianoforte, painfully conscious of Theo standing behind her. Somewhat nervously, she ran her fingers over the keys and determined the instrument was in perfect tune, then glanced over her shoulder, silently requesting him to return to his chair.

With a smile of encouragement, he did so, and she instantly felt herself relax. This was her world—the world of music. A place where she had achieved sufficient mastery that it no longer mattered that her lineage was somewhat questionable or that she was plain of face and small of stature.

But what should she play for an audience such as this? Something light and melodic, like one of Joseph Haydn's delightful sonatas, she decided. Then perhaps the little known piece by Mozart that had always intrigued her.

Poising her hands above the keys, she took a deep breath and began her impromptu concert. As always, with the first notes of the sonata, she lost herself in the subtle intricacies that Haydn had woven so brilliantly into his lovely composition, and beneath her skillful fingers, the music came vibrantly, breathtakingly alive. "Music from your heart" her demanding teacher had called it on the rare occasions when he'd complimented her on her interpretation of the composer's work.

A hush fell on the audience. Maeve was vaguely aware that every eye was riveted on her, every ear avidly listening to the exquisite sounds her fingers were creating. Time stood still—until, with the last poignant note, she bowed her head and dropped her hands into her lap.

A long moment of stunned silence ensued. Then a voice she recognized as Theo's cried, "Bravo!" and suddenly everyone was cheering and clapping and talking to anyone who would listen. Everyone, that it, except the dowager, whose cold, expressionless features resembled that of a marble statue—and

Richard Forsythe, whose mouth-gaping, eye-bulging look of disbelief gave him the appearance of a fish that had landed out of water.

Briefly, she wondered if her taste in music was so far afield from that of her twin that she had given herself away. Then someone shouted, "More!" and she promptly forgot Richard and the countess and launched into the composition by Mozart.

She could never remember the title the composer had given it; she thought of it simply as "Laughter," for the daring, irreverent, almost giddy collection of notes perfectly captured the euphoria of joyous, uncontrollable laughter.

Faster and faster her fingers flew over the keys. Wilder and more wanton the melody grew until in an instant too subtle to pinpoint, the laughter evolved into hysteria, the joy into madness. More than any other music he had written, this obscure little piece paralleled the tragic life of the young Austrian composer, and Maeve never failed to be deeply moved each time she played it.

It had been a great favorite of Lily's, too, and Maeve had performed it many times for her mother's circle of close friends. It was always well received; even the least discerning of listeners had thrilled to the rapid fingerwork the brilliant little composition required. But precious few had ever seen beyond the exacting technique to the tortured passion it portrayed. The "rare ones" Lily had dubbed them, and warned Maeve that to give herself to a man with such insight into the human soul would be asking to have her heart broken.

The sound of the last note died away, and Maeve lifted her fingers from the keys. The applause was even greater than for the sonata. The faces surrounding her, including those of the duke and viscount, were all smiles; even the dowager appeared to have thawed sufficiently to look slightly amazed.

Her gaze flew to Theo. He was clapping with the same enthusiasm as before, but for a few brief moments his dark eyes held a haunted look that proclaimed he had sensed the torment of the young composer.

An instant later, the look was gone, and Maeve told herself she had only imagined it. Surely, the rakish earl was not the type of man to be one of Lily's "rare ones." It was enough that she was beginning to find him likable; she didn't need to endow him with nonexistent sensitivities as well.

She braced herself for the rush of embarrassing praise she had come to expect whenever she performed, but strangely enough, this time the rush went right past her—toward Theo. One and all, the local squires and their wives crowded around their resident earl to congratulate him on having the intelligence to choose a wife who could provide him with such excellent entertainment.

An unaccustomed flush stained his cheeks, and over the heads of the toad-eaters his eyes sought hers in embarrassed apology. But unmistakable humor glinted in their dark depths as well and Maeve's first thought was that Lily would have liked this belted earl who could laugh at the idiocy of the British social system.

She turned her gaze to the corner of the room where she'd last seen Richard. He stood alone, some distance from the crowd surrounding Theo. He was noticeably pale, and the grim expression on his face made him look like anything but the mild-mannered country vicar she had come to know in the past few days. Something was definitely wrong. Heart pounding, she rose and made her way toward him.

"Who are you, madam?" he hissed, grasping her upper arms in a viselike grip.

Maeve stared at him in horror, her first thought that he had noticed the color of her eyes.

"Who are you?" he repeated. "Though you look incredibly like her, I know you are not Margaret Barrington." His grip tightened. "I taught her everything she knows about the pianoforte—a few simple tunes she plays with minimal skill. She can't even read music."

Maeve groaned to herself. What had she been thinking of? She should have realized a shy recluse who rarely stepped outside the boundaries of Barrington Hall would have no chance of studying music with a master teacher.

"I am Meg's twin sister, Maeve," she admitted in a whisper. If nothing else, Richard's look of grave concern told her she must be honest with him.

"Good heavens! I had heard a vague rumor about the existence of such a person when I was a boy . . . I thought it was merely scandalbroth invented by one of the village gossips." His eyes narrowed. "But where do you come from, and why are you here posing as Margaret? And, dear God, where *is* Margaret? I must know if she is well—and safe."

"The squire assured me she is with her aunt in the Scottish Highlands," Maeve said. Over his shoulder, she could see Theo working his way through the crowd toward them. "As for your other questions, I can't answer them here. Call on me at Barrington Hall tomorrow morning; I promise I'll tell you everything I know."

She pulled free of his grasp. "Now leave please before the earl descends on us, demanding to know why you're manhandling me."

Richard's face turned a deep crimson, and he mumbled what sounded like an apology. "I cannot leave without paying my respects to my hostess," he protested.

"I'll make your apologies. Just leave while you have the chance." Maeve gave him a gentle shove, afraid to trust him to keep her secret in his present agitated state of mind.

"Very well then, until tomorrow morning. I shall be there no later than ten o'clock." With a furtive glance in Theo's direction, he disappeared through the nearest open door.

"What was that all about?" Theo asked a moment later, his gaze riveted on the fingermarks Richard had left on Maeve's arms.

"Nothing of consequence." She managed a smile. "Richard and I were simply disagreeing about the . . . the relative merits of Haydn versus Mozart."

"Indeed? Then why did he feel it necessary to skitter away like a cutpurse caught with his fingers in another man's pocket when he saw me approaching?"

"He did not 'skitter.' He simply remembered he needed to make a call on one of his parishioners who . . . who is about to give birth," Maeve said, remembering the excuse Richard had used on Sunday. She had always prided herself on her truthfulness; she was amazed at how easily she'd taken to lying in the past few days. It occurred to her there might be deficiencies in her character of which she had never before been aware.

Theo's scowl deepened. "Very well, Meg, if you say so, I shall accept your word . . . in this instance. But never bother trying to lie to me again about your friendship with Richard— or about anything else. I am an astute judge of character, and you have the kind of face that gives you away every time."

For the life of him, Theo couldn't imagine what he'd said that sent Meg into such gales of laughter. Nor would she divulge her reason, no matter how much he quizzed her. In the end, he chalked it up to her eccentric nature, and let it go at that.

"The party is over, and the guests are leaving, but I'd like a few minutes alone with you before you depart for home," he said, abruptly changing the subject. The truth was, this incredible musical talent of hers made her more intriguing than ever, and he was determined to discover where and how she had learned to play with such skill and passion.

"With the weather as it is, we can't go out on the terrace," he continued, pointing to the streaming window. "But we're very near the family portrait gallery. We can stroll there to our hearts' content."

Without waiting to see whether or not she was in agreement, he picked up a candelabra from a nearby ivory and ebony pier table, propelled her through the door Richard had just exited, and across the hall into the gallery. "My father," he said indicating the first portrait.

Maeve studied the somewhat dissolute-looking former earl. "He was very handsome," she said. "You have his features."

"But not his coloring." Theo made a sweeping gesture with the candelabra. "Nor, for that matter, the coloring of any of my predecessors. I must be a throwback to some distant ancestor who failed to have his portrait painted."

"Like an Italian gardener," she said with what sounded very much like a giggle, then blushed furiously.

"Very possibly," Theo admitted, startled by her surprisingly earthy sense of humor. He stifled the laugh rising in his throat. "But I must say, Miss Barrington, I consider it most unladylike of you to suggest such a thing."

She sobered instantly. "I know. I keep forgetting."

"Forgetting what, Meg?"

"That I am supposed to act like a lady."

"Ah, yes, that." He surveyed her flaming cheeks. "For some reason I cannot begin to explain, your rather amazing admission reminds me that I haven't kissed you since Sunday morning. How are we ever to become sufficiently acquainted to enter comfortably into marriage at that rate?"

"How, indeed?" She regarded him with solemn, trusting eyes, and Theo felt a twinge of guilt. She had naively accepted his claim that engaged couples were expected to do a great deal of kissing. With no one but that vulgar old housekeeper and a maid or two at Barrington Hall, who was there to tell her differently? He was free to kiss her whenever he wished.

He placed the candelabra on a nearby credenza and drew her into his arms. The sweet little ninny obviously knew nothing of the ways of the world outside the borders of her father's estate. Just thinking about all he would have to teach her after they were married lent a fervor to his kiss that would have seriously shocked most innocent virgins. But Meg Barrington was not the average innocent virgin—a blessing for which Theo sincerely thanked his Creator.

As always, she responded to him with an eagerness that made him curse the fact that he must wait a decent interval after the engagement announcement before setting their wedding date.

He found himself wondering if she realized what a temptation she was offering with her daring decolleté, and how she would react if he should kiss the two alluring mounds that were all but popping out of the neckline of her gown. Bending his head, he pressed his lips to her creamy flesh, and felt a shock of awareness ripple through her.

She burrowed her heated face into his shoulder and clung to him as if seeking his protection against . . . what? The lustful beast that was himself?

This time the guilt that assailed him was considerably more than a twinge. With firm determination, he put her at arm's length, lest the feelings she aroused in him should drive him to lose all sense of decency. The one thing he hadn't counted on when he entered into this agreement with the squire was that he would lose his head over—and possibly his heart to—the very woman he had been so reluctant to offer for.

He might not be in love with Meg Barrington; he had never really believed in that elusive emotion. But he was most certainly in lust, and propriety be damned, he would speak with the squire in the morning. He could see no practical reason why he should put himself through the torture of waiting until autumn to claim the little temptress as his bride.

Some moments later, having walked her to her carriage, he watched her driven away through the rainy night. "Hell and damnation!" he exclaimed, suddenly remembering he'd completely forgotten to quiz her on how she had managed to gain such expertise on the pianoforte while hidden away in a place as devoid of culture as Barrington Hall.

Ah, well, tomorrow was another day and he'd already planned to call on the squire. He would seek her out and quiz her about it once he'd concluded the business of setting a wedding date.

Sketchbook in hand, Maeve seated herself on one of the garden benches to wait for Richard's arrival the following morning. A brisk southerly wind had blown away the last remnants of the rainstorm during the night. The air felt delightfully fresh, and every leaf and blade of grass sparkled in the warm sunshine.

Her spirits lifted. Surely, nothing too disastrous could happen on a glorious morning like this. She would tell Richard the truth as she knew it—except, she quickly amended, for the payment she was demanding for her part in the madcap scheme. She salved her conscience with the thought that men of the cloth were notoriously dense where business transactions were concerned, and she would only confuse him by revealing the arrangement between the squire and herself.

No, she decided, the mild-mannered vicar was no problem. She could handle him. But as for Theo . . . now there was a magus with a different bag of tricks. Every time she came in contact with him, she felt less in control of her mental and emotional faculties. If she had a grain of sense, she would make certain she was never again caught alone with the annoying fellow. For sooner or later, she was bound to say or do something she would seriously regret.

Frustrated by the very thought, she resolutely dismissed him from her mind and opened her sketchbook. Leafing through the pages, she came to the half-finished cartoon that was the next in her series about the men who were known as the Regent's inner circle. This one, at the request of her editor, was on that fascinating fellow, Beau Brummell.

Thanks to the Regent's slavish admiration, Brummell had enjoyed a good many years as fashionable London's most influential arbiter of dress and etiquette. But he and the prince had recently had a falling out, and Brummell's star was rapidly descending.

Maeve knew the Beau well. He had been a close friend of Lily's for many years, and one of the few people to attend her funeral. Brummell's caustic wit and irreverence for the dictates of polite society had always fascinated Maeve. Like him, she didn't suffer fools gladly, even if they were titled fools.

Now she was torn between loyalty to a friend in trouble and the need to keep her means of employment. For she hadn't the slightest doubt that her editor would replace Marcus Browne in an instant if she failed to satisfy his urge to join the rest of the bloodthirsty media who were thrusting their *literae scriptae* swords into the fallen hero. She had started the piece a dozen times, only to give it up in disgust.

Flipping to a blank page, she began the sketch once again. But to her surprise, instead of Brummell's fashionable form, the figure emerging beneath her pencil had unruly black hair, amused dark eyes, and a torso rippling with powerful muscles.

She stared in disbelief at what she'd drawn. Was she becoming so obsessed with Theo, he was beginning to control her innermost thoughts? And why? Because his kisses made her heart pound and her blood race through her veins?

The old fear that she'd kept buried deep within her since the day she'd realized she'd reached womanhood rose to haunt her. There was no longer any doubt about it. *She had inherited her mother's promiscuous nature.* Thoroughly disgusted with herself, she closed the sketchbook and laid it facedown beside her on the bench.

Just in time, as it turned out. For a moment later, Richard stood before her wearing the same fierce scowl as when she'd last seen him some twelve hours before. "You promised me an explanation of this havey-cavey business you're involved in. It had better be a good one, or I shall be forced to inform my benefactor, the earl, of your duplicity."

Patiently, Maeve related all that had transpired since the squire sought her out in London. "So you see," she concluded, "I absolutely must maintain my masquerade until I know for certain what my twin's wishes are concerning the earl."

"I agree. Under the circumstances, you can do nothing less." Richard frowned. "But I find it most surprising that Margaret would run away as the squire claims. It is true, she's painfully shy, but I'd swear that for all her timid ways, she's pluck to the bone."

His brow furrowed. "You said the squire assured you she was with her aunt in Scotland. But how do you know he was telling the truth? The evil old reprobate is, among other things, an inveterate liar."

That same thought had occurred to Maeve when she'd been unable to pin the squire down as to when Meg would return, but hearing it on Richard's lips gave it a frightening credence. "I wish I knew how to communicate with my sister," she declared. "I doubt she is even aware of my existence. I certainly knew nothing about her until the squire sought me out in London a few days ago."

Richard's smile had an air of triumph about it. "I have Lady MacDougal's direction. Margaret and I corresponded when she visited her aunt two years ago. If you write to her, I will personally see that it's posted. Better yet, I'll hire one of the village lads who's an expect horseman to take it to Scotland for me."

It was the first encouraging thing that had happened since Maeve had begun her madcap masquerade. She immediately wrote a letter describing everything that had occurred since her fateful meeting with the squire. It covered two full sheets of paper from her sketch pad, and with the exception of Theo's kisses and her bewildering reaction to them, was accurate down to the last detail. She ended it with, "Dear sister, let me know your wishes. We are neither of us helpless pawns in this scheme of our father's as long as we stand together."

Folding it into a neat square, she handed it to Richard, who left immediately to send it on its way. His parting words were, "It could take a fortnight or more to receive a reply, so you might be obliged to pose as your twin longer than you'd planned."

Maeve's heart sank. Under no circumstances did she dare stay one day beyond the fortnight to which she'd originally agreed. Come what may, she would collect the money due her and travel to London by mail coach if her father refused her the use of his carriage.

But she held her tongue. The earnest young vicar was the last person to whom she could explain that she was desperate to leave Kent, because every day she stayed at Barrington Hall, her resistance to Theo's subtle but persistent seduction grew weaker.

She was too aware of her own deficiencies of face and form to believe he desired her as passionately as his kisses suggested. She strongly suspected the rakehell was "hedging his bet" as her gambling-mad mother would say. For how could his heiress of choice refuse to marry him once she was well and truly compromised?

Her duty was clear. For Meg's sake, as well as her own, she must stand firm against Theo's magnetic charms—and against her own wanton nature.

So engrossed was she in her grim thoughts, she failed to notice the tall, black-haired man approaching along the garden path. Not until he stood so close his broad shoulders blocked out the sun did she look up.

By then it was too late to raise her guard, and she could see that Theo had the same wicked glint in his eyes that had been her undoing in the portrait gallery the night before.

Instinctively, she braced herself, certain she was about to face the first test of her brave new resolve.

Chapter Eight

"**W**as that Richard I saw leaving the garden as I came across the terrace?" Theo had that look on his face again—the one he'd worn when he'd accused her of "dangling Richard like a puppet on a string."

Maeve shrugged. "As a matter of fact, it was."

"I thought we agreed you should discourage his attention."

"That, my lord, was your idea. I agreed to no such thing. Richard is my vicar, my confidante, and my friend; I refuse to tell him he cannot call on me."

Sparks of anger flashed in Theo's dark eyes. "Devil take it, Meg, I will not be disobeyed in this. I have no intention of allowing my wife to keep a cicisbeo in tow, even if the spineless fellow is her vicar."

"Richard is not spineless, as well you know," Maeve declared, "and luckily, since I am not your wife, I am under no obligation to obey you in this or any other matter."

Theo's smile was triumphant. "That, my dear termagant, is a situation which will soon be rectified. I have just this morning informed the squire that I want our wedding date moved forward to the first day of June—a plan with which he is in full agreement. That should give us ample time to post our banns and prepare for a simple country wedding, since you've already shopped for your bride clothes."

Shock propelled Maeve to her feet. The first of June was just a little over a fortnight away. Chances were she would not have heard from Meg by that time, much less formulate her plan to thwart this latest scheme hatched by their wily father and the earl. It was becoming more and more obvious that the squire didn't care which daughter he married off to the earl, so long as the conditions of the Barrington Hall land grant were fulfilled.

She felt momentarily gripped by panic, until she remembered a piece of advice Lily had given her not long before she died. *If ever you find yourself cornered by some man, silly goose, strike back. It's the last thing the fools expect a woman to do, and it throws them off guard every time.*

Maeve raised her chin to a defiant level and stared Theo straight in the eye. "How dare you make such a decision without consulting me, you unconscionable tyrant!" She clenched her fist and waved it in his face. "I hadn't yet convinced myself I'd be ready to marry you in September; I know bloody well I won't be in June. You and the squire will simply have to make other plans."

The haughty arrogance Theo was so adept at assuming slid over him like a familiar mantle. "You forget yourself, my dear," he said with icy disdain. "The truth is a woman has little to say in such matters."

His feisty betrothed tossed her head. "Unless that woman is two and twenty. Then, by English law no man, including her father, can force her to marry. And if you think the evil old devil can bring me to heel by threatening to withdraw his support, you are dead wrong, my lord. My aunt has offered me a home in the Scottish Highlands should the squire's domineering ways become unbearable."

Theo felt a stab of something closely resembling fear. He couldn't believe Meg would actually consider breaking their engagement. Was it possible she hadn't yet realized how perfectly they suited each other?

Catching hold of her shoulders, he drew her to him. "Are you saying you would prefer living with your old aunt to living as my wife?"

She offered no resistance, but her little pointed chin rose yet another inch. "That is exactly what I'm saying, my lord. If this latest bit of business is any example of the treatment I could expect at your hands, I would simply be exchanging one tyrant for another if I married you. Anything would be preferable to that."

Now he was a tyrant. Theo felt consumed with rage that this insignificant country miss should judge him, the Earl of Lynley, and find him wanting. "Of all the charges you could level against me, tyranny is the most unjust," he declared indignantly. "You have only to inquire of my servants and tenant farmers to learn I am a scrupulously fair master. I would certainly be no less to my wife."

The cheeky miss actually sneered at him. "A benevolent tyrant is still a tyrant, my lord."

Theo loosed his hold on her arms. *Deuce take it, she was serious.* It had never before occurred to him that a woman might desire such things as freedom and independence. Those were male ideals; females were supposed to be content with comfort and security and a babe or two to dandle on their knees. He was beginning to think this woman he'd chosen to marry was not only eccentric—she was downright unnatural.

She was also, unfortunately, correct about the legal status of a single woman over one-and-twenty. Neither he nor her father could force her to marry him. Theo took a deep, calming breath, but his heart still thudded painfully in his chest. The truth was he found it absolutely unthinkable that Meg Barrington, and her sizable fortune, would not one day belong to him.

Furthermore, the most disquieting aspect of the bizarre situation in which he found himself was that her fortune was no longer his primary reason for wanting her. He wanted Meg, herself, with every fiber of his being, and the very fact that she rebelled at his normal male dominance made her appear more intriguing than ever—and more intensely feminine.

It was almost laughable. The stubborn, pigheaded woman was threatening to take up permanent spinsterhood in some godforsaken homecroft in the Scottish Highlands, when he had but to touch her to turn her into a quivering mass of female passion.

Like all women, she was totally illogical, which was undoubtedly the reason why English law was so clear as to the absolute rights of a husband over his wife. Ergo, all he had to do was get his wedding ring on the chit's finger and his troubles would be over. But until he'd accomplished that feat, he would have to play his cards close to his chest.

"Very well," he said, his tongue firmly lodged in his cheek, "I apologize for not consulting you about the change of wedding date. It was, as you say, inexcusably high-handed of me. I can only plead that I was carried away by my intense admiration for you."

She raised a skeptical eyebrow. He ignored it and favored her with a smile sincere enough to melt the heart of the most hardened cynic. "Tell me your wishes on the subject, dear lady, and perhaps we can agree on a compromise."

Maeve answered Theo smile for smile. But she didn't trust his motives. He'd backed down much too easily to her way of thinking. Still, he had given her the opening she needed to postpone the wedding long enough to hear from Meg and to collect the money due her from the squire.

"My wish is . . ." She stared into the distance, pretending to contemplate the weighty subject. "My wish is to have enough time to really get to know you before we marry. Not just how you kiss"—she felt a flush creep into her cheeks—"but how you think about . . . about important things. I believe a happy marriage must be built on a foundation of trust and respect. Two weeks is not long enough to create such a relationship."

Theo clasped his hands behind his back and rocked onto his heels. "Ah, I see. In other words, you want to be properly courted. I should have known a woman who played the pianoforte with such passion was a romantic at heart."

"Romance is not what I had in mind," Maeve protested. A sinking feeling in the pit of her stomach warned her he was purposely twisting her words to suit himself.

He silenced her with another devastating smile. "Very well, we will set our wedding date for the first week in July. I am in the midst of repairing the damage that years of neglect have wrought on my estate, but I shall arrange my work so I may spend an hour or two each day with you. Surely, with a routine such as that, we can become sufficiently acquainted in six weeks' time to marry as friends, not strangers."

"That is too much to ask of you. I would feel guilty interrupting your work," Maeve sputtered, aware she'd gotten much more than she'd bargained for. The last thing she needed was to spend part of each day in Theo's company. The rake was too charming by half. She'd be lucky if her poor beleaguered bluestocking heart wasn't smashed into a million pieces by the time she returned to London.

"Not to worry. My reward will be the satisfaction of knowing I have put your mind at ease about our future life together." Theo gently clasped her right hand and raised it to his lips. "And what better time to begin my campaign to win your approval than right now. I drove over in my curricle in the hope you would enjoy a ride on this fine spring day. Would you do me the honor of accompanying me on my inspection tour of my estate, my dear? I'll wait here while you fetch your bonnet."

Maeve opened her mouth to say no, but nothing came out. Her fingers tingled where Theo's lips had touched them, and her heart pounded so loudly against her ribs, she couldn't hear herself think. In the end, she simply nodded and fled toward the manor house to do as he bid.

Not until she reached her bedchamber and donned one of Meg's prettiest chip straw bonnets did she remember she had left her sketchbook lying in plain sight on the garden bench.

Theo was sitting with the sketchbook on his lap, staring at the drawing she'd done of him, when she returned. He looked up, amazement stamped on his handsome features. "You are a woman of many talents, Meg," he said gravely.

Maeve gulped. "Only two, actually, and now you've seen them both."

Theo glanced down at the drawing in his lap. "I'm curious. How did you gain such expertise living in a provincial area like Kent all your life?"

"I taught myself to draw as a means to—" She almost said "make a living," but luckily stopped herself in time. "As a means to pass the time," she finished quickly. "As you can see, I have much to learn before I could be called an expert."

"On the contrary, this likeness of myself is quite accurate, and the drawings of the dandy on the other pages look amazingly like my friend George Brummell. But how could a country recluse become acquainted with the infamous Beau?"

Maeve managed a shaky laugh, but quickly sat down before her legs gave out beneath her. "I am not acquainted with him, of course," she said, "except through cartoons I've seen drawn by that clever fellow George Cruikshank."

"From the number of unfinished drawings of him in this book, you would appear to be obsessed with the fashionable fribble." Theo's eyes narrowed. "What, may I ask, is the attraction he holds for you?"

"There is no attraction. Only frustration that I cannot seem to capture his wonderful arrogance, as Mr. Cruikshank did."

"I see. How interesting that you find Beau Brummell's arrogance 'wonderful' when I distinctly remember your declaring the same trait in me 'monstrous' and 'disconcerting.'"

Maeve smiled in spite of herself. "I do not have to deal with Mr. Brummell."

"Touché, little termagant." Theo chuckled. Setting the sketchbook beside him on the bench, he rose to his feet. "Which reminds me, it's time we began our program of learning to deal with each other."

With a graceful bow, he captured her hand and drew her up beside him. "You may begin by telling me how you learned to play the pianoforte with such skill—and don't try to tell me you taught yourself, for I know that's impossible."

"My teacher was a French emigré who lived with us for four years," Maeve said, deciding the closer she could stay to the truth, the safer she would be.

"Was he really?" Theo offered her his arm, and they strolled along the garden path to the waiting curricle, where he helped her into the passenger's seat. "I find it strange that I've never heard mention of him in the village. I should think such a fellow would be prime fodder for the local gossip mill."

"Henri never went into the village. He was an even greater recluse than I," Maeve said, frantically trying to think of a way to change the subject. It came to her with her first glimpse of Theo's curricle and pair. Lily had often claimed that men of title were notoriously horse mad and prone to bore one to death expounding on the virtues of their prime cattle.

"What a gorgeous pair of bays," she exclaimed. "You must be prodigiously proud of them."

"I can take no credit for them. They were my father's." Theo's narrowed eyes told her he knew exactly what she was doing, but to her relief, he obligingly dropped the subject of her musical training.

"So, Meg, I take it you are an enthusiastic horsewoman—as all true country women are," he said as he guided his pair of bays through the gateway and onto the road beyond.

Maeve swallowed hard. "I'm not certain 'enthusiastic' is the proper word to describe how I feel about horses," she ventured. In truth, she had never ridden one of the beasts and found the very idea utterly terrifying.

"I ride every morning at sunrise," Theo said. "I shall look forward to your joining me . . . maybe tomorrow."

"Maybe," Maeve agreed weakly, wondering what excuse she could come up with short of dying in bed to avoid beginning her morning in such a hellish way. She shivered, despite the warm sun beaming down on her. How much longer, she wondered, before her luck ran out and the house of lies she'd constructed came tumbling down around her ears?

They rode in companionable silence through the lush, spring-green countryside, first on Barrington land, then on Ravenswood, until, as he'd planned, Theo saw the first of the cottages belonging to his tenant farmers come into sight. He had an ulterior motive in bringing Meg to this particular cottage. Annie Jennings had given birth to her fourth child two days earlier, and he wanted to see how Meg reacted to the newborn.

So far, everything he'd learned about her had convinced him she was the woman with whom he wanted to spend the rest of his life. Except, of course, for her tendency to stretch the truth about such odd things as her mysterious music teacher. A French emigré indeed! Didn't she realize servants carried tales? Everyone in the village would have known within the hour if such a fellow had arrived at Barrington Hall.

Ah, well, he thought, that one shortcoming was of little consequence compared to her many virtues. He felt certain that once they were married, he could convince her she no longer needed to make up ridiculous stories to gain his attention.

This test today would be the most important of all. If she displayed the kind of maternal instincts he suspected she had, she would indeed be the perfect wife for him and the perfect mother for the children he longed to sire.

"I thought we'd begin our inspection by stopping to congratulate John and Annie Jennings on the birth of their new daughter," he said.

His betrothed's eyes instantly lighted up, just as he'd hoped they would. "A new baby? How exciting," she exclaimed. "Oh, I am glad you thought to share this with me, Theo."

A few moments later, he drew up in front of a neat little cottage surrounded by a garden in which the tops of early spring vegetables were just poking their heads above the carefully tilled soil. The young father answered their knock—the sleeping baby in his arms, a worried look on his face, and three small children clinging to his trousers.

He blinked as if the sunlight hurt his eyes. "How kind of you to come, my lord, and with your lady, too." He stepped aside to let them enter. "Annie will be that proud."

Maeve watched Theo's black brows draw together in a frown. "Is everything all right, John?" he asked. "You look a bit pulled."

John Jennings gave a heartfelt sigh. "We've a collicky one this time. I was up all night walking the floor with the wee mite." He hesitated, a furtive look on his thin, young face. "And I'm that worried about my Annie. She's not getting her strength back as fast as she did with the other babes. It's not that she's sick with the childbed fever or anything like that, but she just . . . she just cries all the time, and I don't know what to say to make her stop."

Maeve studied the three tow-headed stairsteps clustered around him, the oldest of whom couldn't yet be five years, and decided the poor woman was probably crying from sheer exhaustion.

"May I hold the baby?" she asked, and a moment later cuddled the blanket-wrapped babe to her breast while the young farmer left to inform his wife of the arrival of their distinguished visitors.

It was the first newborn infant Maeve had ever held, and she found the sensation so overwhelming she felt as if her heart would burst. The tiny girl-child smelled indescribably sweet and milky, and her little rosebud mouth worked as if she were dreaming of suckling at her mother's breast. Maeve buried her nose in the silky curls atop the baby's head and gave herself up to the pure joy of the moment.

"You look very natural with a babe in your arms, Meg. You will make a wonderful mother for our children," Theo said, and there was no mistaking the emotion in his deep voice. Startled, Maeve raised her head and stared into a pair of dark, fathomless eyes, whose tender expression warmed her to the very depths of her soul—until she remembered that if he knew the truth about her, she would be the last woman on earth he would want as the mother of his children.

"Annie can see you now, my lord." John Jennings's voice snapped her out of her painful reverie and, with the babe still in her arms, she followed the two men into the one other room of the tiny cottage. Theo drew a gold sovereign from his pocket and laid it on the crude table beside the bed. "Congratulations on your lovely daughter, Annie."

"Thank you, my lord," the young mother said, but tears spilled from her eyes, and she turned her head and stared at the wall. John Jennings exchanged a puzzled look with Theo, and as if on cue, the two men tiptoed from the room.

Gently, Maeve laid the sleeping baby in her cradle and prepared to follow them until she glanced toward the bed and saw that Annie Jennings's tear-filled blue eyes were following her every move. The forlorn look in those eyes told her the young mother desperately needed to talk to another woman.

She closed the door behind the men, then stepped to the side of the bed and took Annie's hand in hers. "You have a beautiful baby," she said because she could think of nothing else to say.

Annie nodded, spreading a wealth of golden hair across the coarsely woven pillow cover. "Aye, and three more, and barely a full year between any of them."

"Four children in less than five years. You must be worn out."

Annie nodded again. "I am that, my lady," she whispered, and Maeve saw a look of abject terror in her eyes.

"But that's not why you're crying. What is it that's troubling you? Tell me, Annie. I promise nothing you say will go beyond this room, and maybe I can help."

The girl's fingers tightened on Maeve's, and she closed her eyes as if attempting to shut out the specter that haunted her. "I don't want to die and leave my brood for another woman to raise. I want to see my children grown. I want to live to hold a grandchild in my arms."

"Of course you do," Maeve soothed. "But why should you think you won't?"

"Because next year there'll be another babe, and the year after that another—and another and another without ever a chance to gain back my strength in between—until a few years from now I'll be so worn out I'll just give up and die. I've seen it happen time and again with women I've known."

Annie choked back a sob. "It's not that I don't love my babes, for I do with all my heart, and I'd not take all the gold in England for a hair off one of their dear little heads. But we've scarce enough food to fill the bellies of the ones we have now. God only knows how we'll feed the ones to come."

"I can understand your dilemma," Maeve said. "Maybe you should talk to your husband about it. He seems a kindhearted fellow."

"John's a good man, and that's the trouble. I can't turn him away when he comes to me for comfort after working so hard all day in the fields. But every time he touches me . . . you know, that way . . . there's another babe on the way."

Maeve gave Annie's hand a comforting pat. "Perhaps there's another way around your problem." She hesitated, wondering if she dare pursue this line of conversation with a young woman who but a few moments ago had been a complete stranger to her. The utter despair she read in Annie's face decided her.

"I understand," she began hesitantly, then cleared her throat and started again. "I've heard tell there are ways to prevent having babies."

"I've heard so, too," Annie said, her eyes wide and solemn. "And 'twould be the answer to my prayers, but I daren't ask any of the village women if they know how 'tis done, for my mam said 'tis a thing only a whore would know about." Her mouth twisted in a bitter smile. "I wish some whore had told my mam the secret. She died in childbirth with her tenth babe the year I married John."

Two bright spots of color flamed in Annie's cheeks, but her steadfast gaze never wavered from Maeve's face. "I got to tell you, my lady, there's gossip in the village that the titled and the gentry look at such things different from us ordinary folk."

"I suppose that's true in some cases," Maeve agreed.

Annie searched Maeve's face hopefully. "Then I got to ask—do you know how to keep from having a babe every time a man and wife does . . . that?"

Maeve was sorely tempted to tell her no. Regardless of what Annie had heard, it was not the sort of information a proper lady should have at her disposal. But the girl was obviously desperate, and understandably so.

Maeve cleared her throat again. "Mind you, I've no firsthand knowledge of such things, but I once knew a lady who was a very forward thinker. She believed every woman should have such knowledge in case she found herself in a situation such as you're in now."

Annie took a death grip on Maeve's fingers. "And did she tell you, my lady?"

Maeve nodded. "As a matter of fact, she did, and if you promise never to divulge where you heard it, I'll tell you what she said."

Annie gave her solemn promise, and for the next few minutes, Maeve related everything she could remember that Lily had told her about how to prevent an unwanted pregnancy. It was information that, at the time, she protested she neither needed nor wanted. She was glad now that Lily had insisted on educating her about such matters. For Annie was right. At the rate she was producing offspring, she'd be lucky to live long enough to see her oldest child reach the age of ten.

When at long last Maeve opened the door and stepped into the other room, she couldn't bring herself to meet Theo's questioning gaze. Her frank discussion with the troubled young mother had left her feeling unusually shy and embarrassed around him—not to mention considerably more guilty than she'd already felt about deceiving him. She had, after all, shared information with one of his tenants that only a hardened

Cyprian would normally know. She doubted even an inveterate rake like Lynley would countenance behavior that unconventional.

It was all too apparent their frank discussion had neither embarrassed Annie nor turned her up shy. Glancing over her shoulder, Maeve saw her sitting up in bed, grinning from ear to ear. "Thank you again for the gold sovereign, my lord," she called out. "I shall add it to the three others you gave me when you returned from the wars."

John Jennings stared first at his wife, then at Maeve, a look of wonder on his face. "Will you look at what your lovely lady's done, my lord," he marveled. "A few words of kindness from her sweet, innocent mouth, and here's my Annie, her old happy self again."

Chapter Nine

Theo returned in high spirits to the Ravenswood manor house some two hours later. His tenants had all responded to Meg's quiet charm with the same enthusiasm as the Jenningses. She'd held their babies and admired their gardens, shook hands with the men and chatted with the women, and generally deported herself in a restrained but friendly manner that had obviously won the respect of one and all.

She'd even ducked her head in that demure way she had, and admitted she'd often longed to speak to the women after Sunday service in the village church, but she'd always been too shy to do so. This, of course, had only endeared her more to the plainspoken people whose families had worked the land for as long as his family had owned it.

Yes, indeed, Meg would make a fine mistress for Ravenswood and for his two lesser estates. With her at his side, there would be none of the barely concealed animosity his tenants had shown toward his mother on the rare occasions when she'd accompanied him on his inspection tours.

Things were looking up—or so he thought until he handed his horse to a solemn-faced groom and entered the door of the manor house to find utter bedlam. Two of the maids were huddled at the foot of the staircase, weeping copiously; a young footman appeared about to do the same; and Mrs. Heatherwood, the housekeeper, stood above them on the landing, looking for all the world like one of the fire-eating dragons of ancient mythology.

The dragon advanced on Theo, eyes blazing, the moment she saw him. "Just like that, she sacked him, my lord, because his hand shook when he served the tea and a mite sloshed on the sour-faced duke—and him serving the Earls of Lynley for more than forty-five years. No disrespect to my betters, but it's not right, and it fair broke the old man's heart."

It took no imagination on Theo's part to figure out who had sacked whom. His mother had apparently flown into one of her rages and discharged Doddsworth, the ancient butler who had served three generations of the Hampton family through triumph and tragedy with quiet distinction.

What in God's name was the woman thinking of? Doddsworth was as much a fixture at Ravenswood as the bronze lions at the gate and the Gobelin tapestries and Baccarat chandeliers that decorated the drafty entryway.

"Where is Doddsworth?" Theo asked. Repairing the old man's injured feelings was the important thing at the moment; he would deal with his mother later.

"In his chamber, packing his things. If you've a mind to speak to him, my lord, I'll show you the way."

Theo raised a hand to forestall her. "I know the way, Mrs. Heatherwood." Many's the time he'd sought refuge from his mother's rigid discipline in Doddsworth's neat little apartment when he was a lad. The one place the countess would never demean herself to enter was the servants' quarters.

He knocked on the butler's chamber door to find, as reported, that Doddsworth was indeed packing a battered brown valise—probably the same one he'd brought with him when he'd begun his service at Ravenswood nearly half a century before.

Theo clasped the old fellow's hand in his, shocked to see how uncontrollably it shook. No wonder he'd spilled the blasted tea. "So, Doddsworth," he said, "what's this I hear about you and my mother having a run-in?"

"It was all my fault, my lord. I should never have tried to pour, what with my hands shaking as they do nowadays. I'm just a pride-foolish old man, too stubborn to let loose of the reins." His rheumy eyes glistened with unshed tears. "I should have retired when the old earl died, but I convinced myself you needed me until you settled in."

"And so I did, Doddsworth."

"But now, look what I've done. Disgraced myself and dis-

graced Ravenswood as well, to my everlasting shame. Did they
tell you it was the Duke of Kent I spilled on?"

"The Duke of Kent be damned. I thoroughly despise the
pawky fellow. I hope he'll be gone in a day or two, and this
sorry business will be forgotten. I'll smooth things over with
my mother and—"

"No, my lord. You've enough on your plate as it is without a
doddering old fool like me to worry about. The number one
footman can take over my duties. The kindhearted fellow's
been quietly relieving me of more than half of them for the past
year, though he thinks I don't know it. I'm tired, my lord, and
more than ready to spend the summer sitting in the sun outside
my sister's cottage in Surrey. She's been after me to move in
with her ever since she was widowed five years ago."

"Are you certain that's what you want, Doddsworth? I wish
you'd reconsider. It won't seem like Ravenswood without you
at the helm."

"I'm certain, my lord, now that I know you've found yourself a fine lady to be your countess. Anyone with eyes in his
head can see yours will be a happy marriage, unlike that of your
poor father, if you'll pardon my saying so."

"I doubt my parents' unhappiness was a secret from the
staff—certainly not from you," Theo said dryly. "Neither of
them made any effort to hide the fact that they despised each
other, as well as the only issue that came of their hell-spawned
union."

"Never think that, my lord. Your father loved you in his fashion. If he hadn't, he wouldn't have gone to such lengths to protect your claim to the earldom. If he spent little time with you
when you were a lad, it was more than likely because you were
too painful a reminder of . . . of the unhappy past. But forgive
me, my lord, I've said far more than I've a right to."

Snapping the ancient valise shut, he straightened up and
smiled fondly at Theo. "I've watched you grow from a wee
babe into a strong man worthy of the title and responsibilities
you've come into, and I'm proud to have served you and your
father and your grandfather before you. But it's younger hands
you'll be needing for what's ahead of you now, so if you'll be

kind enough to give me the loan of a carriage to carry me to the coaching inn at Maidstone, I'll be on my way."

"The carriage and John Coachman with it are yours for as long as it takes to carry you to your sister's cottage in Surrey," Theo declared. "And if you'll leave her direction with my man-of-affairs, I'll instruct him to send your pension to you there each quarter from now on."

Overcome with emotion, Theo abandoned all thought of social decorum, clasped the frail old butler in his arms, and gave him a fierce hug that left them both close to tears. "God bless you, Doddsworth," he managed in a strangled voice, "and don't be surprised to find me dropping in for a cup of tea the next time I'm on my way to London."

The old man pulled a square of linen from his pocket and blew his nose. "I'll be looking forward to it, my lord."

"Well, that's that then," Theo said, and without further ado, he marched down the three flights of stairs to the entryway and sent a footman to the stables with orders to his coachman to ready his crested traveling coach. Then, through the myriad hallways of Ravenswood he strode to where Nigel Farnham, the man-of-affairs he'd inherited from his father, maintained his cluttered little office.

"Doddsworth is retiring," he announced as he threw open the door. "You'll need to set up an adequate pension, to be paid quarterly, so he can live out his remaining years in comfort."

Farnham looked up from the account book on which he was working, a smile on his heavily jowled face. "Yes, my lord. Luckily, that will be no problem since I received notification from our London banker just yesterday that the squire has already transferred a sizable portion of Miss Barrington's dowry into your account. I shall simply start a new sheet in the pension ledger."

"We have other servants currently on pension? I don't recall seeing any such accounts when I went over the books with you last winter."

"You would not have, my lord. The pension accounts are in a separate ledger that is locked in my safe. Only the total quarterly amount is entered in the general ledger."

"Are there any other accounts kept in *your* safe that I may have missed?" Theo asked, struggling to control his temper. Farnham was a good man and kept meticulous records, but prying information out of him was like pulling hens' teeth.

"No, my lord. There is nothing else in my safe except the oilskin packet Doddsworth gave me for safekeeping the day your father died."

"What is in the packet?"

Farnham looked insulted. "I wouldn't know, my lord. It is sealed."

Theo took a deep breath and began again. "Would you be good enough to explain why the pension accounts are secreted away in such a manner?"

A dull red flush darkened Farnham's pasty complexion. "I cannot say, my lord. Your father gave me explicit instructions on my first day of employment, two years ago last March, on how the pension ledger was to be handled. He did not, however, explain why."

"I see," Theo said, but, in truth, he saw no reason whatsoever why something so simple and straightforward need be locked away in a safe. Furthermore, he had a strong suspicion that his man-of-affairs was not being entirely candid with him about this particular matter. He scowled darkly at the portly fellow. "Please retrieve the ledger from the safe, and the oilskin packet as well. I would like to examine them."

Farnham instantly leapt to his feet and sprinted across the room to where the small metal safe was tucked in between two tall wooden file cabinets—not an insignificant accomplishment for a man of his bulk.

"Here they are, my lord," he said breathlessly a moment later, handing the two items to Theo. "As you will see when you look at the ledger, we currently have three pension accounts—Eudora Thistle, your former nanny; Joseph Hogg, the head gardener, who retired four years ago after thirty years of service." He hesitated, and his flush unaccountably deepened.

"And the name of the third pensioner?" Theo asked impatiently.

"Rosa Natoli." Farnham's tongue slid over the name so rapidly, Theo nearly missed it. "There have, of course, been others over the years," he continued, "but their accounts were closed out when they died."

Theo remembered Eudora Thistle and Joseph Hogg very well. They had both been an integral part of his childhood. But who the devil was Rosa Natoli? The name sounded Italian, and offhand he couldn't recall there ever having been an Italian servant at Ravenswood, or, for that matter, even an Irish, Scottish, or Welsh one. What he could recall very clearly was his mother's often expressed horror of having any servants in her house who did not have staunch English blood flowing through their veins.

There was something havey-cavey here if his father felt it necessary to go to such lengths to keep the pension ledger away from prying eyes—something he felt certain his man-of-affairs knew more about than he was willing to admit. Furthermore, now that he thought about it, Doddsworth had made some rather odd allusions to his father's conduct as well.

He thanked Nigel Farnham for his help, tucked the account book and packet securely under his arm, and declared, "I'll take these with me and look at them when I find time." If, as he suspected, they contained some dark family secret, the last thing he wanted was an audience when he came upon it.

All the way to his bookroom, he speculated on who this woman, Rosa Natoli, might be. Probably some doxy his father had kept as a mistress; even in his fifties, the earl had been a virile man, and few had condemned him for his philandering ways once they'd met his frigid countess.

But why so secretive? His father wouldn't be the first nobleman who'd chosen to support a mistress of whom he was particularly fond. If such an act were seriously frowned upon by society, most of the royal dukes would have been ostracized years ago.

After pouring himself a brandy, Theo settled into the chair behind his desk and opened the account book to the place marked by a strip of wide white ribbon that had yellowed with age. It was the quarter just passed, and Farnham's neat figures clearly showed that the three pensioners he'd mentioned had been duly paid their stipends.

One ledger sheet was allocated for each quarter, and Theo

leafed back through them to where the gardener's name first appeared, then farther yet to when his old nanny had been pensioned off after being replaced by the tutor who'd prepared him for enrollment in Eton. Even that far back, the mysterious Rosa Natoli was listed on each sheet.

One by one he turned the sheets, back fifteen years, twenty years, twenty-five years . . . thirty. Other names appeared and disappeared, always with their occupation and length of service to the Hamptons recorded next to the first listing of their names, but Rosa Natoli's name still headed each ledger sheet.

Finally, toward the front of the book, he found the sheet on which her name first appeared. Her occupation was listed as ladies' maid, her length of service at Ravenswood a mere seven months. Her first quarterly stipend was entered in the ledger on the thirtieth day of June in the year seventeen hundred eighty-two.

Theo's jaw clenched. He was born on the twenty-first day of June in that same year.

The coincidence was so glaring no one, including the village idiot, could come to any conclusion other than the obvious one. Now he understood why Farnham had found the subject of the pension accounts so embarrassing.

"Bloody hell, I'm my father's bastard," he muttered, and an icy chill crept through him that not even the finest French brandy could dispel.

For a long, painful moment he simply stared at the telltale entry in the ledger, his mind too shocked to accept what his eyes had already verified as an indisputable fact. Finally, with shaking fingers, he broke the seal on the oilskin packet.

If he'd had any lingering doubts about his dubious parentage, the folded parchment contained within it quickly dispelled them. Apparently a copy of a document filed with the Master of the King's Records, it stated that the fifth Earl of Lynley acknowledged his son, Theodore Edward James, while born out of wedlock, to be his rightful heir with full legal claim to all titles and lands belonging to the Earls of Lynley. The king's official seal was affixed to the document, and it was witnessed by the Earl of Stamden and the Marquis of Blandford.

Theo stared with unbelieving eyes at the signatures of the

two men he had known since childhood. Neither one had ever given the slightest hint that they were privy to such information about him. He shook his head, hoping to clear the cobwebs from his befuddled mind, but none of what he'd stumbled upon made any sense. Why, of all the bastards his father must have sired in his long career as an unconscionable rake, had he chosen to acknowledge the illegitimate son of an Italian maid as his legal heir? And why had his wife countenanced the bizarre act?

Theo knew instinctively he would receive no answers to these questions from the proud, cold woman he had called "Mother" all his life. Nor did he dare, at this particular moment, confront her concerning her cruel treatment of Doddsworth. Between that and the mind-boggling information he'd just unearthed, he doubted he could keep from strangling the cold-hearted bitch. It was enough that he finally understood why she had never shown him the slightest scrap of tenderness or affection.

But answers he must have, no matter how painful they might be. He made note of Rosa Natoli's direction—the village of Hawkshead in the Lake District. His heart skipped a beat. He'd made a pilgrimage to that very village in his eighteenth year to view the place where his idol, William Wordsworth, had lived in his youth. For all he knew, he might have passed Rosa Natoli on the street and never known she was the woman who'd given him life—then given him away in exchange for a quarterly stipend.

A terrible bitterness welled within him. Most men had only one mother. He apparently had two. One was as cold and brittle as a statue carved from a block of ice—the other a greedy Italian trollop whose only legacy to her abandoned child was the hot blood that flowed in his veins. He knew the one woman all too well. He would make an effort to know the other so he could put a face on the shadowy creature he already despised. Then he would consign them both to hell and get on with his life.

The first shades of evening were creeping over Barrington Hall when one of the Ravenswood grooms delivered Theo's note to Maeve. It was brief and to the point. He would be unable to ride with her the following morning as he'd been called away for a few days on family business.

She clutched the piece of paper to her bosom and offered a prayer of thanks for the reprieve she so desperately needed. Then quickly, she penned a note of her own and directed one of the kennel boys to deliver it to the vicar. He sent his reply back with the same boy. He would be happy to meet her at dawn, and though he doubted it could be accomplished in such a short time, he would do his best to teach her to ride a horse before Theo returned to Ravenswood.

True to his word, Richard arrived shortly after sunup the next morning, driving a donkey cart with two young mares tied to the back of it. The most docile-looking of the two had a sidesaddle on its back. With a curious groom looking on, Maeve quickly climbed into the passenger's seat. A moment later, they were off to a remote section of her father's estate where they could secure the donkey to a tree or fence post and proceed with the riding lesson with no one the wiser.

"This is the pommel," Richard said once it was safe to begin the lesson. He indicated a knob protruding from the front of the saddle. "When I give you a boost up, you must wrap your right leg around it, grasp the reins, and put your left foot into the stirrup iron."

That sounded easy enough. Maeve put her left foot in Richard's cupped hands, grabbed what she could reach of the saddle, and said a small prayer. An instant later, she shot upward and landed with her head hanging down the other side of the horse and her stomach across the saddle seat.

From its spot beneath a nearby tree, the little donkey brayed "Hee-haw, hee-haw, hee-haw." Maeve would have laughed out loud if she could have gotten her breath. It was, she had to admit, a singularly apt pronouncement, considering her present situation.

"Are you all right?" Richard asked anxiously, grasping her around the waist and pulling her back to the ground.

"I . . . I think so," she gasped, pushing the mangled feather on Meg's jaunty little hat out of her eye and straightening the skirt of Meg's emerald green riding habit. She'd halfway suspected the act of riding a horse could prove somewhat difficult, but she'd had no inkling that merely mounting one of the beasts would present such problems. Still, if the silly, vacant-eyed incomparables she'd seen riding in Hyde Park could do it, then devil take it, so could she.

The next two attempts were as fruitless as the first, but on the fourth try, she managed to get her bottom onto the saddle. Unfortunately, her legs were so tangled in the flowing skirt of the riding habit, she could neither hook her right knee over the pommel nor her left toe into the stirrup. Once again, Richard had to lift her down.

"This time we'll try a different approach," he said in the patient tone of voice she suspected he used when teaching the tenant farmers' children their letters. "I'll grasp you around the waist and lift you into the saddle. All you have to do is—"

Maeve grimaced. "I know, hook my right knee over the pommel and put my left toe into the stirrup iron."

"Correct." Richard's hands circled her waist, he gave a mighty heave, and Maeve found herself sitting in the saddle. Instinctively, she hooked her right knee over the pommel, stuck her left toe in the stirrup, and smiled triumphantly down at her teacher, who appeared a bit breathless from his exertion.

The mare shifted restlessly beneath her, nearly unseating her. Maeve flailed her arms helplessly, suddenly remembering there had been a third thing she was supposed to do when mounting.

"The reins," Richard shouted. "For God's sake, catch hold of the reins."

Ah, yes, that was it. Maeve did as he instructed, then wriggled into a slightly more comfortable position in the saddle and asked, "What do I do next? I'm ready to begin riding."

The expression on Richard's face said he had his doubts about that, but he promptly mounted his horse, took the leading rein, and handed her a whip like the one he carried in his right hand. "Just in case you need it," he explained, "though the mare you're riding is trained to voice command, as is Meg's mare."

He smiled reassuringly. "Put your tongue behind your teeth and give a clucking sound to start her off. After that, she'll respond to the words 'walk,' 'trot,' or 'canter.' A gentle 'whoa' or even a strong exhalation through your mouth will bring her to a stop."

So saying, he did something with his knees that set his own horse in motion and started off across the open meadow that lay before them. Maeve made the clucking sound he'd suggested, and the little mare immediately began a slow walk, leaving her with the strange, but not unpleasant, sensation that the very earth itself was moving beneath her.

She smiled to herself. Riding a horse was obviously much easier than she'd thought it would be, once one managed to mount the beast. Theo had said he'd be gone four days or more; by the time he returned, she should have sufficient expertise to carry off her role of a country squire's daughter most convincingly.

"Hee-haw, hee-haw, hee-haw," the little donkey brayed again. Maeve tossed her head defiantly. What did a donkey know?

"Now let's try trotting," Richard said half an hour later. "You can either give a voice command or brush the mare's right shoulder with your whip while you nudge her with your left foot."

Maeve did both, just to be sure, and the mare instantly changed her gait. But what had previously been a gentle, swaying motion now turned into a torturous collection of uneven bumps and jolts that had Maeve hanging onto the reins for dear life. For some reason she could not begin to explain, her body had assumed a rhythm diametrically opposed to that of the horse. With every hitch in the mare's gait, she felt herself rise in the air, only to plop back down with a force that set her ears ringing and her teeth rattling.

"The trot is the most difficult gait for a new rider," Richard declared cheerfully as he fell back to ride beside her. "Once you're adept enough to try a canter, you'll find it much smoother—more like the action of a rocking chair. But I think we should leave that for another day. Walking and trotting are enough to master your first time out."

He cast her a surreptitious look. "You're turning red as a beet. Don't, under any circumstances, forget to breathe. The mare can feel your agitation. You don't want to frighten her."

"God forbid. The last thing we want to do is cause the blasted

horse any discomfort," Maeve said, clamping her teeth together
to keep them from chattering.

Richard chuckled. "Tomorrow will be easier, although you
may find yourself a bit stiff when you first get out of bed. But
with persistence and determination, we'll make a horsewoman
out of you yet, Maeve Barrington." With a nudge of his knee
and a gentle tap of his whip on his horse's shoulder, he again
moved ahead of her.

Maeve's backside was beginning to feel the effects of the
merciless pounding, and her right leg had definitely fallen
asleep, as had the left toe she'd jammed so forcibly into the stirrup iron. Tears of frustration blurred her vision, but she had no
trouble seeing the ease and grace with which her nauseatingly
competent companion was riding—a grace that made him and
the horse beneath him appear as one fluid being.

Another bump, another plop, and she found herself seriously
wondering if under circumstances such as these, throttling a
country vicar would still be considered a hanging offense.

The Lake District was every bit as beautiful as Theo remembered. Despite his tumultuous state of mind, he was keenly
aware of the majestic hump-backed hills, or fells as the locals
called them, and the picturesque lakes and valleys nestled beneath them.

He vowed that come what may, he would not let the bitterness he held toward the woman who dwelt here destroy his love
of the richly varied region. One day when the anger and be-
trayal he felt at this moment were only dim memories, he would
bring his bride here.

Together they could explore the ancient and mysterious
stones of Castlerigg and the remains of the Roman fort atop
Hardknott Pass. Together they would stand in the courtyard of
the Castle of Carlisle, where a hundred pipers once heralded the
arrival of Bonnie Prince Charlie, and walk in the footprints of
the warrior-craftsmen who'd erected the Emperor Hadrian's
wall. Together they would experience firsthand all the breathtaking beauty of the region Wordsworth and Coleridge had
made immortal.

With her keen wit and sharp eyes, Meg would be the ideal

companion with whom to explore this fascinating corner of England. More important, her compassionate heart would make her the ideal friend and wife and lover once he'd convinced her he no longer wanted her for her money—but for herself.

When he returned to Ravenswood, he would court her as she deserved to be courted. He would ply her with flowers and poetry and all the other things that touched a woman's heart. He would demand the dowager relinquish the magnificent emerald ring that for the past three centuries every Earl of Lynley had presented his bride-to-be, and place it on Meg's finger—something he should have done the day he offered for her.

Somehow, some way, he would make her see that in the short time he'd known her, he had come to treasure her as he had never treasured any other woman. He was firmly convinced Meg and he were ideally suited to each other in all ways—mentally, physically, emotionally—and he determined to convince her of that happy truth as well.

And one day, years from now, when he felt very sure of her, he would divulge the truth about his parentage. Surely, a woman who had agonized over the injured feelings of his discarded mistress would be broad-minded enough to overlook the revelation that the father of her children was an earl's legalized bastard.

He was still thinking of her—longing to feel her slender body pressed to his, daydreaming of her warm, eager lips opening to his hungry exploration—when late in the afternoon he entered the outskirts of the town of Hawkshead.

The first person he came upon was the village blacksmith, hard at work at his anvil. "Tell me if you please, my good man," he said, "do you happen to know the whereabouts of a woman named Rosa Natoli?"

Chapter Ten

The giant smithy paused in the act of hammering into shape what looked to be part of a carriage frame. "Miss Rosa? Now where would the sweet lady be at this time of day but at the Rose and Thistle, serving a meal to the travelers who're biding the night in Hawkshead. And as fine a meal as you'd be finding in any inn in England it is, too."

Stunned, Theo gripped the reins so tightly, the weary stallion beneath him gave its sleek black head an angry toss. With a few gentle strokes, he quieted the testy animal while he gathered his wits. "Do you mean to tell me the woman I seek is a common serving wench at an inn?"

The blacksmith gave a roar of laughter that echoed in Theo's ears like a clap of thunder. "There's nothing common about Miss Rosa, as anyone in Hawkshead will tell you. And she's not the serving wench, but the owner of the Rose and Thistle."

So, the heartless jade had set herself up in business with the "pieces of silver" she'd collected over the years. He might have known a woman callous enough to exchange her newborn son for a lifetime sinecure would put the money to practical use.

"Where may I find this inn?" he asked, squinting against the heat rising from the blacksmith's forge and the stench of his sweat-soaked body.

"At the other end of the village. You cannot miss it, sir, for 'tis the only inn inside the village proper. Just follow this street you're on. 'Twill lead you to the very spot." Like all true natives of the county of Cumbria, the smithy's words were thick with the guttural sounds his Viking ancestors had added to the already colorful dialect of northern England. Theo had to listen carefully to determine what exactly he was saying.

The burly fellow pulled a grimy rag from his belt, wiped away the sweat dripping into his eyes, and peered closely at Theo. "I take it you be kin to Miss Rosa. I can plainly see you've the look of her about you."

Theo stiffened. "The kinship is a distant one." Once he'd learned of Rosa Natoli's existence, he'd had to assume he'd inherited his dark coloring from her. But the knowledge that his resemblance to her was so strong a complete stranger could instantly see it came as a shock.

He thanked the smithy for his help and rode on into the village, glad to be out from under the fellow's scrutiny. But it was soon obvious, from the curious looks on the faces of the villagers he passed, that the blacksmith wasn't the only one who recognized his similarity to the woman who'd borne him.

His plan had been to take a room at one of the inns in the district and remain incognito while he made discreet inquiries about the woman he sought. He could see now that was impossible. In a town the size of Hawkshead, the news that her lookalike had arrived on the scene would probably reach her before he had time to travel the length of the street. There was nothing for it but to walk boldly into the inn she owned, take a room under his own name, and let her make the next move.

The ostler who relieved him of his horse in the courtyard of the neat brick-and-timber inn was a stocky, gray-haired fellow of middle years. Like the blacksmith, he studied Theo with narrowed eyes. "So you've come at last, my lord," he said in a voice heavy with disapproval. "What took you so long? Rosa has looked for you every day since word came of the old earl's death. 'Twas almost more than I could bear to see her rush to the window every time a horse and rider approached."

The ostler jerked a thumb toward the wide oak plank door that stood beneath a wooden sign embellished with carvings of the rose and thistle for which the inn was named. "Hurry now, my lord. She'll be in there waiting for you, her great foolish heart pounding in her breast. A lad from the village came running with the news a good five minutes ago that a young gentleman as looked to be her kin was asking after her."

Silently, Theo collected his saddlebag and tossed it over his shoulder. He felt bewildered by the obvious affection in which

Rosa Natoli was held by the blacksmith, and now this man—and at the same time consumed with rage at the thought that a common servant was aware of his relationship to her. Had the woman no sense of decency, that she should so freely discuss the fact that she'd borne and then abandoned an illegitimate son?

Grimly, he opened the heavy door and stepped into the inviting, low-beamed entryway of the inn. He blinked, momentarily blinded by the light of a dozen candles shining down at him from wrought-iron sconces lining the pristine white walls.

Once his eyes adjusted, he became aware of the tall, regal-looking woman standing in the center of the well-scrubbed flagstone floor. Her hair was jet black with a single streak of silver at her right temple and pulled back into a severe chignon at her nape. Her eyes were as dark and unreadable as he knew his own to be, the tilt of her head as proud. A subtle scent of lavender clung to her fashionable black gown. He had expected a coarse Italian peasant; he found, instead, a beautiful woman with the bearing of a duchess.

He took a step closer and saw, to his surprise, that her eyes glistened with tears and her lips trembled like those of a child awaiting punishment for a bit of naughtiness. Against his will, he felt a subtle shift in the knot of hatred he'd carried deep within him since the moment he'd discovered the truth of his birth. Rosa Natoli was not at all as he'd pictured her.

"I am Theodore Hampton, Earl of Lynley. I seek shelter for the night," he said in his haughtiest tone of voice to hide his confusion.

"Your chamber is ready, my lord, and a private room where you may take your evening meal as well." Her voice was low and throaty, her accent a mixture of the Cumbrian dialect and the musical tones of her Latin heritage. She brushed away the single tear that spilled down her cheek. "We will talk after you've bathed and supped. The matter between us is too weighty to be discussed on an empty stomach."

She raised a hand, and an apple-cheeked elderly woman in a snowy mobcap appeared out of nowhere. "Lydia will show you to your chamber. Your meal will be ready whenever you are."

Just like that, she dismissed him, as if she were indeed his mother and he a green lad to be ordered about. He opened his mouth to protest, but she'd already turned away. A moment later, she disappeared through a door at the far end of the room, leaving him no choice but to follow Lydia's stout, black-clad figure. Up the winding stairway he traipsed behind the silent maid, who led him to the neat, little chamber assigned him by the woman he couldn't bring himself to think of as his mother.

An hour later, after a much needed bath, a shave, and a change of clothing, he descended once again to the main floor of the inn, ready to face his betrayer. But the tantalizing smell of spices and roasting meat wafted his way, and his stomach rumbled with hunger. Grudgingly, he conceded she'd been right on one point; their discussion would be better conducted after a good meal.

Again, the silent maid appeared to lead him to a private parlor off the taproom, where, as promised, a crusty loaf of bread and a plate of something closely resembling the highly seasoned ragouts he'd enjoyed in France awaited him. With the fervor of a man too long on the road, he tucked into the hot, savory repast. He'd just wiped up the last drop of wine-laced gravy with the last crust of bread when Rosa Natoli walked through the doorway, carrying a tray bearing a bottle of brandy and two glasses.

Theo automatically stood up and remained standing until she seated herself in the chair on the opposite side of the table. Too late, he realized she might construe his simple act of proper manners as a show of respect, and fervently wished he'd had the sense to remain in his chair.

She poured two stout glasses of brandy, placed one in front of him, and raised the other to her lips. After a swallow healthy enough to have laid out most men he knew, she lowered the glass to the table and regarded him with her unfathomable dark eyes. "I see, from the scowl that knits your brow, you come armed with anger and resentment. Perhaps if you tell me why, we may get this long overdue discussion under way."

"Why?" Theo choked on his brandy. "You dare ask why I feel anger and resentment toward a mother who, until a few days ago, I never knew existed? A mother who willfully abandoned me within a se'enight of my birth in exchange for a quarterly stipend?"

Rosa Natoli's pale cheeks blanched to a chalky white, but the gaze she'd leveled on Theo never wavered. "I accepted my stipend and 'abandoned you,' as you choose to put it, to a life of luxury and respectability, an education at Eton and Oxford, and a claim to one of the oldest titles in all of England. Would you rather I'd kept you as my bastard and took to whoring to keep the wolf from the door? For those were the only two choices I had—and the one only because it suited the countess's purposes."

"Are you saying this incredible deception was the countess's idea?" Theo shook his head in disbelief. Once he'd realized the truth of his birth, he'd reasoned that the woman's unremitting coldness toward him had stemmed from the humiliation of a barren wife who'd been forced to recognize another woman's son as the legal heir to her husband's title.

Rosa Natoli nodded. "She is a beautiful woman with ice in her veins. Phillip fell in love with her exquisite face—she with his title. But she hated the physical side of marriage. The deception was a means of securing an heir without having to submit to the intimacies necessary to produce a child of her own.

"I was her personal maid. Thinking back on it, I realize she took every opportunity to throw the earl and me together. Phillip being the rake he was, and I a hot-blooded young innocent of sixteen years, whom she'd hired in Florence when they were on their wedding trip, the result was inevitable."

Theo cringed. Knowing the frigid dowager as he did, he could well believe she would go to such extremes to avoid the necessity of having to share a bed with his father. She had made it very clear that she abhorred any form of physical contact. In all the years he had thought her his mother, she had never once hugged him or even patted him on the head as he'd seen the mothers of his friends do.

"Of course, she planned to send me back to Italy once the babe was born," Rosa Natoli continued. "The pension and the Lake District were both Phillip's ideas for, oddly enough, he did love me in his fashion."

A hint of some emotion Theo couldn't identify flashed in her dark eyes. "The countess was furious, of course. She didn't want him herself, but she didn't want any other woman to have him either. In the end, she forced him to give her his solemn promise he would never see me again if she agreed to raise you as her own—and the heir to the title."

She sighed. "At the time, I was young and deeply in love and I despised her for her cruelty. I know now she did both Phillip and me a favor. Had we continued as we were, he would soon have tired of me as he did every woman who gave herself to him.

"The truth is, I'd have had a better chance of capturing a sunbeam in a bottle than turning your father into a faithful lover. But since I was forever forbidden to him, I think I became the one and only tragic love of his life—something he desperately needed to maintain the illusion that despite his rakehell ways he was actually a man of great emotional depth."

Remembering his lonely, confused childhood, Theo sensed the core of truth in her insightful analysis of his father's shallow character. How often, after months of seeming indifference to his very presence, had the earl suddenly taken to gazing at him with tear-filled eyes and pressing his hand to the place where his heart should have been. At long last, he understood his father's strange behavior. It had been nothing more than a reaction to his own uncanny resemblance to his natural mother.

He raised his head to meet a pair of luminous dark eyes in which he spied the same look of ironic humor that often stared back at him from his shaving mirror. Absentmindedly, Rosa Natoli ran her finger around the rim of her empty glass. "Did you know that Doddsworth kept me informed of all the major happenings in your life?"

"No, I didn't. But I'm not surprised."

"And did you know your father and I exchanged letters every month for more than thirty years? Though I must say, his were not nearly as newsy as Doddsworth's."

Theo shook his head, utterly dumbfounded by this latest bit of information about a man he now realized he had not known at all. "I had no idea."

"I kept every one he sent me. Some of them are really quite touching." Her smile was tinged with sadness. "And he kept mine as well. Doddsworth returned them to me when he wrote me of the earl's death. So you see, we each in our own fashion kept faith with the other."

Theo swallowed the last of his brandy, and Rosa Natoli poured him another glass. Quietly, he said, "I take it you've never married, since you're known in the village as 'Miss Rosa.'"

She shrugged. "I couldn't very well, could I? It would have spoiled my beloved rake's grand illusion—and I owed him my loyalty since he'd provided for both my son and me."

The wicked twinkle he'd glimpsed earlier returned to her eyes. "But that's not to say I've lacked the pleasure of male companionship. You met my ostler, I assume."

"I have, and a cheeky fellow he is." To his embarrassment, Theo registered the note of prudish disapproval in his voice.

"That he is." Rosa Natoli's warm, throaty laugh danced between them. "And a patient fellow as well. Claude's been waiting nearly twenty-five years for me to make an honest man of him. I may just do that now that I've settled things with you."

Theo stared at the still-beautiful woman who sat across the table from him, unable to believe he was actually having such a frank conversation with her. He'd come to Hawkshead prepared to find a greedy trollop on whom he could vent his bitterness over her cruel abandonment of him. He'd found, instead, a warm, intelligent woman who, when no more than a child herself, had protected the babe she'd born out of wedlock in the only way she knew how.

The thought occurred to him that of the three parents he had known, she was the only one he could claim with pride. He wondered if he would have been able to recognize that truth so easily if Meg hadn't forced him to comprehend the plight of fallen women like Sophie. Thanks to the two unorthodox women who'd recently entered his life, he would never again look at the soiled doves of society with the same eyes.

He found himself smiling for no reason. "Did Doddsworth, by any chance, tell you I am betrothed?"

She smiled back. "He did. What's more, he said that in his opinion, the young woman will make you the perfect countess."

"That she will, and once I've explained the situation to her, I'll want you to meet her."

"No!" His mother shook her head vehemently. "That is not a good idea. Young ladies tend to be easily shocked, and you must admit ours is not a relationship that's readily explained."

"But Meg is not an ordinary young lady. She's eccentric, unconventional, extremely liberal-minded. There's not a petty nor a deceitful bone in her body. In truth she's far more forthright and honest than most men I know. You will like her, ma'am . . . and she'll like you."

The smile returned to Rosa Natoli's face. "I take it you are in love with this paragon."

"I don't know if I can call what I feel for her 'love.' I've only really known her for a few days." Theo frowned thoughtfully. "But I like her—and desire her—more than any other woman I've ever known."

"And how does she feel about you?"

"At the moment, I fear she distrusts me—and for good reason. She knows I originally offered for her solely because I desperately needed her huge dowry to save Ravenswood. She also knows I have a reputation for being my father's son where women are concerned." Theo took a fortifying swallow of brandy. "But I'm determined to win both her trust and affection by the time our wedding vows are spoken in July."

The dark eyes studying him widened noticeably. "And how do you propose to do that?"

"I intend to court her in all the romantic ways women like to be courted. I'm not certain I'll be successful, but—"

"Never fear, my son, you will be," Rosa Natoli interrupted. "If, that is, you truly put your heart into your courting." She regarded him with obvious pride. "I may be prejudiced, but I doubt there's a woman on earth who could resist you once you set out to win her."

Theo sat back in his chair and basked in the warmth of his newfound mother's approval. It was a unique experience—one that gave him a feeling of profound contentment. He knew he was grinning from ear to ear. He couldn't help it. In less than a fortnight, he'd progressed from a lonely, disillusioned rake to a man who had both a sweetheart and a mother he could cherish and trust.

What more could any man ask of life?

Three days later, he arrived back at Ravenswood, exhausted from his long ride, but more at peace with himself than he could ever before remember. His memories of the time he'd spent with his natural mother were all happy ones, albeit a trifle frustrating.

She'd asked him to call her "Rosa," since calling her "Mother" would give away their secret. He'd readily agreed, but not to safeguard a secret he was tempted to shout from the steps of Carlton House. It simply went against his grain to call her by the name he'd used for the frigid countess.

He'd asked her to return to Ravenswood with him. She'd flatly refused, claiming anyone who saw them together would guess the scandalous truth of their relationship, and her thirty-two years of sacrifice would be for naught. He'd finally agreed after she'd pointed out that not only he, but his wife and children as well, would be tainted with the scandal of his birth.

She'd begged him to stay in Hawkshead long enough for them to become better acquainted. He'd explained he had to defer that pleasure until a later date since he needed to get back to Ravenswood and begin seriously courting Meg. Despite Rosa's encouragement, he would never feel entirely certain of Meg until he had his wedding ring on her finger.

He'd begged her to come to his wedding. She'd declined, citing the same reasons she'd had for not returning with him to Ravenswood.

In the end, he'd simply acknowledged there was no changing the mind of a stubborn woman who believed herself in the right—and ridden away, pledging to write her weekly. Ironically, his strong-willed mother reminded him very much of the woman he planned to marry. This rather shocking observation started him thinking he probably deserved a medal of valor for daring to welcome two such women into his life.

The third woman in his life was waiting for him when he stepped through the manor house doorway. The dowager accosted him before he could so much as set foot on the stairway leading to the third floor and his private apartment. "Where in heaven's name have you been this past week?" she demanded in scathing tones. "How dare you disappear without so much as an explanation to our distinguished guests."

Theo struggled to control his temper. "They were your guests—not mine, madam."

"Nevertheless, your conduct was inexcusable. Between your rudeness and that dreadful cartoon in the *Times* ridiculing him so cruelly, my poor brother's visit was a complete disaster. You should have been here to offer him your support and comfort. I swear, I do not know what has come over you lately. Despite all my efforts to turn you into a proper peer of the realm, you consistently display the breeding of a peasant."

"Not surprising. I've heard blood will tell," Theo said without thinking, then immediately cursed his careless tongue. He fully intended to confront the dowager with what he knew of her devious manipulations, but he'd planned to wait until he was rested from his journey and able to do the subject justice.

She gave him a look that could have frozen boiling water. "What exactly is that obscure comment supposed to mean?"

Theo glanced about him to make certain no servants were within earshot. "It means, madam, that I have spent the past few days visiting my mother at her home in the Lake District. If her charming manners are representative of those of the Italian peasantry, then I sincerely thank you for the compliment you just paid me."

The dowager gasped. "How did you . . . who told you . . . ? It was Doddsworth, wasn't it? I often suspected your father had taken that old fool into his confidence. Lynley was always an idiot."

Theo didn't bother to correct her. In a roundabout way, it was Doddsworth who'd started him digging into ancient records.

"I cannot say I am sorry you know the truth," the dowager admitted in her usual chilling tones. "It will be a relief to no longer be required to pretend a maternal affection for you I have never felt."

Theo laughed in spite of himself. "It is a lucky thing you were born to a title, madam, and not forced to pursue a career on the stage. If the affection you pretended for me is any example, your acting ability is indeed minimal."

A glance at her outraged countenance sobered him instantly. "I, too, am happy there need be no more pretense between us. I shall be even happier when I never have to look on your face again."

"How dare you speak to me in such a manner, you ... you common upstart."

"I have given the matter much thought on my long ride back from Hawkshead," Theo continued. "I believe my small estate on Lambourn Downs in Berkshire will be the ideal place for you to spend your remaining years. I shall direct your maid to begin packing your clothes and my man-of-affairs to set up your account in the pension ledger—along with the rest of the pensioners I support."

"You forget to whom you speak," the dowager said, her jaw rigid. "I have no intention of leaving Ravenswood. I am the only woman qualified to be its mistress. If you persist in this madness, I shall be forced to publicly divulge the fact that you are a bastard with no legal claim to the title of Earl of Lynley. I am certain the heir presumptive, your cousin Edgar Hampton, will be sufficiently grateful to accord me the respect due me."

Theo shrugged. "Divulge all you wish, my lady. I care not a whit what scandal you create amongst members of the *ton*— which is the only harm you can do. My father was not quite the idiot you imagined him to be. He saw to it that papers stating I am the legal heir were duly signed, witnessed, and filed with the Master of the King's Records."

The dowager literally collapsed before his eyes, her face the color of the marble statue to which he'd so often likened her. Theo could almost bring himself to feel sorry for the old besom. Until he remembered that had she had her way, he would never have known he had a mother who loved him with the selfless kind of love the dowager was incapable of feeling.

"For the sake of appearances, I shall agree to move to the dower house for the duration of the summer," she bargained through tight lips. "Surely, not even you can be so foolish as to think you can exclude me from your wedding without causing a scandal that would turn the affair into a circus. I have to believe even a bride as common as yours would despise you for that."

Theo cringed. She was right, and he knew it. Like a bird of prey circling its victim, she had intuitively sensed his weak spot. Meg and he had enough problems to overcome; the last thing they needed was to begin their life together with a wedding marred by scandal.

"Very well," he agreed grudgingly. "You may make your home in the dower house until after the wedding, providing you remove yourself and your personal possessions from the Ravenswood manor house before this day is ended and make certain you never cross my path until the day of the wedding. Once the ceremony is over, you may go to Berkshire, or if that doesn't suit you, any place else you may choose. Leave your direction with my man-of-affairs. He will see that your quarterly stipend reaches you wherever you may be."

Without a backward glance at the woman he had called "Mother" for the first thirty-two years of his life, Theo took the stairs to his chamber two at a time and gave orders to his valet he was not to be disturbed for the remainder of the day.

Maeve had already finished her evening meal and retired to her bedchamber for the night when Lucy knocked at her door to tell her a note had been delivered by a Ravenswood footman and he was to wait for an answer. From the sparkle in the maid-servant's eyes and the bright spots of color in her cheeks, Maeve deduced said footman was none other than Ben Flynn, and that Lucy would appreciate her taking her time composing her answer.

The very masculine handwriting left no doubt as to the identity of the writer of the note. The name that Theo always called her scrawled in his bold script made Maeve's heart pound and her hands tremble as she opened the folded missive.

It was an invitation to accompany him, if she so desired, on his ride early tomorrow morning, and signed simply "Theo." The short postscript scribbled at the bottom of the page was barely legible, but it looked very much like "I missed you."

Maeve's breath caught in her throat. She had missed him, too—more than she cared to admit. Richard was pleasant company, but there was nothing exciting about him—and she appeared to have acquired an addiction to the kind of excitement Theo exuded. Just thinking about kissing him again started her pulse racing.

She penned a brief note telling him she'd be delighted to ride with him. In truth, she could scarcely wait to show off her newly acquired equestrian skills. Even Richard was amazed at how quickly she'd learned the basic technique of riding sidesaddle. She would have no problem portraying the country girl Theo believed her to be—something she had to do until she heard from Meg and collected the money due her from her father.

She told herself she would be glad when the masquerade was over and she could return to her quiet life in London. She told herself she could never be attracted to an admitted rake and fortune hunter. Ergo, she felt no guilt over her cleverly calculated masquerade, since the pawky fellow deserved whatever trouble came his way.

The thought seemed plausible enough. If it hadn't been for the terrible ache in her heart, she might have deceived herself as thoroughly as she'd managed to deceive Theo.

Chapter Eleven

Theo was waiting for her when Maeve arrived at the stable shortly after dawn the next morning. Dressed all in black and astride a huge black stallion, he made a striking picture, albeit a somewhat menacing one. As if to corroborate Maeve's impression, the stallion reared onto its hind legs and snorted ominously when she approached. An omen of things to come, she suspected, screwing up every last ounce of courage to keep from running back to the manor house as fast as her legs would carry her.

"A punctual woman! Will wonders never cease!" Theo's dark eyes scrutinized her with a shocking intimacy she found almost as unnerving as the stallion's reaction to her presence.

"Good morning, Meg," he continued in a silky voice that raised the hairs on her nape. "I took the liberty of asking your groom to saddle your favorite mare. He tells me she's liable to be a bit frisky because she hasn't been ridden since before you went to London."

His smile was slow and entirely without humor. "According to your father's groom, this particular mare won't tolerate anyone but you in her saddle. Perhaps, my love, you should have thought of that when you abandoned her for one of Richard's nags these past four days."

Maeve ignored his gibe. She was too busy praying the persnickety mare would settle for an identical twin.

Theo raised a questioning eyebrow. "Do you think you can handle her? I, myself, think it's rather risky, but the groom seems to have great faith in your ability as a horsewoman."

Maeve gulped. "Of course I can handle her," she declared,

relying desperately on what she was beginning to suspect might be fool's courage to carry her through the ordeal ahead.

Theo's smile warmed a fraction. "Then we should have a challenging ride, since my stallion seems especially spirited today, as well."

"How propitious," Maeve murmured as she walked to the mounting block, where the groom held the reins of the restless dapple gray mare. Luckily, Richard and she had found a large rock in one of the Ravenswood meadows, on which she'd practiced mounting on her own, so the block was no problem. She wished she could say the same for the horse.

It had never occurred to her that two mares could be so different in temperament. But this lively, prancing creature upon which she'd managed to perch herself precariously bore no resemblance whatsoever to the docile mount Richard had provided her. Furthermore, it was all too obvious the mare was not as easily fooled by the physical resemblance between Meg and herself as most humans were.

One backward look when she attempted to mount, and the wild-eyed horse gave a warning snort that fairly chilled her blood. Then no sooner had she settled onto the saddle and grasped the reins than the fey creature took off at a jolting trot. Across the stable yard, down the long, curving driveway, and through the arched entryway the little mare trotted with Maeve bouncing up and down like a cork riding a choppy sea.

"The road," Theo called out. "Guide her onto the road outside the gate."

Maeve did her best; the mare would have none of it. With a toss of her elegant head, she bounded across the road and over a low hedge to the wide, flat meadow that stretched beyond as far as the eye could see. There, to Maeve's despair, the horse took off at a full gallop, nearly unseating her.

"Whoa, you stupid beast," she cried as the reins slipped from her hands. In desperation, she bent over the saddle, grasped handfuls of the mare's flowing mane, and held on for dear life.

Over the pounding of her horse's hooves, and the pounding of her heart, she heard Theo shout from behind her, "Hell and damnation, Meg, slow down before you kill yourself." How she was supposed to accomplish that feat, she had no idea. She was too terrified to do anything but hang on with fingers frozen to their task and pray for deliverance from her nightmare.

Across the seemingly endless meadow the mare galloped with Theo's stallion thundering close behind. They splashed through a shallow stream, across another stretch of meadow, and up a grassy slope toward a small stand of birch trees.

Maeve vaguely remembered Richard's warning to stay away from trees until she'd gained sufficient experience in the saddle to have complete control over her mount. There was, he claimed, that odd horse perverse enough in nature to deliberately try to brush its rider off by galloping beneath low-hanging branches. A sinking feeling in the pit of her stomach told her the mare was one of those horses.

"Watch out for the trees!" Theo yelled. It was too late. With an unbelievable burst of speed, the mare plunged into the very heart of the thicket. Instinctively, Maeve let go of the mane and raised her arms to protect her face. A low branch caught her shoulder-high, and the next thing she knew, she'd catapulted backward off the horse and landed in a breathless heap on a grassy mound at the base of one of the larger trees.

"Ugh," she gasped, trying to draw air into her tortured lungs. But between the impact of the branch and the force with which she'd hit the ground, the act of drawing a deep breath was beyond her.

Damn and double damn, she silently cursed when she heard Theo crash into the thicket behind her. She couldn't face him. How could she explain why a supposedly accomplished horsewoman was sitting here on her bruised backside with that miserable mare nowhere in sight? With a groan, she closed her eyes, lay back against the grassy mound, and prayed she'd either die on the spot or he'd go away and leave her alone.

He didn't, of course. She heard him murmur her name as he dropped to his knees beside her, and the anguish in his voice was nearly her undoing. She should, by rights, open her eyes and assure him she was uninjured—and she would—just as soon as she got up the courage to look him in the face. For if he'd never before doubted she was born and bred in the country, he would most certainly doubt it now.

Theo had galloped into the thicket just in time to see Meg fly off the back of her horse. He'd thought at first she'd merely landed on her rump on a soft, grassy mound; in fact, he could almost swear she had. But by the time he'd tethered his horse and rushed to her side, she was lying flat on her back with her eyes closed, looking as crumpled and lifeless as a doll that had been carelessly tossed aside by a thoughtless child.

He knelt beside her, studying her chalk white face and feeling utterly helpless—afraid to move her lest something inside her slender body was broken. "Meg," he said softly. "Speak to me if you can."

Her eyelids fluttered momentarily, but remained firmly closed. As he watched, her gently rounded bosom heaved with the exertion of drawing air into her lungs. A good sign, he decided. At least she was breathing, however laboriously.

The heaving gradually slowed, her breathing eased, and a touch of color returned to her cheeks—more than a touch. If he didn't know better, he'd swear she was blushing. Slowly, her eyes opened, their startling emerald hue echoing the vivid green of the grass on which her head was cushioned.

Her lips moved, and Theo leaned forward to hear her. "I guess I should have listened to what Richard said about trees," she murmured weakly. Then pressed her fingers to her lips as if surprised by her own words.

A surge of pain and anger raced through him at the idea that her first thought on regaining consciousness should be of a man he strongly suspected was his rival for her affections. Grimly, he stifled his desire to shake some sense into the stubborn little minx.

"Richard isn't here," he said tersely. "I'll have to do."

"You'll do just fine, Theo." She turned her head and fastened her somewhat unfocused gaze on his face. He breathed a sigh of relief, thankful the foolish woman hadn't broken her neck. Maybe the good Lord was handing out miracles today, and she'd merely knocked the wind out of herself.

"Can you tell me where you hurt?" he asked softly.

She sighed. "Everywhere. But I feel better now that I can breathe again."

She struggled to sit up, but Theo grasped her shoulders and

gently laid her back down. "Not yet. Rest a minute. You've had a bad fall. I want to make sure nothing is broken."

Maeve felt relatively certain the only serious injury she'd sustained was to her pride, but she shifted slightly to find a more comfortable position and gave herself up to his painstaking examination of her arms, her legs, her ribs, her aching head. A mistake, she soon discovered, for every nerve in her body sprang to life beneath his gentle probing.

She closed her eyes again, lest they reveal that she was literally melting beneath the touch of his long, elegant fingers. "That's enough," she said finally, pushing his hands away when she could stand no more of the sensuous torture. "I'm perfectly all right. Just a little out of breath."

"I do believe you are. I can find nothing broken," Theo agreed in a voice that sounded oddly unsteady. "Which makes me think you are either made of stronger stuff than you appear to be or you've a guardian angel watching over you. Whatever, my love, you just took ten years off my life. I swear I feel as weak as a newborn kitten."

Without further ado, he stretched out beside her on the grassy mound, rolled to his side, and propped himself on one elbow.

"What . . . what are you doing?" she stammered.

"I'll ask the questions," he said, staring down at her with narrowed eyes. "Question number one: What made that idiot groom think you were an accomplished horsewoman? I've half a mind to rearrange the stupid fellow's face when I get back to the stable."

He scowled. "Question number two: Why in the name of heaven would you willingly mount a horse you had to know was too skitterish for you to handle? Devil take it, Meg, I've seen rank beginners ride better than you just did. I don't blame the mare for throwing you."

Maeve felt as if the ground had just dropped from beneath her. This was it, she told herself—the moment of truth when her madcap masquerade was at last unveiled. Question number three would undoubtedly be, as Richard had asked before him, *Who are you, madam?*

Theo removed a twig from her hair and impatiently tossed it over his shoulder. "You constantly surprise me, Meg Barring-

ton." His tone of voice made the statement an accusation. "How
is it you are so marvelously accomplished in ways no country
woman should be—yet, abysmally lacking in the one skill in
which I would have expected you to excel?"

Maeve stared at him, her heart pounding. Anger and bewilderment clouded his dark eyes, but still he circled around the
truth, almost as if he were loath to face it.

"You constantly surprise me, too, Theo," she said in a desperate attempt to divert his attention. She managed a halfhearted smile. "Any other man I know would be sympathetic
when I came so close to breaking my neck. For some reason I
cannot fathom, you appear angry."

She struggled to sit up, but once again he pinned her down—
this time with a none too gentle hand across her ribs. "Angry is
too mild a term for what I'm feeling at the moment," he stated
grimly. "If you ever pull another harebrained stunt like the one
I just witnessed, you needn't worry about breaking your neck.
I'll wring it."

The hand across her rib cage edged a fraction higher until his
fingers touched the swell of her breast, and a warm glow spread
from the point of contact throughout her entire being. If the
glow spread through him as well, he managed to hide it. "Do
you have any idea how I felt when I saw you fly off the back of
that horse?" he asked through tight lips.

The tremor in his deep voice startled her. He really was
upset. Instinctively, she reached up to stroke the rigid line of his
jaw.

He turned his head and kissed her palm. "My heart nearly
stopped beating. In case you've failed to notice, my dear,
you've become very precious to me."

Maeve felt herself respond to his unexpected endearment
with a warmth that both surprised and frightened her. Dear
God, surely she couldn't be losing her heart to the charming
rogue. "You flatter me, my lord. My dowry must be even larger
than I'd realized," she quipped, hoping to dampen his ardor
with cynicism.

"Your dowry be damned!" Theo's eyes blazed. "I admit it
was my initial reason for offering for you. But now that I know
you—now that I've seen your courage, your compassion, your

honesty—give or take a fib or two about something as ridiculous as your French emigré music teacher—it's you I desire."

He cupped her chin with his strong fingers and stared deep into her eyes. "God help me, you stubborn, headstrong, impossible woman, I think I've fallen in love with you."

As if to prove his point, he shifted his body to where she lay beneath him, lowered his head, and kissed her with a passion that left her almost as breathless as her fall from the horse.

"Tell me, my love," he said in a throaty whisper, "is that the kiss of a man whose only interest is money?"

"No," Maeve whispered back, too stunned by the passion Theo's kisses awakened in her to be anything but honest.

But much more than his passionate kisses drew her to him now. He was not the same arrogant aristocrat who'd greeted her at the ball; nor was he the conscienceless rake who'd used the Widow Whitcomb so shabbily. Something had changed him—made him more thoughtful, more caring . . . and sadly, more vulnerable.

His declaration of love had touched her heart as nothing else ever had, and at the same time, left her feeling sick with guilt. He'd called her courageous, compassionate, honest. She was none of those things, least of all, honest. But he believed she was. He believed so strongly, he'd managed to blind himself to all the clues that should have warned him of her deceit. If he only knew what a fraud she was, he'd hate her.

He stared down at her, his face suddenly grim. "Have you nothing to say to me, Meg? Am I the only one whose heart is in jeopardy?"

She closed her eyes, unable to face the hurt she saw in his.

"Is it Richard who stands between us?"

Her eyes popped open. "Richard? Why do you ask that?"

"Anyone can see the man is hopelessly in love with you."

She'd told him so many lies that had seemed necessary at the time. The least she could do was tell him the truth about her friendship with the vicar. "Richard is hopelessly in love all right," she agreed, "but not with me. We are friends who confide in each other. Nothing more."

The relief she saw on Theo's handsome face made her feel more guilty than ever. Why hadn't she realized that in telling him that one truth, she'd merely given more strength to all the other lies on which he was building his hopes for the future.

Three more days, she reminded herself. Then the fortnight she'd pledged her father was over, and with it, her hateful masquerade. In three more days she could collect her money, pay Lily's debts, and go back to living her own life.

But not before she'd told Theo the truth. Not before she'd disillusioned him so thoroughly, he would feel nothing but relief that he need never see her again. Not before she'd set him free to find a truly courageous, compassionate, and honest woman with whom to share his life.

She owed him that much for falling in love with her—something she'd thought no man would ever do—and for a dozen other reasons she wasn't sure she could define.

But most of all, she owed him the truth because she'd just this moment realized, fool that she was, she'd fallen in love with him as well.

There were three more days in May—three days until the date he'd originally chosen as his wedding day. Theo rode slowly back to Ravenswood, deep in thought. Meg's accident had made him realize how deeply he cared for her and how desperate he was to make her his own in every way possible.

He would, he decided, put everything else aside and devote every waking minute of the next three days to his courtship. He'd be so tender, so considerate, so charming, he just might convince her that June fifteenth would be as acceptable a date for their wedding as July first.

She might not yet realize she loved him. She'd kept disappointingly silent on that subject when he'd declared himself to her. But she desired him every bit as much as he desired her. Her response to his kisses had told him that, as had the way her body had melded to his when he'd lain above her on that grassy mound, or held her before him on his saddle when they rode to Barrington Hall.

He just hoped he could convince her of that truth in the next few days. He needed to get this courting business behind him and establish Meg as his loving wife and the new mistress of

Ravenswood. He was neglecting important work that must be finished before another winter was upon him.

All of his tenants' houses needed repairs, and there were fences to be built for the cattle he'd ordered the day he and the squire signed the marriage agreement. They'd be delivered soon, and he'd been warned they couldn't graze the same pastures as the Ravenswood sheep.

The west wing of the manor house needed a new roof. It had leaked badly last winter. Another such winter and all the priceless furnishings that section of the house contained would be nothing more than moldy rags.

All of these things could be accomplished now that Meg's dowry was added to the depleted Ravenswood coffers. He felt a twinge of guilt over that, but only a twinge. She would benefit as much as he from every cent he spent once she was his wife.

Stepford, the newly appointed butler, greeted him at the door when he arrived at Ravenswood. "A note arrived for you from the village this morning, my lord," he said in his usual aloof manner. He held out a small silver tray on which reposed a piece of folded paper, and Theo spied the words "His Earlship" in a childish scrawl he knew all too well.

With sinking spirits, he carried the note up to his chamber to read in private. So much had transpired since last he'd seen her, he'd almost forgotten about Sophie. Like the countess, she was a part of his past he must put in place before he could look to his future.

The note was short and in Sophie's usual semiliterate style.

Dear Theo
I have thot about what you sed and no you are rite. Our tim together is over. I am moving to Wembley in Middlesex and hop to open a dressmaker shop if you can see yur way to lone me the blunt. Two hundred pounds will do me nicely.
                                                 Yur frend Sophie

Theo breathed a sigh of relief. One more problem solved. If two hundred pounds was all it took to rid him of the guilt he felt over his part in aiding Sophie's fall from grace, it was money well spent. He made a mental note to instruct his man-of-affairs to deliver the sum to her that very afternoon along with his best wishes for her success in her new venture.

Grinning from ear to ear, he tore Sophie's note into minute pieces and dropped them into the cold ashes in the fireplace. So that was that. Sophie's practical nature had won out over her romantic fantasies after all. He was not surprised. Every woman he'd ever known had been practical to the core when push came to shove.

The countess—he would never again think of her as his mother—was the epitome of practicality; she'd stopped at nothing to protect her role as Mistress of Ravenswood. Even Rosa had managed to negotiate herself a lifetime sinecure along with the legal status she'd sought for her illegitimate child.

The possible exception was his bride-to-be. As far as he could determine, Meg Barrington hadn't a practical bone in her body. Neither title nor money meant a thing to her—which was undoubtedly why his pressing need for her large dowry gave her such a distrust of him.

Somehow he must find a way to gain her trust and win her heart. The task wouldn't be an easy one. The only thing he had in his favor at the moment was the passion he stirred in her each time he touched her.

His smile broadened. Then passion it was, and there was no time like the present to begin seducing the fascinating lady he intended to make the next Countess of Lynley.

Theo's note addressed to Meg was delivered shortly before noon by Ben Flynn. It informed her that he would call on her at one o'clock to take her for a drive into the countryside. A postscript added that he would have his cook prepare a picnic lunch.

Maeve read the note a second time and decided it sounded more like a summons than an invitation. What had made her think the Earl of Lynley was anything but arrogant? Still, she could almost forgive him since the proposed outing sounded most appealing—far more appealing than either the formal ball or the lavish dinner she'd attended at Ravenswood.

The truth was, she had never before been on a picnic. Lily had considered partaking of a meal anywhere but at a properly appointed dining table positively barbaric. Maeve, on the other hand, had always secretly thought dining alfresco would be great fun.

The idea of doing so with Theo sounded especially intriguing at the moment. She'd given her situation some serious thought since returning from her disastrous early morning ride, and had come to the conclusion she should put aside her feelings of guilt and enjoy every minute of the last three days she would spend with him.

Her reasoning was both simple and logical. Foolish though it might be, she had given her heart to a man she would probably never see again once she returned to London—a man who would thoroughly despise her once he knew the truth about her. Since there was nothing she could do in three days that would make him despise her even more, she might as well store up memories for the long, lonely years ahead.

She was waiting, parasol in hand, when he arrived promptly at one o'clock in a shiny black tilbury drawn by a powerful-looking bay. "What did your cook prepare for our picnic?" she asked, eyeing the intriguing cloth-covered basket on the seat of the carriage.

Theo grinned. "Who knows? Whatever took her fancy."

She grinned back. "A surprise. I love surprises."

Meg was a surprise herself this afternoon, Theo decided, flicking the reins to set the bay in motion. There was a brightness in her eyes, an eagerness in her voice he hadn't noticed before.

"Where will we eat our picnic lunch?" she asked, peering at him from beneath her flower-trimmed bonnet. "Will it be by a lake? Oh, I do hope it will be by a lake."

"Of course it will. Picnics should always be by lakes," Theo assured her, congratulating himself on his brilliant selection of a way to amuse her. Picnicking must be one of her favorite pastimes. She looked almost childlike in her excitement.

They drove for a good half hour, chatting companionably, and still hadn't reached their destination. Theo could have shortened the trip by half had he wanted to. He'd decided instead to take the longest possible route to the spot he'd chosen, simply because he was enjoying himself so much seeing the familiar countryside through Meg's eyes. She had the same look of wonder as on their last drive. One would think she'd never before seen the countryside, from the way she exclaimed over every tree and flower, every grazing lamb and waddling duck. Even a field of common daisies drew gasps of pleasure from her.

They passed a spindly wild rose bush growing by the side of the lane, and reverently, she touched the pale pink blooms with the tips of her slender fingers. He watched, aching to feel those fingers touching him.

Finally, when the sight of an apple tree in full blossom brought tears to her eyes, he could stand it no longer. He pulled the carriage to the side of the lane, took her in his arms, and kissed her. It was not a kiss of passion as the others he'd shared with her had been, but rather a profoundly tender kiss, celebrating the pure, undiluted joy of life that this moment, this place, this woman generated in him.

Maeve slowly opened her eyes when he finally raised his head. "All your kisses have been lovely, but this one was the loveliest of all," she pronounced solemnly. "I shall remember it forever."

"There are plenty more where that came from," Theo said, and to his surprise, watched her happy smile fade to but a pale version of its former brilliance.

Automatically, he picked up the reins, his mind anywhere but on what he was doing. He found himself wondering what he could have said to cause the mysterious sadness he'd glimpsed in her eyes. She was obviously a woman given to quixotic changes of mood.

He quickly dismissed that fact as irrelevant. With all he found to like in her, he could learn to live with an occasional mood. A moment later, she was once again chattering blithely, and he found himself so caught up in the pleasure of her company, he all but forgot her brief, inexplicable lapse into melancholy.

The lake, when they finally reached it, was a perfect oval sapphire glistening in the bright May sunshine. Clumps of wild violets and sweet clover dotted the grassy slope that led to the water's edge. A gentle breeze, fragrant with the scent of wild thyme from the meadow across the lane, stirred tiny ripples on the water's surface.

"It's called Jewel Lake," Theo said. "There are three other small lakes on Ravenswood property, but this is my favorite." He spread the carriage robe beneath a huge old oak, set the basket on one corner of it, and smiled at Meg. "Now you can see what cook considers proper picnic fare."

She dropped to her knees beside the basket and began rummaging through the contents. "Let me see, we have a bottle of wine, two small roasted chickens, fresh scones with strawberry preserves, and I do believe . . . yes, they are . . . cucumber sandwiches," she said, laying each serviette-draped plate on the carriage robe as she took it from the basket.

"A veritable feast," Theo declared, dropping down beside her as she uncovered the last dish. It contained two perfect golden peaches.

She beamed with delight. "What a treat. But where would your cook find peaches so early in the season?"

"They're from the Ravenswood orangery. One of my grandfather's better ideas. Because of it, we have fresh fruits and vegetables all year round, no matter how foul the weather."

He frowned. "But shouldn't we lay the cloth before we unpack the basket?"

"Oh!" A flush stained her cheeks. "How stupid of me. Of course we should."

While Theo watched, she painstakingly returned all the food to the basket, then removed the snowy cloth that was folded into one corner. She sat with it in her hands, a puzzled look on her face. "Are we supposed to lay it atop the carriage robe or beside it?"

Theo chuckled. If he didn't know better, he'd swear she'd never been on a picnic before—at least not one where she was expected to sit on the ground. "As I recall, my nanny used to spread the cloth beside the robe," he said, "probably because it left more room to sit down that way."

"That makes sense," she declared and promptly spread the cloth adjacent to the robe. "You picnicked with your nanny?"

"Almost every day in the summer. In this very spot, in fact." Theo sat down, his back against the tree trunk, while she once again removed the food from the basket and arranged it on the cloth with careful precision. "Some of my happiest childhood memories are of reading my books beneath this old oak or sculling about on the lake under Nanny Thistle's watchful eye."

He accepted the plate, serviette, and utensils she handed him and watched her seat herself rather gingerly on the edge of the robe. "I apologize for the lack of formality. It's what I'm used to because this is how Nanny Thistle and I always picnicked. Are you accustomed to a more formal type of picnic?"

She looked startled by his question. "No. I've never been to a formal picnic. I can't even imagine one."

"I have." Theo pulled a blade of grass and chewed it thoughtfully. "Three summers ago, when I was on leave from the Peninsula, I was invited to a 'picnic' at the home of the Duchess of Manchester. It was quite an affair.

"Twenty tables, complete with crystal, silver, and three-foothigh epergnes, set beneath striped canopies. Plus a butler and a hundred or so liveried footmen. A dead bore as far as I was concerned. As the dowager has often been heard to say, I have the taste of a peasant."

He grinned. "Not that I don't like service." He handed Meg his plate. "I'll have one of everything if you please, ma'am. I need to build up my strength if I'm to row you across the lake once we finish eating."

Maeve's eyes widened with obvious astonishment. "You're going to take me out on the lake . . . in a boat?"

Surreptitiously, he crossed his fingers. "It's an ancient Ravenswood tradition. Whenever two lovers picnic on one of the Ravenswood lakes, the man must row his lady back and forth across that lake three times."

"Why?" Maeve passed him the plate of food he'd requested.

Theo demolished one of cook's dainty cucumber sandwiches in a single bite. "To assure them the blessings of long life, true love, and a brood of happy, healthy children. Of course, it also gives the fellow a chance to show off his manly muscles."

Maeve's smile was disturbingly enigmatic. "But, as you may remember, I've already seen your manly muscles. And since we're not lovers—"

"Ah, but we are!" Theo leaned forward and brushed her lips

in the gentlest of kisses. "In spirit, if not yet in actuality. And I give you fair warning, Meg Barrington. I fully intend to change the nature of our relationship before much more time has passed."

Chapter Twelve

After enough grumbling to lodge a protest at what she saw as another of his autocratic summonses, Maeve finally agreed to let Theo row her back and forth across the lake. Not that she had any choice in the matter. He flatly refused to take no for an answer, so obsessed was he with this Ravenswood lovers' tradition of his.

She wondered if adhering to it had brought any of his sour-faced ancestors whom she'd viewed in the portrait gallery the "long life, true love, and many children" it promised. As far as she could see, his father had come up short on all three counts. But the very idea of the austere countess sitting in a rowboat seemed so ludicrous, Maeve couldn't help but laugh at the picture she conjured up.

She sobered fast, however, when it occurred to her that if it was truly a traditional Ravenswood ritual, she'd be participating in it under false pretenses. She was superstitious enough to wonder if such irreverence would bring a new epidemic of bad luck crashing down on her head.

Still, it was almost worth the risk. It would be her first time in a boat—another first to which Theo would introduce her. She'd never realized, until she'd met him, how narrow and restricted a life she'd led. If nothing else, she'd gained a taste for adventure from their brief association.

Theo watched the laughter come and go on Meg's expressive face and wondered what had occasioned it. Had she guessed the Ravenswood lovers' tradition was merely something he'd thought up to introduce a little romance into his seduction plan? He wouldn't put it past her, clever minx that she was. But at least she was going along with it.

With her hand in his, he headed for the spot at the water's edge where he remembered the boat was always moored. To his surprise, it was gone. "Somebody's moved my boat," he complained, searching the grassy area in vain. Meg stifled a grin, and he had to admit, that considering the fact that some twenty years had passed since he'd last looked for it, he did sound a bit ridiculous.

"Maybe that's it," his betrothed suggested, pointing to a small, grayish object half hidden in the reeds.

Theo shrugged. "I sincerely doubt it, but I suppose we should take a look." With Meg trailing close behind him, he worked his way through another twenty feet of high grass and reeds, and sure enough there it was—the boat that had once been his pride and joy. To say the relic was a shock would be the understatement of the century. In truth, had it not been for the faint outline of the word *Starfire*—the name he'd lovingly dubbed it so long ago—on the weather-beaten hull, he'd have never recognized it.

With disbelieving eyes he stared at the sorry little craft. If he didn't know it was impossible, he'd swear the blasted thing had shrunk since last he'd seen it.

"It's somewhat smaller than I remember," he said apologetically.

"You're undoubtedly somewhat larger than when you and your nanny picnicked here." Maeve studied the decrepit little boat. "It looks to be mired in the mud, as if no one has used it in years. Are you thinking you can't wrench it free?"

"No, I'm thinking of the dressing down I'll get from my valet when I return home with my boots covered with mud."

She raised a questioning eyebrow. "I wasn't aware a mere valet was allowed to dress down an earl."

"Albert Figgins is not the ordinary run-of-the-mill valet. He was my batman on the Peninsula. I owe my life to the stout-hearted fellow. Twice, old Figs dragged me off the battlefield and patched me up when I'd been left for dead. Naturally, I felt duty-bound to keep him with me when I sold out my commission, and I've never regretted it. He's my most loyal friend, as well as my employee. To be truthful though, he's not much of a valet. Can't tie a decent cravat to save his soul. His only talent lies in keeping a mirror sheen on my boots."

Theo gritted his teeth. "Well, I'd best get on with it." So saying, he waded into the gooey muck surrounding the little boat, though, if the truth be known, the idea of rowing on the lake was fast losing its appeal.

He'd come up with the myth of the "lovers' tradition" on the spur of the moment. Now he was stuck with it. His romantic fantasy had been of his ladylove reclining in the stern, parasol in hand, while he rowed her across the sparkling blue waters of the lake. There was no room for her to lounge in this dilapidated little dinghy; she'd be lucky to find enough space to sit bolt upright—and he'd seen mackerel boats plying the murky water of the Thames that looked more romantic.

Muttering increasingly vile obscenities under his breath, he tugged and pulled at the mired boat, which in turn made odd, creaking sounds as if protesting being roused from its long slumber. With a final monumental effort, he freed it from the tenacious mud and dragged it into the water.

"There," he said, as he removed his handkerchief from his pocket and wiped off the plank on which he intended his betrothed to sit. Wading through the shallow water, he lifted her in his arms and settled her in the stern of the boat. Then, taking his place on the plank spanning the midsection between the oar locks, he dipped the oars in the water and began rowing.

Meg instantly opened her parasol and gazed about her with a look of pure, unadulterated pleasure. He'd forgotten what joy she took in the little things that a woman of his own class would despise. Maybe this impromptu excursion would turn out all right after all . . . if he could just master the knack of rowing.

He'd assumed it was one of those things that automatically came back to one, no matter how long one was away from it. Apparently, it wasn't. He'd never before realized his right arm was so much stronger than his left. He had the choice of zigzagging across the lake like a demented dragonfly or making two dips of the left oar for every dip of the right—neither of which action projected the aura of manly prowess with which he'd hoped to gain Meg's admiration.

Luckily, the lake was relatively small, and somehow he managed to cross to the other side in his lopsided fashion. He kept waiting for Meg to tease him about his lack of skill as an oarsman. She never did. In truth, from the excited gleam in her eyes when she pointed out the giant willow at the far end of the lake and the pair of black swans floating beneath its trailing branches, he began to think she was blissfully unaware of his embarrassing ineptitude.

He silently congratulated himself. Once again the phenomenal luck with which he'd always been blessed was standing him in good stead. Despite all odds, this romantic interval he'd arranged looked to be a happy success.

Rowing in a straight line was difficult enough; turning around was even trickier. Somehow, someway, he managed to swivel the boat around and head back without too much trouble toward the spot from which they'd embarked. He was beginning to get the hang of this rowing business after all. At this rate, he'd be plying the oars like an expert by the end of the next lap.

No sooner had he come to that comforting conclusion than the right oarlock tore loose from the rotting wood of the hull, leaving no place to anchor the oar. Cursing under his breath, he decided there was nothing for it but to haul in the left oar and use the right one as he might a canoe paddle. "We have a little problem," he said tersely.

"We have a big problem," Maeve corrected him. He glanced up from his thankless task to find her look of rapture had mysteriously changed to one of utter dismay. "Are you a strong swimmer?" she asked somewhat warily.

Grimly, he wielded his oar cum paddle first on one side of the boat, then the other. "As a matter of fact, I am, but why do you ask?"

"Because I can't swim at all, and I think it entirely possible the boat may be sinking. My feet are beginning to get very wet."

He surveyed the inch or so of water sloshing around his boots. "Not to worry. There's always a little water in the bottom of a rowboat," he said reassuringly.

But even as he watched, the water rose to two inches, then before he had time to blink an eye, to ankle deep. "What the

devil?" he exclaimed. "You're right. The blasted boat is leak-
ing like a sieve, and there's not a thing in sight we can use as a
bailing bucket."

"Oh, yes there is." Meg dropped her parasol, whipped off her
bonnet, and began frantically scooping up water and throwing
it over the side. He could see it was a losing battle, but he
blessed her for trying, and for abstaining from the usual female
hysterics.

"Good girl," he said approvingly and immediately began
plying his makeshift paddle with a vengeance. Their only
chance of avoiding a dunking was to reach shore before the
boat took on so much water, it could no longer stay afloat. For
a few hopeful minutes, he thought that between her bailing and
his paddling, they might make it, but just when he needed it
most, his luck failed him.

They were still some fifty feet from the lakeshore when the
little boat sank. He made a lunge for Meg as she went under,
tucked her into his left arm, and, keeping her face above
water, swam for shore as best he could with one free arm, and
feet encased in boots that had suddenly grown as heavy as
lead anchors.

A few breathless moments later, he planted his feet on the
bottom and stood waist deep in the water, cradling her shiver-
ing body in his arms. He waded ashore, carried her to where
they'd eaten their picnic lunch, and wrapped her in the carriage
robe.

She was shaking in earnest now—a delayed reaction, he suspected, to the terror she'd just endured. Cursing himself
soundly for conceiving of such a harebrained scheme, he
wrapped his arms around her in a desperate attempt to warm
her chilled body.

"I'm so sorry," he said contritely. "I should have known better than to take you out in that miserable excuse for a boat." He
fully expected her to push him away, or at the very least, berate
him for his stupidity. She did neither. She buried her face in his
shoulder and made odd little snuffling noises while her body
shook even more violently than before.

Tenderly, he brushed away a lock of lank, wet hair that was

dripping water down the front of her bodice. "I'm so sorry," he said again. "It was supposed to be a—"

"A romantic interlude," she interjected, peeping up at him with eyes brimming with mischief. "I can't say it was terribly romantic, but it was by far the most fun I ever remember having." Her shoulders still shook, but he suddenly realized she was laughing—not sobbing, as he'd believed.

"Fun? You think that . . . that catastrophe we just experienced was fun," he sputtered, stepping away from her, only to find his boots so full of water, he made an odd, squishing sound with each step he took.

"Fun! And funny!" she declared. "Funnier by the minute, in fact." Wrapping her arms around her middle, Maeve laughed until tears ran down her cheeks. "Are you aware you squish when you walk?" she gasped.

Theo gritted his teeth. He had no choice but to drop down on the ground beside her, pull off his boots, and pour out the collected water—a process that immediately sent her into new gales of laughter.

"You find the destruction of a pair of Mr. Hoby's handmade Hessians amusing?" he asked sourly.

"Not the Hessians, the look on your face. It's almost as funny as when you got your first good look at that impossible little boat you'd claimed was part of an ancient Ravenswood legend." She wiped her brimming eyes. "But the funniest look of all was when you realized we were actually sinking."

"Bloody hell, woman," Theo growled. "Must you rub salt in the wound? I'm having a little trouble at the moment, seeing the humor in this miserable situation." He was having even more trouble cramming his feet back into his wet boots.

"Oh, don't be such a stick in the mud. Granted, you have a rather unique method of courting a woman, but there's no harm done except to your pride—and you've such a surfeit of that, you can afford to lose a little."

Her brows knit in what might have passed for a thoughtful frown if he hadn't caught the twinkle in her eyes. "Still, you should do something about your appearance before you return home. You are a member of the nobility, after all, and have certain standards to maintain. To put it bluntly, my lord, you are a soggy mess. The dowager will probably faint dead away at the sight of you, and your valet will have more than your boots to complain of this day."

Theo laughed in spite of himself. "I'm a soggy mess? Have you taken a good look at yourself, Meg Barrington?"

The pins were gone from her hair, and it hung, a dripping mass, down her back. The robe had slipped from her shoulders, revealing a gown that was molded to her slight figure like a sheet of wet paper. Beneath the muddy hem, he could see two equally muddy stocking-clad feet. God only knew where her slippers might be. Yet, the crazy woman proclaimed her unexpected dunking "the most fun" she could ever remember having.

He couldn't believe his ears.

He couldn't believe his luck.

He could face anything life had to offer with a woman like this at his side.

There was nothing for it but to kiss her. Leaning forward, he grasped her shoulders, and pulled her from her perch beneath the tree and onto his lap.

"Laugh at me, will you, little hoyden? I'll teach you to show some respect for your lord and master." He captured her soft, laughter-parted lips in a hot, possessive kiss that branded her wholly and unconditionally his. Her response was a mixture of laughter and passion, tenderness and teasing, that sent waves of heat rippling through his chilled body.

Long, mind-shattering moments later, he raised his head. "I love you, Meg," he said softly. "I always will."

"No, don't say such a thing." She scrambled from his lap, her luminous emerald eyes clouded with some disturbing emotion he couldn't define.

He reached for her, but she evaded him, once again pressing her back to the tree trunk and covering herself with the carriage robe as if by hiding her body from him she could will it to resist the response his touch elicited in her.

Perplexed, he propped his elbows on his knees and stared at her. "What is it that troubles you, Meg? Why are you so afraid to believe I've come to care deeply for you?"

"Fear has nothing to do with it."

"Oh, but it has. It's all too obvious you're afraid to trust your heart to me. But why? I'm not the irresponsible rake you believe me to be. I swear I'll treasure your heart and protect it from everything and everyone that could hurt it—even from myself if needs be."

Maeve heard the sincerity in Theo's voice and felt a great, painful crack open in her heart. Never, in all her life, had she wanted anything as much as she wanted the future he promised—the future she could never have.

She knew as sure as the sun above her would set this evening, that she would spend the rest of her days grieving for the fulfillment she would never find in his arms, the beautiful black-haired babies she would never suckle at her breast.

She closed her eyes, unable to bear the intensity of his gaze. With all her heart, she wished she could end her torturous masquerade here and now before she risked hurting him—and herself—even more. If it were only her future at stake, she would break her silence and consign the squire and his plans to the devil, no matter what it cost her.

But what of Theo? He admittedly needed to marry an heiress to save his precious Ravenswood. If not Meg, then whom?

And what of her sister? Until she knew Meg's wishes, her lips must remain sealed.

"If you don't mind, I'd rather finish this discussion at another time, when I'm not so cold and wet," she said wearily. "There are things about me you should know—things that will make you realize I am nothing like the image you've formed of me—and I promise to divulge them. But right now, I can think of nothing but a hot bath and a soft bed."

Theo blinked as if emerging from a dream. "Good Lord, what am I thinking of? I should have rushed you home the minute I carried you out of the water. I'll never forgive myself if you end up with lung fever because of my stupidity."

He quickly rose to his feet, gathered the four corners of the picnic cloth together, and dumped the entire contents into the picnic basket. "Wait here. I'll come right back and carry you to the carriage, since you've apparently lost your slippers," he said, starting toward that vehicle, basket in hand.

"You'll do no such thing. I'm perfectly capable of walking."

Maeve took a tighter hold on the robe and followed Theo toward the tilbury. Once again she'd managed to stave off the inevitable. But her luck couldn't last much longer. Sooner or later, her frayed nerves or her guilty conscience would give her away.

Mrs. Pinkert met them at the door when they arrived at Barrington Hall. "Lord a'mighty, whatever have you done to yourself, missy," she squealed when Theo lifted Maeve from the carriage and insisted on carrying her into the manor house.

"It's a long story, which I'm sure Miss Barrington will tell you in good time," Theo said before Maeve could get a word out. She managed a broad wink at Mrs. Pinkert, which let her know he was not in the best of moods. Apparently, belted earls took injuries to their pride very seriously.

He started up the stairs, a determined look on his handsome face. Maeve opened her mouth to protest, but instantly thought better of it. In some mysterious way, carrying her about as if she were an invalid seemed to bolster his flagging self-esteem. Very well, so be it. Lily had often complained that men were unpredictable creatures; Theo was certainly proving the point.

"My chamber is the first door to the left of the stairs on the second floor," she directed and received a curt nod for her effort.

"Miss Barrington is in need of a hot bath," Theo called over his shoulder to the gaping housekeeper. "Please arrange for one to be brought to her chamber immediately, and notify her abigail her services are needed."

Maeve cringed, fully expecting Mrs. Pinkert to respond in the same surly fashion as when the squire issued an order. To her surprise, the rotund housekeeper mumbled, "Yes, your lordship. Right away, your lordship," and sprang into action as fast as her swollen feet and unwieldy body would allow.

"I'm impressed, Theo." Maeve laughed. "I doubt Mrs. Pinkert has moved that fast in the last ten years."

His only reply was a grunt, which reinforced her suspicion that he was beginning to find his water-soaked burden a bit heavier than he'd expected.

The door to the bedchamber was ajar. Theo pushed it open,

strode through the doorway, and stopped dead, obviously searching for someplace to deposit a woman in her condition without doing irreparable damage to the furnishings. He settled on the pretty little ruffled stool sitting before Meg's pretty little ruffled dressing table.

Maeve watched him straighten up and gaze about the very feminine pink-and-white room—at the lacy canopy above the narrow satin-covered bed, the partially embroidered altar cloth in its tambour frame, the doll collection.

"I'd never have guessed this was your bedchamber," he said, a puzzled look on his face. "Somehow it doesn't look like you."

Maeve swallowed hard. "I tried to tell you that you didn't really know me. You wouldn't listen."

"I can see now that I should have." Theo frowned. "Maybe tomorrow we can have that talk you mentioned. If you're up to it, I thought we might visit an ancient Roman-Christian church that's not too far from here. I think you might find it interesting, and I hesitate to say it—romantic."

A touch of his usual cynical humor tinged his smile—something Maeve realized she'd sorely missed in the past hour or two. "At least it has the advantage of being on dry land."

Maeve knew she should beg off. Her plan to store up memories for the future had backfired on her. She knew now that every moment she spent with Theo would simply make it that much more difficult to return to the lonely life awaiting her in London.

She couldn't bring herself to refuse him. As a dying woman might cling to the last faint breath of life, so she clung to these last hours with Theo, painful though they might be. "It sounds delightful," she said somewhat breathlessly.

He gave a stiff little bow. "I'll plan on calling for you around one o'clock then."

He hesitated in the doorway as he was about to take his leave. "Are you in the habit of praying, Meg?" he asked.

He took her by surprise. "I . . . can't say I've actually formed a habit of talking to God on a regular basis," she stammered. "But yes, I do pray on occasion."

"Good. I believe this might qualify as one of those occasions. I'd do so, myself, but I seem to have lost the knack."

Once again, the ironic smile played across his strong, chiseled features. "All things considered, it might be well if one of us prayed that the blasted roof doesn't cave in on us while we're nosing about the 'romantic ruin.' "

The "romantic ruin" was everything Theo had claimed and more. It was, in fact, not a ruin at all, but a solid little church with both walls and roof intact.

The printed plaque at the entrance announced that it had been constructed during the time of Constantine, and Christian worship had continued in the chapel through the Dark Ages and even beyond the departure of the Romans from Kent in the early part of the fifth century.

It went on to say that this had been a favored chapel of the devout Frankish Queen Bertha, consort of the heathen King Ethelbert of Kent, who was converted to Christianity by St. Augustine in the late sixth century.

Maeve had had no formal religious training. Lily considered the clergy a bunch of pious hypocrites; they, in turn, considered her a fallen woman beyond redemption. As a result, Maeve had developed an unorthodox kind of faith through her own reading, which was a far cry from either the Church of England or the Church of Rome. But the thought of walking in the footprints of St. Augustine still sent shivers down her spine.

Without thinking, she slipped her hand into Theo's and felt his strong fingers encircle hers in a way that told her he felt the same sense of timeless awe as she. "Notice the brick," he said, indicating the unique, narrow bricks that formed all four walls of the little church. "They were hand-fashioned by the Romans who invaded this area sometime in the fourth century. It's a lost art now."

"And the roof is the same beautiful silver gray slate I've been admiring on the local farmers' cottages," Maeve added.

Theo ducked his head, and together they stepped through the low, arched entryway into the silent, musty-smelling chapel. Heavy oak beams, darkened with age, crisscrossed the ceiling above them. Four rough-hewn benches of the same native wood faced a small, crudely carved altar, on which a lighted candle testified to the existence of a caretaker.

"Am I seeing things, or is that a painting above the altar?" Maeve asked. "Surely, no painting could survive four centuries in such a place as this."

"Of course it couldn't, even though it's painted on wood, not canvas. But it's been here as long as I can remember, and none of the locals could give me a clue as to the identity of the artist."

With her hand still in his, Theo led her around the benches to stand at the chancel rail and stare at the painting of a sweet-faced madonna with dark eyes and raven hair, holding a plump, dark-haired baby. "It's a crude rendition of a familiar subject, and the figures are slightly out of proportion, but I've been strangely fascinated by it since the first time I saw it—as if something deep inside me recognized a kinship with the lady."

Maeve nodded. "She does resemble you—certainly more than your own mother does. Whoever the artist was, I think he must have empathized with the lonely Roman soldiers who built this chapel so far from their homeland, and endowed the holy pair with the features and coloring of the wives and babes they'd left behind."

Theo smiled down at her, the light of the single candle gleaming in his dark eyes. "You think I took Italian then?"

"I do, indeed." Maeve chuckled. "You would look very much at home in the uniform of a Roman soldier, thanks to that Italian gardener we agreed was somewhere in your background."

"Actually, she was a maid."

Maeve stared at him, startled by the solemn note in his voice. "I'm not sure I understand what you're saying."

"I'm saying my mother—my real mother—was an Italian maid who was my father's mistress. I met her for the first time a se'enight ago. She looks very much like the madonna in this little painting, which is why it seemed appropriate to bring you here to tell you about her."

"But that makes you—"

"A bastard. A legalized one, but a bastard nevertheless. I can see, from the look on your face, how deeply I've shocked you. But, believe me, you can't be any more shocked than I was when I first learned the truth of my birth."

"I'm not shocked, just surprised," Maeve lied, though, in truth, her knees were trembling so badly she had to grip the chancel rail with both hands to steady herself. It was not the fact of his illegitimate birth that shocked her, but rather that Theo would entrust her with knowledge that could bring scandal and disgrace to the noble house of Hampton should it become public.

She took a deep, calming breath and turned to face him. "Why have you told me this?"

"I'm ashamed to say I hadn't planned to until after we were married, and I was absolutely sure of you. But yesterday, when I saw how worried you were about divulging what you apparently consider some deep, dark family secret, it occurred to me you might find it easier to trust me with your secrets if I trusted you with mine. I want no lies between us when we begin our life together, Meg. Not even lies of omission."

Maeve couldn't bring herself to look at him. How it had come about that this incredible man should fall in love with a plain, bookish sort of woman like her was more than she could fathom. But love her he must; she no longer doubted it. If God was seeking to punish her for her sinful ways, he had found the cruelest of methods.

"I am not as courageous as you, and the tale I have to tell is far more ugly than the one you've told me. I think I must write you my truth in a letter," she said in a hoarse whisper, and watched his beautiful, sensuous mouth form a protest.

She stopped him with a finger to his lips. "No, it is best this way. I give you my solemn promise I will begin writing my letter tonight and have it in your hands no later than the day after tomorrow—the first day of June."

The truth was she couldn't endure the anguish of being near him a moment longer. Nor could she bear to see the tenderness in his eyes turn to hatred, the passion to disgust.

She could wait no longer to hear from her twin. This heart-wrenching situation between Theo and her had to be resolved. He wanted there to be nothing but truth between them. Very well, she would give him that truth, sordid though it might be. Then, like the coward she was, she would run back to London to lick her wounds in the privacy of the little house she'd paid for with a broken heart.

But first . . . She reached up to cup his beloved face in her hands for the last time. "Tell me, Theo," she whispered, "do you think the little madonna who resembles your mother will be scandalized if you kiss me in this house of God?"

Chapter Thirteen

Maeve woke to gray skies and the sound of rain pelting her window on the morning after the excursion to the little Roman-Christian church. A fitting ambience for the mood she was in, she decided, too exhausted from her restless night to rise from her bed. She was still staring aimlessly into the ruffled canopy above her when Lucy arrived half an hour later with a large pitcher of hot water and a cup of steaming chocolate.

"Good morning, miss, and what have you planned for today, so's I know what clothes to lay out for you?" she asked with a cheerfulness that grated on Maeve's tender sensitivities like a fingernail on a slate.

Maeve hunkered deeper into the bedcovers. "Any old thing will do. I don't plan to leave the house."

"Aye, the weather's that fearful now, isn't it?" Lucy threw open the door of the armoire and started leafing through the gowns hanging inside. "But just in case his lordship should call, you'll want to look your best." She held up a yellow dimity gown with white ruffles at the neck and wrists. "How about this one? And if you don't mind my saying so, miss, a touch of bloom of ninon for your cheeks wouldn't be amiss. You're pale as a ghost this morning."

Somehow Maeve found the energy to sit up and dangle her legs over the edge of the bed. "The dress is fine, the rouge is not necessary, and if the earl should call, you're to tell him I have a sick headache and cannot see him."

"Oh, miss, I'm so sorry you're unwell. I'll ask Mrs. Pinkert for one of those tisanes she makes up for the squire when he's suffering from his sick headaches, so you'll be up to snuff when his lordship arrives."

Maeve glared at the nauseatingly cheerful maid. "Go away, Lucy," she said more sharply than she intended. "I do not need a tisane, and I do not want to see the earl. Furthermore, I am perfectly capable of dressing myself without your help."

"Yes, miss." The young maid's face crumpled, and her full, pink lips trembled noticeably. "I was just trying to be helpful, miss."

Maeve sighed. "I know, Lucy, and I apologize for my rudeness. I'm in a foul mood this morning. I just need some time to myself to finish an important letter I'm writing." She'd started the dreaded missive, as promised, the previous evening and gotten as far as, "Dear Theo."

With Lucy pacified and on her way to the kitchen for her breakfast, Maeve washed her face and hands, dressed herself in the gown the maid had chosen, and started in on her letter. For the balance of the morning, she sipped her chilling chocolate and labored over her letter to Theo—changing a word here, a sentence there—more often than not, scratching out more than she kept.

Recounting her monstrous lies and deceit was difficult enough; explaining her reasons for doing what she did was close to impossible. But finally, after a dozen tear-soaked handkerchiefs, a like number of discarded sheets of paper, and nearly as many broken nibs, she was satisfied with what she'd written.

It was all there, every damning word of it, including the exact sum of money she'd persuaded the squire to pay her for her nefarious masquerade. Two things only were left out—her mother's profession, which she couldn't bring herself to mention, and her own profession, which she dare not make public.

All that remained was a decision as to if and how she should tell him that in spite of everything, she did truly love him. For more than an hour, she pondered the question of whether or not he would take comfort in such knowledge, and finally decided to end the letter without mentioning her feelings. After three pages of foolscap on which she'd detailed all the ways in which she'd lied and cheated and deceived him, she could scarcely expect him to believe her capable of any honest emotion.

Theo came to call on her, as she'd known he would, once the sun broke through the clouds—and Lucy turned him away, as directed. Heartsick, Maeve observed him from behind the drape as he cast a troubled glance toward her chamber balcony before riding off.

She watched him until the final moment when he disappeared from sight down the tree-lined drive, knowing it might well be the last time she ever saw him. One more memory to add to her painful collection, she reminded herself, dabbing at her teary eyes with a fresh handkerchief. After all the wonderful "firsts" she'd shared with Theo, such an ignominious "last" seemed particularly sad.

But if there was one thing of value she'd learned from Lily, it was that grieving over what could never be was beyond futile. She folded her letter into a neat square and slipped it into the drawer of the dressing table. She'd drop it at the vicarage tomorrow morning with instructions to Richard that he should deliver it to Theo once she was safely on the coach that would take her to London.

That accomplished, she marched down the stairs to settle her business with the squire while they shared the noonday meal. She fully expected the wily old fox to demand she stay until Meg returned, maybe even balk at paying her the money due her. She would have none of it; when push came to shove, she could be just as obstinate as he.

He was not in the dining room. Nor was Mrs. Pinkert, who had given up eating with her employer now that the staff had been enlarged. Maeve ignored the covered dishes laid out for her on the sideboard and hurried to the kitchen.

"Where is the squire?" she demanded.

Mrs. Pinkert looked up from her plate of food. "Where else but out with the hounds."

"At this time of day? He never misses a meal unless . . ." Maeve stared at the rotund housekeeper in horror. "Oh, no! Don't tell me he's off on one of his—"

"The sickness is upon him," Mrs. Pinkert interrupted, waggling her eyebrows to remind Maeve the two maids sharing the meal with her were listening, wide-eyed, to everything they said.

"Sickness, my eye!" Maeve was too angry to care who heard her. The squire knew very well tomorrow was her last day at Barrington Hall. He was hiding out in the kennels to avoid facing her. She clenched her fists in frustration. "If that old reprobate thinks he can bamboozle me, he has a surprise in store for him. I'm going out there."

Mrs. Pinkert paused in the act of slicing her mutton, her eyes wide with shock. "I wouldn't do that if I was you, missy. He's meaner'n a snake when he's taken with the sickness."

"I'm going after him," Maeve repeated, heading for the door that opened on the kitchen garden and beyond it, the kennels.

"Well, don't say I didn't warn you. And mind you watch your head. He's been known to throw things at times like this."

Maeve circled the rows of Mrs. Pinkert's carefully tended early vegetables, which were obviously thriving in rich, black soil damp from the morning rain, and opened the garden gate. Two kennel boys were sunning themselves side by side on a bench outside the half-timber building in which the squire kept his prize hounds. One of them had a bandage wrapped around his forehead. The door to the kennel stood open, and two cinnamon-colored hounds lay sprawled across the entrance, sound asleep.

"Is the squire in there?" Maeve asked.

"Yes, ma'am," the boys answered in unison.

Maeve strode forward, determined to have it out with her father before he got too far into his cups.

The older of the two kennel boys jumped up and barred the door with his thin body. "Ye'd best not go in there, ma'am. He's liable to wing ye wi' a bottle or such. His temper be somethin' fierce when the sickness is on 'im. Why, young Timmy here got a knock on the head not an hour ago as near laid 'im out, just for tiptoeing in to see iffen the yellow bitch had whelped 'er pups yet."

"Well, he'd better not try such a thing with me, or I'll raise a knot on *his* head he won't soon forget."

The kennel boy, who was a half a head taller than Maeve,

smiled tentatively. "No disrespect, ma'am, but you're kinda puny to be tacklin' a fella the size of the squire."

"Size isn't everything." Maeve pushed the boy aside and entered the kennel. Instantly, a powerful smell of dog assailed her nostrils, as well as another more pleasant smell of fresh straw emanating from the bales stacked just inside the door.

She blinked as her eyes adjusted to the dim light in the large windowless enclosure. From somewhere deep in the murky interior came the undeniable sound of snoring, but even when her vision cleared, she could see no sign of the squire.

What she could see was a pile of brownish-colored fur in the middle of a large straw pallet. On closer inspection, it turned out to be six or eight sleeping hounds sprawled atop each other like a litter of newborn pups she'd once observed in the window of a used-book store in London's East End.

The loud, rhythmic snoring continued unabated. Led by the sound, she ventured farther into the kennel and promptly stumbled over a bucket of water sitting in the middle of the plank floor. The horrendous racket woke the hounds, and the three on the top of the pile lazily detached themselves and wandered over to sniff at Maeve's skirt. She patted their sleek heads somewhat gingerly, but they seemed friendly enough.

As she watched, the remaining hounds shifted positions, revealing the source of the rhythmic snoring. At the bottom of the pile, flat on his back, with an empty brandy bottle clutched to his chest, lay the squire. Mrs. Pinkert hadn't exaggerated; the disgusting man actually did sleep with his dogs.

Maeve stepped closer and kicked the sole of his boot. "Wake up, blast you, we have business to transact."

The squire snored on, his eyes closed, his mouth slack, his bulbous nose red as a new-picked cherry.

Maeve kicked the other boot. Once, twice, three times. Not so much as an eyelid flickered, but now, after each snore, he emitted a sound reminiscent of a brisk wind whistling through a broken shutter.

Maeve was in no mood to wait patiently while her annoying parent slept off his waltz with John Barleycorn. She had just survived one of the most miserable mornings of her life. She'd painstakingly put every sin she'd committed to paper, wept until she had no tears left, and watched the only man she would ever love ride away from her. Her nerves were as raw as open wounds, her temper as short as a burning fuse.

She looked about her for something suitable to crown the sleeping squire. There was nothing in sight . . . except the bucket on which she'd barked her shins. Without another thought, she picked it up and dumped the contents on his head.

He exploded from the tangle of hounds like an erupting volcano—sputtering, spitting, turning the air around him blue with his cursing. With a violent push, he dislodged the dog draped across his stomach, wiped the water from his eyes, and stared up at Maeve. "I might've known 'twas ye," he fumed. "Misbegotten spawn of yer hell-born mother." He winged the brandy bottle at her. Maeve ducked, and it shattered against the wall behind her.

"That was smart," she said scathingly. "Now you can spend your spare time picking chips of glass out of bleeding paws."

The squire ignored her comment. "What the devil are ye doing in me kennel? No female's ever set foot in here before ye dared foul it with yer fishwife's tongue."

Maeve tossed her head. "I came to settle up my account with you. Tomorrow is the end of my promised fortnight. I'm leaving for London on the mail coach that stops at the village inn at noon, and I want the money due me."

"The agreement was ye stay till yer sister returns."

"The agreement was I attend the betrothal ball and stay one fortnight beyond, and I've a written contract to prove it."

"And what am I supposed to tell folks—like say, the earl—when they asks where ye be?" The squire settled back on the straw pallet, a bulldog look on his face. "It won't do, ye scrawny scarecrow, and I ain't paying up, so best ye play the cards as was dealt ye. Don't ask me why, but Lynley, poor fool, is besotted with ye, and it don't matter a whit to me which of me daughters he marries."

"As long as he gets one with child before she's five and twenty so you don't lose everything you own to the crown."

"So ye knows about that, do ye? Thanks to that blabbermouth, Emma Pinkert, no doubt. Well, don't make no matter down the road. I'll not pay ye so much as a brass farthing, and that's me final word so ye'd best feather yer nest where ye can, missy."

"What makes you think the earl would marry me once he knew how I'd deceived him?"

"What the cloth-head don't know won't hurt him."

"But he will know. I've already written him a letter telling him the whole sordid story."

"Ye done what?" The squire bolted upright, clutched his head, which was obviously paining him sorely, and stared at Maeve through narrowed, bloodshot eyes. "Why'd ye do a bird-witted thing like that, ye silly goose?"

"Because . . ." Maeve felt a traitorous sob rise in her throat. "Because Theo's not the rake I thought him to be. He's a kind, decent man who deserves to know the truth. Because . . ." She swallowed hard. "I love him with all my heart." What did it matter if she admitted the truth to this evil old scoundrel. She would never see him again after today.

"Ye *love* him?" The squire's tone of voice made a mockery of the word. "Then why, when ye had him practically slavering at your feet, would ye write him a letter bound to turn him against ye?"

Maeve felt tears well behind her eyes. She willed herself to remain dry-eyed. She would not—simply would not—let her heartless father see her cry. "I told you why. I love him. I couldn't bear to live with him as his wife if I'd won him by trickery."

"Ye're a fool, Maeve Barrington, and ye're no true daughter of Lily's after all. She would have seen her main chance and taken it, no matter what."

Maeve pulled herself together and stared him in the eye, hating him for what he was—hating herself for letting desperation force her to sink to his level. "I may be a fool," she said coldly, "but I'm a fool who holds a signed and witnessed contract, and if you think I won't take you to court to collect my money, just try me, old man. When it comes to collecting what's due me, I am very much like my mother."

For a change, Maeve instructed Mrs. Pinkert to open a bottle of the squire's best wine to serve with dinner that evening. It

was her last night at Barrington Hall, and though she was dining alone, she intended to do so in style.

The squire was still in the throes of his current "sickness,"
but she felt certain she'd put the fear of God in him with her
threat to face him in the London courts with his signed agreement. Luckily, he had no way of knowing she was bluffing, or
that she would never dare risk such notoriety for fear of revealing the true identity of Marcus Browne in the process.

He had grudgingly promised to travel to London sometime in
the month of June to arrange transfer of the stipulated funds to
her account. She could only pray he kept his word. After her
last encounter with him, she felt no compunction whatsoever
about forcing him to pay Lily's debts. It seemed an ironic justice, considering what the two of them had done to Meg and
her.

Despite her flagging appetite, she ate heartily of Mrs.
Pinkert's perennial mutton and potatoes. This might well be her
last good meal until she managed to sell another cartoon or the
squire made good his promise, whichever came first.

After dinner she wandered out to the kitchen to spend a few
moments chatting with Mrs. Pinkert and Lucy, surprised at how
fond she'd grown of them both in but two weeks' time. There
would be no one to chat with in London; Bridget had left for
Yorkshire to live with her married sister the same day Maeve
had departed for Kent.

The snug little house in which she'd once felt so contented
would seem terribly empty and lonely without Lily and Bridget—almost as lonely as her life would be without the excitement and passion Theo had brought to it. The very thought
triggered a pain so intense, she said a hasty good night to the
two servants and fled from the kitchen before she turned into a
watering pot yet again.

She stopped at Meg's music room on her way to the bedchamber, and let her fingers wander idly over the keys of the pianoforte, playing bits and fragments of compositions she loved.
Her music had always seen her through difficult times before;
tonight it failed her miserably. Every note she played reminded
her of Theo's voice, Theo's laugh . . . Theo's kiss.

There was nothing left to do but retire, though the thought of enduring yet another interminable sleepless night was almost more than she could bear. Wearily, she trudged up the stairs to the pretty bedchamber that belonged to her identical twin—a woman who was her exact image, yet as much a stranger to her as any she might pass on a London street.

The truth was there was no one in the whole wide world who cared if she lived or died—except Theo—and by tomorrow at this time, he would despise her. She had lived with loneliness and isolation all her life. She'd thought she knew them well. She realized now she'd only just begun to comprehend the meaning of the words.

The French windows were standing open when she reached the bedchamber, and a pale spring moon cast a silver glow over the small balcony beyond them. Maeve placed the lighted candle she'd carried with her on the bedside table, stepped out of her slippers, and onto the balcony.

The wood beneath her stockinged feet was still warm from the sun, the night breeze fragrant with the scent of spring flowers. A thousand stars shimmered in the heavens. Somewhere a cricket chirped; a nightingale trilled its lonely, exquisite song.

Tomorrow she would return to the smell of fresh pasties warmed over charcoal braziers and soot from thousands of smoking chimneys—to the sound of carriage wheels on cobblestones and the cries of street whores selling their bodies to the dandies exiting a performance at the Drury Lane theater. But tonight she would give herself over to the sights and sounds and fragrances of the Kent countryside.

Removing the pins from her hair, she invited the friendly breeze to play through the heavy tresses as Theo's fingers had done the day he'd carried her from the lake.

Closing her eyes, she let the memories of the moments she'd spent with him during the past two weeks parade through her mind, one by one. She could almost feel his presence, almost sense the magic that sparked between them whenever he was near.

So real was her lovely dream, she even imagined she heard music in the background. Strange, hedonistic music like nothing she'd ever heard before—music that made her woman's body ache for a fulfillment she could only begin to imagine.

A moth, drawn to the candle flame, brushed by her cheek, and she opened her eyes, expecting the pain of reality to erase the last remnants of her brief, beautiful phantasm. Oddly enough, the music played on, the lilting melody seeming to rise from beneath the very balcony on which she stood.

She held her breath, waiting for the music to slip away on the night breeze like the rest of her fantasy. It grew louder, more poignant, and someone began putting words to the music— strange foreign words sung in a rich, throaty baritone.

Puzzled, she leaned over the balcony railing and spied a familiar tall figure lounging against the trunk of a white birch in the garden below her. His song finished, he stepped forward into the moonlight.

"Theo?" Maeve gasped. "Good heavens, is that you? What in the world are you doing down there?"

"I'm serenading my ladylove with my guitar—an instrument I was taught to play by a Spanish nobleman, a *caballero* who fought with my regiment to free his country from Bonaparte's clutches. When Ramon wasn't fighting like a demon from hell, he could always be found standing beneath some senorita's balcony, strumming his guitar and singing his heart out. I thought it a wonderfully romantic custom—one I wanted to share with you."

He was dressed all in black in what Maeve realized must be the costume of a Spanish *caballero*, like the one he spoke of. A short black jacket trimmed in silver embroidery skimmed his narrow waist. Matching trousers hugged his long, powerful legs and flared above the toes of his black boots. A flat brimmed hat cast mysterious shadows across his handsome features. Maeve's breath caught in her throat. She had never seen anything or anyone as beautiful as Theo was at this moment.

Smiling up at her, he languidly strummed his fingers across the strings of his guitar, drawing forth a sound like a plaintive human sigh. "What say you, my love, can you hear my heart speaking to yours through my song? Can you feel my soul reaching out to yours, my body longing to make us one?

"Say the words I want to hear, *querida*—the words you almost said when I kissed you in the little church." His voice rose strong and determined above the soft, provocative notes he coaxed from the melodious instrument cradled across his chest. "I swear I'll not leave here until I hear them."

Maeve stared at his moonlit figure, torn between retreating to the safety of the bedchamber and acquiescing to his demand. The latter won out; she had wanted to say the words for so long, and this would be the last chance she would ever have of saying them. Another "last," and this one would be the most bittersweet of all.

She gripped the railing with taut fingers. "Very well, my lord, I shall say the words you want to hear, but only if I have your solemn vow that no matter what the future brings, you will always believe that at this moment in this place, I spoke from my heart."

"An odd vow to demand of the man with whom you are destined to spend the rest of your life."

"Still, I demand it."

"Very well, little termagant. I swear that no matter what the future brings, I will always believe that the words my beloved spoke on the night of the thirty-first of May in the year of our Lord eighteen hundred and fourteen came from her heart. There, will that do as a solemn vow?"

"It will do." Maeve leaned forward across the balcony railing. "Listen well, for I shall have the courage to say them only once." She drew in a deep breath and exhaled slowly. "I love you, Theodore Hampton, Earl of Lynley, with all my heart and all my soul, and shall until the day I die."

"And I love you, Meg Barrington, with all *my* heart and all *my* soul, and shall until the day *I* die."

Maeve looked down on Theo's handsome face one last time through eyes blurred with tears, and thought what fitting irony that his declaration of love should be to a name that had never belonged to her. "Good night, my love," she said quickly before her trembling lips could no longer form the words.

"*Buenas noches, mi querida,*" Theo replied as she turned and fled into the bedchamber.

To her surprise, Lucy was standing beside the bed, her eyes brighter than the bedside candle. "I just come to help you undress for bed, miss. I didn't mean to listen to you and the earl.

Honest I didn't. But I just couldn't help myself. It was so romantical. Just like a page from one of Mrs. Radcliffe's books."

She clasped a hand to her generous bosom. "La, miss, has there ever in all this world been a woman as blessed as you?"

Chapter Fourteen

One of the village lads delivered a note from Richard early the next morning while Maeve was having her second cup of tea. It said the package she'd been expecting had arrived safely and was waiting for her at the vicarage.

The package? An odd way of putting it, to Maeve's way of thinking. She was expecting a reply to the letter she'd sent her twin. But why would Meg send her a package? She shrugged. Maybe Richard was just being cautious in his wording in case the squire should see his note.

Maeve could have put his mind at ease on that point. She doubted her father would crawl out from under the pile of hounds until he'd drained the two full bottles of brandy she'd seen beside the straw pallet, and slept off the effects.

Still, Richard's note couldn't have arrived at a better time. She had already alerted Mrs. Pinkert that she was leaving, and she'd planned to tell Lucy she was walking to the vicarage this morning to help Richard arrange flowers for the Sunday service—something she understood Meg often did. The note conveniently corroborated her fib.

Half an hour later, with her night rail and a pair of slippers crammed into her reticule, she closed the door on Meg's pretty bedchamber and walked down the three flights of stairs to the vast, two-story entryway of Barrington Hall. She'd dressed in the same long-sleeved dress she'd worn the day before; Lucy had insisted on giving her own drab dresses to the village poor. But absconding with one of Meg's lovely dresses was bad enough; she couldn't bring herself to take anything else. She was, therefore, wearing her own serviceable outerwear that she'd brought from London.

Lucy was just starting up the stairs, her arms full of freshly ironed garments. The young maid gave a shriek of dismay when Maeve passed her. "Why ever are you wearing that awful bonnet and that heavy old brown pelisse on a beautiful day like this, miss? What if you should happen to meet the earl? La, I maybe shouldn't say it, but you don't look your usual pretty self. As I always tell my sisters, clothes do make a difference."

Somewhat curtly, Maeve dismissed the young maid's pleas that it was her reputation at stake as well as that of her mistress, since everyone in the village knew who dressed the squire's daughter. She had no intention of meeting up with Theo; she had, in fact, purposely chosen the time of day when she knew he'd be involved in the work of managing his estate.

She soon realized, however, that Lucy had been right about the pelisse. It was much too heavy for a warm spring day. By the time she reached the neat little two-story brick house adjacent to the village church, she had the garment draped over her arm and was ready to remove her bonnet as well.

Richard himself answered her knock at the vicarage door. "I gave my housekeeper a holiday, for obvious reasons," he said mysteriously as he led Maeve down the hall to his book room.

"I take it, from your note, the letter from my sister has arrived."

"The letter? Oh, no. Something much better than that." With a dramatic flourish that seemed totally foreign to his retiring nature, he threw open the door and stepped aside to let Maeve enter ahead of him.

Sunshine streamed through the windows of the cheerful little book room, and Maeve found herself momentarily blinded after the dimly lighted hall. She heard a soft gasp, and glancing in the direction from which it came, stared at what could easily have been her reflection in a mirror. For a long heart-stopping moment she stared at her twin in stunned silence, vaguely aware that Richard had exited the room and discreetly closed the door behind him.

Meg was the first to speak. "I set out for Kent the day I received your letter. I couldn't believe I actually had a twin sister." Her voice was softer, more hesitant than Maeve knew hers to be, her smile endearingly shy.

"Nor could I when Lady Hermione told her amazing story." Maeve took a step forward. "I believe it now."

Meg's gray-green eyes searched Maeve's face as if memorizing every feature. "I have always had this strange feeling that some part of me was missing. Now I know why."

Maeve took another step . . . and another. "*Oh* Meg, I've had that same feeling so many times. I'd be going along in my usual way, doing my usual thing, then for no reason I could fathom, I'd suddenly have this terrifying sensation that I was somehow incomplete . . . and isolated from everyone around me." Maeve knew she was chattering; she couldn't help it. The shock of meeting her twin face-to-face had thrown her completely off-kilter.

Tears streamed down Meg's face. "It was very confusing. As if I were desperately lonely for someone I had never met . . . someone who, for all I knew, didn't exist."

Maeve could stand it no longer. With a hoarse cry she covered the last few feet between them and clasped her twin in her arms. Long, breathless minutes passed in which they could do nothing but cling to each other and weep for joy.

Finally, Maeve stepped back, a little embarrassed by the intensity of her emotional reaction. "We should have grown up together," she said grimly. "We should have always been there for each other." She clenched her fists as a wave of soul-scorching anger swept over her. "I shall never forgive Lily or the squire for the terrible thing they did to us."

Meg nodded her head solemnly. "I, too, felt terribly bitter when I was first confronted with the revelation that I had a sister I'd never known and a mother who hadn't cared enough about me to keep me with her."

Gracefully, she seated herself on a nearby chair and indicated Maeve should do the same. Folding her hands in her lap, she continued. "On the long ride from the Highlands, I devoted every waking minute to praying for guidance and understanding as to why our parents felt impelled to do what they did. I am happy to say that after much meditation, I was finally able to cast my anger from me. I am at peace now . . . with everything."

"Well, I'm not," Maeve stated flatly. "You're obviously a much nicer person than I am."

"Not nicer—different." Meg's gentle smile made her plain features glow as if they'd been lighted from within. "Richard told me that while we looked incredibly alike, we had completely different personalities. I can see he was right. You are so much more . . . lively than I. Stronger and braver, too, I've no doubt. Maybe if we could have grown up together, I might have absorbed some of your independence of spirit."

And I might have absorbed some of your sweet, forgiving nature. Maeve could see why the young vicar admired her gentle sister.

"I'm not at all brave," Meg continued. "I'm deeply ashamed that I ran away from my obligations. I would hope that had I known I had a twin sister who would be made to suffer because of my cowardice, I would have acted differently."

"I didn't exactly suffer," Maeve protested, her conscience pricking her when she remembered how much she'd enjoyed every moment she'd spent with Theo in the past three days.

"Of course you did. You stood in for me at that dreadful betrothal ball, and Richard told me how the earl has forced his attentions on you ever since." Meg dabbed at her tear-filled eyes with a lacy handkerchief. "You must have hated every minute of it."

"Actually, Theo can be quite charming when he puts his mind to it," Maeve said, leaping to his defense, though she recognized that in doing so, she risked exposing her feelings for him. "He's not the arrogant rake I first thought him to be. He's really very kind and considerate and . . . sincere." She almost said romantic, but she had an instinctive feeling that was not a word that would impress her twin.

Meg frowned. "How can you say the earl's not a rake? Or that he's the least bit sincere? My maid, Betty, told me he keeps a mistress right here in our village—and heaven only knows how many in London—and doesn't care in the least who knows it. That is not my idea of a moral, God-fearing man. I have always found it rather amazing that Richard considers him his friend as well as his patron."

"But people can change. Theo has. My maid, Lucy, heard gossip in the village just two days ago that he'd given the Widow Whitcomb her congé and set her up in a reputable business in another county."

The color drained from Meg's face. "Oh, no, never say such a thing—not when I'm faced with the prospect of becoming his wife. His mother assured me that if I married him, I would only have to endure his attentions until I produced an heir. Then, he would take his carnal pleasures with his mistress and leave me alone."

"The dowager countess told you . . . *that*?" Maeve stammered, to hide her shock at discovering that in spite of all that had happened, Meg still considered herself betrothed to Theo.

Meg nodded. "Those were her very words, and comforting words they were, too. In fact, if she hadn't called on me the day before the earl made his offer, I would never have accepted him, no matter how much Papa insisted I must."

A dark red flush crept into her cheeks, and she leaned closer to Maeve to whisper confidentially, "I know all about the unspeakable humiliations a woman must endure in the marriage bed, you see." She shivered. "It's a lucky thing women of the lower classes seem to like that sort of thing, which is why so many of them become mistresses or"—her blush deepened—"even whores. For how could any lady of breeding endure married life if her husband didn't have such unspeakable creatures on whom to slake his lust?"

"How, indeed?" Maeve raised her eyes to the ceiling and prayed for patience. She was tempted to tell Meg that her own mother had been one of those "unspeakable creatures," but that would have been beyond cruel.

"I suppose it was the dowager, coldhearted witch that she is, who educated you on the horrors of married life."

Meg stared at Maeve in obvious dismay. "As a matter of fact, it was my maid, Betty. And how can you speak so disparagingly of the countess? The woman is kindness itself. Why she even went so far as to promise I needn't worry about becoming the mistress of Ravenswood; I could simply leave the management of the staff in her hands, just as it's always been." She twisted her handkerchief into a tight knot. "It was only when I was in London and couldn't seek her sage advice, that I became frightened and ran away."

Maeve shook her head. She couldn't believe her twin could be so gullible as far as the countess was concerned, or so prejudiced against the man to whom she'd allowed herself to be betrothed by their father. In truth, if any other woman had divulged what Meg just had, she'd have judged her a trifle dimwitted.

But how ironic that she, herself, should be the one to defend Theo so vigorously to her timid, confused sister. Could it really have been only a few short weeks ago that she'd naively convinced herself she despised all males and was, therefore, immune to the passions that controlled the lives of so many other women?

Lily had warned her that when the right man came along, she'd change her mind. She could do no less than give her twin the same warning. But then a thought struck her. Maybe that right man had already come along for Meg.

"What about your good friend, Richard?" she asked. "Do you find the thought of physical intimacy with him abhorrent?"

Meg gave her a look that clearly said she had gone mad. "Richard isn't a man. He's a vicar," she said indignantly. "I cannot believe he would stoop to indulging in the disgusting practices men like the earl enjoy."

Maeve wasn't so positive Richard lacked the normal male instincts. She remembered a certain look in his eyes the night of the ball, when he'd believed her to be Meg. "Vicars have children," she suggested. "How do you account for that?"

"I don't know," Meg admitted, her eyes widening with something akin to horror. "But I'm certain it can't be *that* way."

Maeve could see there was no point in belaboring the touchy subject. That prim and proper governess Mrs. Pinkert had mentioned had obviously kept Meg completely ignorant of the ways of men and women, and this was not the time to attempt to educate her.

In fact, she glanced at the clock ticking away on the mantel and realized there was no time left for anything except the briefest of good-byes. Noon would be upon her before she knew it.

"It breaks my heart to think of leaving you now that I finally have a sister of my very own," she said, though in truth, she was a bit disappointed to find Meg and she had so little in common.

"Leaving?" Meg's face fell. "Where will you go? And how can you consider such a thing when we've only just found each other?"

"I have no choice. I must catch the noon mail coach to London."

Tears puddled in Meg's eyes. "But why?"

"Think on it," Maeve said, determinedly hardening herself against her sister's obvious distress. "Two Megs at Barrington Hall is one too many at the moment. Maybe once you've sorted things out with the earl . . ."

It was a lame excuse, but she would only frighten her timid sister if she explained that her real reason for leaving so hurriedly was her belief that she'd better be as far away from Ravenswood as possible when Theo discovered he'd been the victim of a hoax. She'd seen him turn into an absolute bear over something as trivial as the sinking of a rowboat; she could well imagine how angry and mortified he'd be when he realized he'd declared his love for an impostor—even trusted his darkest secret to her.

"Don't cry, Meg," she pleaded when her twin began to do so in earnest. "I can't take you with me at the moment, for I've just enough money to get myself to London. But if all goes well, I should be able to support us both before long. Then you can come live with me in the little house our mother willed me and forget all about the squire and his scheme to marry you to a man you despise."

She gave Meg's hand a comforting pat. "We'll grow old together—two contented old spinsters puttering about in our garden and reading to each other from the London *Times*."

Meg's smile was wistful. "It sounds lovely and I shall, of course, visit you from time to time. But my . . . our Great Aunt Tansy made me realize where my duty lies when I visited her in the Highlands. I am a lady and a member of a wealthy family, if not a noble one," she said, obviously parroting the words of her venerable relative. "I am obligated to save the Barrington land and fortune for generations to come, and I am equally obligated to honor the commitment I made to the earl—no matter how much I might dread the thought of living with him the rest of my life."

She sighed. "As Great Aunt Tansy so wisely put it, 'A true lady must always put duty before happiness.'"

Maeve felt as if a lead weight had just been attached to her heart. "Are you saying that you intend to marry the earl after all, in spite of how you feel about him?"

"I am. Great Aunt Tansy said anything else would be unladylike . . . and dishonorable as well." Meg's face was pale, but the determined tilt to her little pointed chin left no doubt in Maeve's mind that her twin was determined to martyr herself in the name of duty.

Which was all very well. She had a sneaking suspicion Meg would thoroughly enjoy martyrdom.

But what of Theo? What possible happiness could he derive from marriage to a woman who cringed at the very thought of his touch? A woman who would never return his passion or understand the loneliness that lurked beneath his arrogant facade. A woman who wouldn't care enough to applaud his triumphs—or laugh with him when he made a fool of himself.

Someone once said blood was thicker than water. But Maeve knew now that love was greater than both. Without a second's hesitation, she decided what she must do.

When Richard joined them a short time later, she asked him for the loan of a pen and the use of a stick of sealing wax. Then, extracting her letter to Theo from the pocket of her pelisse, she pried it open.

She had ended the enumeration of her many sins with a plea that he remember her sister was as much an innocent victim of the monstrous hoax as he. She couldn't bring herself to speak ill of Meg or to warn him that if he married her for her dowry, he would be condemning himself to the same kind of loveless marriage his father had endured. After much deliberation, she added a postscript:

On second thought, my lord, if you treasure your peace of mind, you would be wise to wash your hands of the entire Barrington clan. We are, all of us, trouble of the worst kind. Find yourself an heiress whose father is an honest merchant—not a devious country squire.

Theo had risen at dawn and spent the entire morning helping his farmhands fence the pasture for the cattle he'd ordered. Now, well past noon, he sat in a tub of hot water, soaking away the sweat and grime of his labor.

He felt both pleasantly tired and deeply satisfied with what he had accomplished in the past few hours. Unlike most men of his station, hard work agreed with him. But then, what other man of his station carried the blood of generations of Italian peasants in his veins?

Methodically, he lathered himself with the fragrant soap Albert Figgins had provided him, and happily contemplated the afternoon ahead in Meg's delightful company. He smiled to himself, every bit as satisfied with what he'd achieved last evening as with this morning's work.

The serenade had been a stroke of genius. Meg was obviously a romantic, and what could be more romantic than the sensuous strains of a Spanish love song played beneath a lady's balcony? At long last, she'd let down her guard and admitted how she felt about him.

"I love you, Theodore Hampton, Earl of Lynley, with all my heart and all my soul, and shall until the day I die," she'd said in that husky little voice of hers, and made him vow that come what may, he would always believe they were words from her heart. As if he would ever doubt her when he'd had to work so hard to persuade her to say what so many other women had said so readily.

He knew he was grinning from ear to ear just thinking about the silly little widgeon. He'd grinned so much all morning, the men had teased him about being in love—then teased him even more when he couldn't deny it. For the truth was he had never felt more contented with his lot in life, nor more hopeful for the future.

He had finished dressing and was tying his cravat when

Stepford, the butler, knocked on his chamber door and announced the vicar was awaiting him in the small salon off the entryway. With a muttered expletive over Richard's unfortunate timing, Theo put the finishing touches on the simple knot, gave the butler an order to have the tilbury brought round from the stable, and strode down the stairs to see what Richard had in mind. Whatever it was, it had better be something that could be dispensed with quickly. He had taken longer than he'd planned with the fencing, and his time with Meg would be cut short as it was.

Richard was standing by the window of the salon, the grim look on his face more befitting attendance at a funeral than a social call on the lord of the manor. Theo dismissed it as meaningless, reminding himself that while Richard was an altogether admirable fellow, he did tend to take life very seriously. He was, in fact, a dead bore, and had been since the day he'd accepted his position of vicar of the village church.

"What brings you to Ravenswood on this lovely spring afternoon?" Theo asked, determined to be cheerful in spite of the aura of doom and gloom surrounding his guest.

"I have a letter for you," Richard said. "One I think you should read immediately."

"A letter? From whom?"

"From the woman you call Meg Barrington."

"Devil take it, Richard, I call her Meg because I'm of the opinion Margaret doesn't suit her. I'm sorry if you disapprove, but she is *my* betrothed, after all."

He fairly snatched the letter from the vicar's hand, annoyed that the pawky fellow should poke his nose into something that was none of his business, and even more annoyed that Meg should see fit to use him as her messenger. "I'm on my way to call on her now, as a matter of fact."

Richard's expression changed from grim to downright woeful. "All things considered, I strongly suggest you read the letter first."

Theo stared at the sealing wax, which had obviously been broken, then re-applied, and his temper flared. "Are you saying you took it upon yourself to read a letter addressed to me?"

"Of course not. I would hope you know me better than that. But I am aware of its contents." Richard squared his shoulders. "I won't lie to you; it's knowledge I've possessed for some time."

"The devil you say!" Without further ado, Theo strode to a small Sheraton desk, broke the seal with a letter opener, and spread the pages of foolscap on the desktop. His first thought was that Meg's handwriting was bold for that of a woman and beautifully legible. With an inexplicable sense of foreboding, he began reading.

> Dear Theo,
> I offer no excuse for what I've done. For I have none except desperation, and considering the monstrous way in which I've deceived and betrayed you, that is sadly inadequate. To begin with, the woman with whom you have spent so much of your time during the past fortnight was not your betrothed, Meg Barrington, but her twin sister, Maeve.

Theo was aware of his heart thudding dully in his chest and a chilling numbness settling over his senses as he assimilated the shock of her first words. He read on, and slowly the numbness gave way to white-hot anger and humiliation. Like twin serpents, they coiled low in his gut as the full extent of her deceit became clear to him.

He read to the end—through that subtly insulting postscript—and a wave of pain, more intense than any he'd suffered from a Frenchman's sword, washed over him. How, he wondered, could a man who had known as many women as he had have been so incredibly, stupidly gullible?

The answer to that question, when it came to him, was the most shocking thing of all. He had fallen head over ears in love for the first time in his life, and love had blinded him to the obvious truth he hadn't wanted to know. For even the greenest gapeseed from the wilds of Yorkshire should have realized the witty, multitalented charmer he'd found so fascinating couldn't possibly be the simple country miss she and her wily father purported her to be.

He glanced up from his reading, suddenly aware that

Richard still stood by the window, watching him nervously. "How long have you known the woman I was courting was actually Meg Barrington's twin sister, Maeve?"

"Since the night of your mother's dinner. I knew she couldn't be Margaret the minute she began playing the pianoforte. I taught Margaret everything she knew about music; she could play half a dozen simple country tunes, and she played them rather badly."

Theo remembered that night well. He particularly remembered how deeply he'd been moved by her brilliantly sensitive rendition of the two compositions. He stood up and faced the perspiring vicar. "Yet, you, who profess to be my friend, let me go on making a bloody fool of myself," he said bitterly.

The color leached from Richard's face. "It wasn't like that," he protested. "You see, Margaret had . . . and the squire had persuaded Maeve to . . . so you wouldn't . . ." He extracted a handkerchief from his pocket and mopped his damp brow. "The way Maeve explained it, it seemed like the thing to do at the time."

"Did it, really?" Theo clasped his hands behind him to keep from planting Richard a facer. He knew if he allowed himself to hit the little traitor once, he'd hit him again and again. His innate sense of sportsmanship forbade him to do so, since the fellow was a head shorter than he and weighed a good three stone less.

Furthermore, he could scarcely fault a simple country vicar for being taken in by the clever minx when he, himself, had accepted her monstrous lies without question.

Still, the temptation was too great, his rage too overpowering. He had to quit the scene before the very sight of Richard's face drove him to do something he would bitterly regret. "I'll deal with you later," he said. Then, angrily, he wadded up the letter, tossed it in the trash basket standing beside the desk, and headed for the door.

"Where are you going? What are you going to do?"

Richard sounded terrified. As well he should, Theo thought with a certain amount of vindictive satisfaction. "Where the devil do you think I'm going," he growled, ignoring Richard's inane sputterings about its being too late. "And as for what I'm going to do," he added as he strode toward the waiting tilbury, "I threatened to wring that conniving little vamp's neck once before. This time I may just do it."

Chapter Fifteen

"Where is she?" Theo pushed past the slovenly house-keeper who'd answered his knock at the door of Barrington Hall.

"Where's who, milord?" the old harridan asked with undisguised insolence.

"Miss Barrington—Meg—Maeve—whatever the witch is calling herself today."

"In there." The housekeeper wiped her hands on her apron and pointed a plump, flour-speckled finger toward the open doorway to the left of the entry.

Without another word, Theo strode down the hall and into the salon she'd indicated. The object of his search was sitting on a stool before a tambour frame, embroidering what appeared to be an altar cloth.

Puzzled, he stared at the still figure. She looked like the woman he sought. Her face was the one that had haunted his every dream since the night of his betrothal ball, her hair the same fly-away, sable brown, even her gown the one he remembered seeing her wear before. Still, though he couldn't quite put his finger on what it was, there was something different about her—the set of her shoulders, perhaps; the tilt of her head?

He took a step forward. Instantly, she dropped her embroidery needle and stared up at him with pale gray-green eyes blank with terror. He stopped dead in his tracks. The woman he'd courted so ardently had had vivid emerald eyes that sparked with wit and humor, not these colorless orbs devoid of all expression. This must be the mousy creature he'd encountered on his first visit to Barrington Hall.

"Where is your sister?" he asked in his haughtiest tone of voice.

"M-M-Maeve is gone," she stammered through chattering teeth.

"Gone?" His pulse quickened alarmingly. "Gone where?"

Her cheeks paled to chalky white. Her lips moved, but no sound came out.

With monumental effort, Theo managed to keep from driving his fist through the nearest wall. Could no one in this god-forsaken pile of stone give a direct answer to a direct question?

"Where has your sister gone?" he repeated slowly and distinctly. "And for God's sake, woman, stop cowering. I have never yet struck a woman; I'm not about to begin with you."

"M-M-Maeve has gone b-b-back to London." She gulped a breath of air and met his gaze. "And there's no use your asking her direction, for I don't know it. Nor does my father. She seemed disinclined to give it."

The anger that had simmered within Theo on his hell-for-leather ride from Ravenswood accelerated into a full-blown rage that sent his blood boiling through his veins. "All things considered, I can well imagine she was so disinclined," he said grimly. "The trollop's no fool."

The mouse's eyes grew round as teacups. "M-M-My sister is not a trollop, my lord. Nor has she done anything to earn your disgust. She merely stood in for me while I visited my great aunt in Scotland."

"And a magnificent performance she gave, too, for a mere stand-in. She should seriously consider joining the company of actors at Drury Lane." Theo found himself wondering what this timid little prude would think about her sainted sister if she knew about the passionate kisses he'd shared with the heartless little flirt.

"I can understand your anger at being deceived, my lord. But must you be so insulting?"

"Yes, Miss Barrington, I find I must. For above all things, I despise a coward—and you and your sister have both proven to be craven to the bone. First *you* fled to Scotland to escape the 'monster' to whom your father had betrothed you. Now *she* flees to London to escape the consequences of her ill-conceived deceit. It appears cowardice is a trait common to those bearing the name of Barrington."

"Once again you accuse my sister unjustly." Meg Barrington raised her little pointed chin in the gesture of defiance Theo had found so endearing in her twin, and a knife-sharp pain twisted deep in his heart.

"I freely admit to being the worst kind of coward, my lord, but Maeve is nothing of the sort," she said in a surprisingly steady voice. "She is the bravest, most independent woman I have ever known."

"That may be," Theo said, remembering he had once judged her the same. "But your sister is also an unconscionable liar and a conniving shrew. I am at a loss to determine which member of your ill-begotten family I find the most reprehensible. Thank God I learned the truth before I made the mistake of allying myself with such a collection of sneaks and shysters."

The mouse clutched her tambour frame to her as if it were a protective shield. "Are you s-s-saying you're planning to break our engagement, my lord?"

"Need you ask, madam?" Theo glared at his timid interrogator. "What man in his right mind would not, once he'd learned the extent to which he'd been deceived?"

"I feel I must warn you that Papa will be most unhappy. He has his heart set on this alliance." She blushed furiously. "He desperately needs a grandchild, you see."

"The squire and his nefarious schemes be damned. I'll have no part of them. Nor will I make one of his despicable daughters the mother of my children."

"Ah, but ye will, me fine, fancy lord. For I've a marriage contract signed and sealed as says so, and I mean to hold ye to it—at least until I've the grandchild I need as heir to me fortune and estate."

Theo wheeled around to find the squire teetering in the doorway like a drunken windmill. His face was mottled from drink, his jacket and breeches a mass of wrinkles, his hair sprigged with wisps of straw—and a blob of something that looked as if it belonged in a chamber pot decorated the toe of his right boot.

The pungent smell of dog and sweat and secondhand brandy radiating from the old man made Theo's eyes water and his stomach churn ominously. But even more disquieting was the squire's contention that despite all that had happened, nothing had changed concerning the marriage contract.

Ignoring the sickening stench as best he could, Theo faced his disgusting would-be father-in-law. "Under the circumstances, sir, I feel justified in withdrawing my offer of marriage to your daughter," he said tightly.

"Do you now?" The squire regarded him through bloodshot eyes. "Well, milord, I gives ye fair warning. I intends to hold ye to it, if I have to take ye before a magistrate to do so."

"There's not a magistrate in the county who would hold me to such an arrangement once I recounted the deceit I've endured at the hands of you and your madcap daughters."

"I begs to differ with ye, milord. I rides to the hounds with every one of them, and a more practical lot ye'll never meet. I think they'll find it downright shameful that ye're trying to weasel out of our 'arrangement' when ye've already dipped deep into me daughter's handsome dowry."

Theo felt an icy chill travel his spine, remembering the substantial sums his man-of-affairs had withdrawn to set up both Doddsworth's and the dowager's retirement funds—and the even more substantial draft he had promised the farmer delivering the cattle in the next day or two.

Dear God, he was trapped, and in the final analysis, he was as much to blame as those who'd set the trap for him. For once he'd authorized the spending of the dowry monies, he'd effectively locked the door of his own prison.

It had seemed of little consequence at the time because he'd believed the woman to whom that dowry belonged was everything he could want in his wife and the mother of his children. He should have known better than to believe in miracles. Now he must spend the rest of his life paying for that moment of stupidity.

He gripped the back of a nearby chair to steady himself as a wave of bitterness and despair swept over him. He'd spent a lifetime hiding his feelings from those around him; he was not about to give this evil old man the satisfaction of seeing the anguish he felt over the collapse of his dream.

But how could he bear to spend a lifetime with this pale facsimile of the intriguing woman who had stolen his heart? Every time he looked at her, he'd be reminded of the clever little green-eyed cat and her cruel deception.

"Very well, sir, I will honor the bargain I made, no matter how onerous it might be," he declared while he could still make himself do so. "A gentleman could do no less."

"I never thought for a minute ye wouldn't, milord." A gargoyle grin spread across the squire's face. "It won't be as bad as ye think. I'm not an unreasonable man. I'll not expect ye to keep Meg at Ravenswood forever, for I can see ye've no liking for the spineless chit. Ye've my permission to send her back to Barrington Hall once ye get her with child, for 'tis only me proper, legal grandchild I'm interested in."

Theo watched Meg Barrington shrivel before his very eyes beneath the squire's crass, unfeeling words. Remembering her sister had proclaimed her the only innocent in this sorry affair, he felt a twinge of guilt, knowing he had contributed to her humiliation. He could relate all too easily to how she was feeling at this moment. The countess might have couched her venom in more subtle terms, but in her way, she had been every bit as cruel as the brutish squire.

"Watch your language, sir," he warned. "You're discussing your daughter, not some bitch hound you're breeding."

"Well, I like that!" The squire cast an indignant look at Theo. "What call have ye to rail at me, milord, when I was only thinking of yer feelings when I made me offer to take Meg off yer hands. For any fool with eyes in his head can plainly see the very sight of her puts ye in mind of the other one."

He shook his head dismissively, rendering the air around him thick with straw and dust. "Though why ye was so goggle-eyed over that hell-born shrew is beyond me. Ye've an odd taste in women, milord, and that's a fact. Once I settles me account with her later this month, I plans to wash me hands of her forever."

Theo knew he would only fuel the squire's speculations about his infatuation with "the other one" if he showed any curiosity. He couldn't help himself. He had to ask, "How will you find her, pray tell. London is a big city, and I understand she didn't divulge her direction when she left."

The squire nodded. "That's true. She didn't. But I can always find her. Me friend Hermione knows where that little house her mother willed her stands—and I happens to know the chit hasn't so much as a farthing to her name, so where can she go until she collects the money I promised her?"

He emitted a vulgar sound halfway between a belch and a sigh. "Aye, milord, if ye're interested—and I can see ye are— I can find me daughter, Maeve whenever I wants to. For didn't I lure the she-wolf from her den once before, to me everlasting regret!"

Theo rode slowly back to Ravenswood, his mind in a turmoil. What, he wondered, was the squire up to now? On the one hand, the slippery old scoundrel had badgered him to set a date for his wedding to Meg; on the other, he'd as much as offered an invitation to accompany him to London to visit Maeve.

Theo grimaced. The first thing was something he had no choice but to do eventually; the second was something he had no intention of ever doing. For why would any intelligent, right-thinking man want to seek out the heartless flirt who had led him on such a merry pace for a fortnight—then calmly walked out of his life forever? The motto "Once burned, twice cautious" had taken on a whole new meaning in the past few hours.

He could remember every word in Maeve Barrington's infamous letter. He just couldn't understand why she'd written it, knowing her confession proclaimed her the worst kind of fraud and liar.

Likewise, he could remember every word she'd ever said to him, including those fateful ones that had sent his spirits soaring. "I love you Theodore Hampton, Earl of Lynley, with all my heart and all my soul, and shall until the day I die." He just couldn't understand why she'd bothered to mouth them or to demand he make that solemn vow to believe her, when she had to have already made plans to leave for London the next day.

The woman was a mass of confusing contradictions. An acknowledged liar, who was the most truthful and straightforward person he'd ever encountered. A witty and talented Londoner, who was moved to tears by the sight of an apple tree in blos-

som. A cold-blooded fraud, paid for masquerading as his betrothed, who responded to his kisses with an innocent, eager
passion that left his heart pounding and his knees weak.

Would he ever discover who and what the real Maeve Barrington was? Would he ever find another woman who intrigued
him as she did? And what would it matter if either thing came
to pass, when he was hopelessly trapped into marrying her
spineless and incredibly boring sister?

Leaving his horse in the care of a groom, he marched into the
house and went directly to the small salon where Richard and
he had met a scarce two hours earlier. At some moment on the
ride home, it had occurred to him that his rage over Maeve Barrington's confession had caused him to do something extremely
foolish. Her letter was much too personal and revealing to be
left where a nosy servant might find it.

He stepped through the doorway of the salon and stopped
short. A faint but unmistakable scent of rosewater lingered in
the room—a sure sign the dowager had but recently departed it.
He'd been aware for some days that she frequently visited
Ravenswood manor house when he was gone. Figgins had
warned him she had a paid spy among the servants who kept
her informed of his comings and goings.

He'd done nothing to prevent these secret visits of hers. As
long as she kept out of his sight, he had no quarrel with her visiting her old home. But visiting this particular salon on this particular afternoon was almost too coincidental.

He hastened to the trash basket, only to find it empty. *Damn
and blast!* Had some overzealous servant emptied it the moment Richard and he quit the room? Or, as he suspected, had
the dowager's snooping rewarded her with a juicy bit of scandal regarding the Earl of Lynley and his future countess?

With a shrug, he left the salon and headed to his chamber.
Speculating on what his stepmother would do with the information Maeve's letter contained—if indeed she had that letter—would yield him nothing but a headache. He had other, far
more serious things to worry about, not the least of which was
readjusting his thinking about his upcoming marriage.

Wearily, he climbed the stairs to his suite of private rooms, determined to do that very thing before the depressing happenings of the past few hours completely overwhelmed him.

The first thing he saw when he entered his sitting room was a silver tray holding a decanter of fine French brandy and a small cut-crystal glass. He smiled to himself. Good old Figs! How could the remarkable fellow know that was just what he needed?

But then, why should he be surprised by this latest proof that his batman cum valet had a sixth sense where he was concerned? Figs had proven it time and again during the hellish years they'd shared on the Spanish Peninsula.

He sat down, poured himself a glass of the smooth, amber liquid, and forced himself to think about the problem at hand. It wasn't as if it were something with which he'd never before wrestled. He reminded himself that he'd been fully resigned to a loveless marriage no longer than a fortnight ago.

It was only after he'd come to know Meg—nay, Maeve Barrington—that he'd wanted more. One glimpse of the passion, the excitement . . . the soul-satisfying contentment the right woman could bring to his life, and he'd foolishly begun to believe he might be one of those rare men who was privileged to enjoy a truly happy marriage.

Now the masquerade was over. The dream was dead. There was nothing for it but to get on with his life. But first, he'd try a dose of Albert Figgins's remedy for what ailed him.

He downed the glass of brandy and promptly poured himself another. Then he stoppered the decanter and set it aside. Liquor might be an effective painkiller for some men; it only intensified the ache in *his* heart. Nor would bedding every light-skirt from here to London lessen his desire for the green-eyed cat who'd sunk her claws in him.

Work and his beloved Ravenswood were all that would save him from the black despair in which he was drowning. And work he would. All day, every day, he'd immerse himself in the business of making Ravenswood the profitable estate it once was before his foolish, profligate father drove it to the brink of destruction.

Then every night he'd fall into bed, utterly exhausted—too tired to think and, he hoped, too tired to dream of Maeve's funny little face and Maeve's wicked, laughing eyes and Maeve's warm, passionate lips.

Somehow, he would conquer his despair. All was not lost simply because he'd fallen in love with a woman who was not what she'd appeared to be. So his foolish dream was shattered; he'd survive the disappointment. He'd survived plenty of others in the years he'd lived under the countess's thumb.

He would have a busy and productive life, and a rewarding one in many ways. God willing, he might even have a child on whom to lavish his love. There were only two things he could think of that would be missing from his life from this day forward—passion and laughter.

Albert Figgins was in a quandary. His young lord was bitterly unhappy, and he wasn't certain what he could do to make things right for the lad. He was, however, certain of one thing. He hadn't twice dragged the wounded earl off the battlefield, patched him up and sat up nights wrapping him in wet sheets to control his raging fever, only to watch him work himself into an early grave.

The lad never stopped. From sunup to sundown he was astride that wild-eyed black stallion of his, supervising the placing of every fence post or the planting of every seed on Ravenswood land. Then, from the time he finished his solitary dinner until he crawled into bed at midnight, he worked on the estate books. Albert found himself wondering how the earl's estate manager and man-of-affairs had the nerve to keep on drawing their handsome salaries when their employer was doing all their work for them.

Now Squire Barrington had forced him to set his wedding date for two weeks hence—a sad mistake in Albert's opinion. For he'd carried a certain letter on his person for over three weeks, which, he felt certain, if he could read it, would verify his suspicion the earl was being coerced into marrying the wrong woman.

He was already sure of one thing: The shy, brown-haired daughter the squire had had in tow when he'd called at Ravenswood last evening was not the woman who'd put the sparkle in the earl's eyes and the laughter on his lips the night of the dowager's dinner.

Oh, she could pass for the lady he'd favored, except for her hangdog look and the fact that she'd never once stared dreamy-eyed at him, the way the other one had. But then, he'd never stared at her either. In fact, from Albert's vantage point in the hall outside the salon where the meeting took place, he could see the two of them made a point of looking everywhere but at each other.

He heaved a heartfelt sigh. If only he could think of a way to save his young lord from wasting his life in this ruinous marriage, the way he'd saved him from losing it to a Frenchman's bullet.

But therein lay the rub. How could he, a simple fellow who could neither read nor write, talk a fellow as smart as the earl out of making such a mistake? For one thing, valets weren't supposed to give advice to earls. For another, he didn't relish admitting he'd been listening at the keyhole the day the vicar had delivered the fateful letter, nor for that matter, that he'd snatched it from the trash basket to keep that witch, the countess, from getting her hands on it.

He wished Doddsworth were still around. The old man might be a bit forgetful, but he was still smart as tuppence, and he'd been at Ravenswood since before the earl was born. He'd surely know what to say to make the lad change his mind before it was too late. But Doddsworth was gone, and that stiff-rumped fellow Stepford was in his place.

But wait! What was it Doddsworth had whispered to him when he'd helped the old fellow into the carriage the earl had provided him? "Watch over our young lord," he'd said in that wavery old voice of his. "For I know you're as fond of the lad as I am. And if ever you need help with the task, call on Stepford. There's a good man behind all that starch and polish."

That evening in the upper servants' dining room, Albert rose from the table when Stepford did and followed him into the hall that ran the length of the servants' quarters. "I'd like a minute of your time, Mr. Stepford, if you please," he said quietly.

The younger man stopped, a frown darkening his gaunt features. "What can I do for you, Mr. Figgins?" he asked in that high-and-mighty way he had of talking that made a fellow feel about two inches high.

Albert pondered a moment, trying to decide how best to broach the subject. "It's not for me I'm asking, but for my young lord," he said finally. "He's mighty unhappy, you see, and I'm the only one as knows why—but I don't know what to do about it." He paused for breath. "Mr. Doddsworth said if ever I was to need help watching over the lad, I should call on you."

Stepford looked momentarily taken aback, but he quickly recovered. "Rightly so," he said. "Mr. Doddsworth admonished me to tend to his lordship's welfare as well. But best we discuss this in my private quarters." To Albert's surprise, the elegant fellow took him by the arm and walked him down the hall to the butler's sitting room.

Albert followed him through the door and stared about him at the room where he'd spent many an evening playing cribbage when old Doddsworth was the major domo of Ravenswood. It looked much the same. The cribbage board even sat on the same small table, though Albert knew for a fact Stepford never invited anyone to join him for a game after the evening meal.

The butler offered Albert a chair, took one himself, and got right to the point. "I, too, have noticed his lordship was distracted recently. Perhaps if you tell me what you think is worrying him, I can be of some help."

Albert withdrew the sheets of foolscap from his pocket and handed them to Stepford. "I haven't read this letter, on account of reading and writing is about the onliest things I can't do. But I know pretty much what's in it." He didn't feel it necessary to explain how he came by such knowledge, and luckily Stepford didn't ask.

The butler withdrew a pair of spectacles from his pocket, perched them on his eagle's beak of a nose, and quickly scanned the letter. Then he read it again more slowly, a look of utter astonishment on his usually impassive face.

Carefully, he folded the sheets of foolscap into a neat square and handed them back to Albert. "Good Lord," he exclaimed in hushed tones, "there are two Miss Barringtons! Identical twins!"

Albert nodded. "And unless I misses my guess, his lordship's marrying the wrong one."

"How can you say that? The young lady who called with the squire last evening seemed extremely shy, but in no way disagreeable."

"Except anyone could see she could scarce stand the sight of our lad—nor him of her."

"There did appear to be a bit of constraint between them," Stepford said thoughtfully. "Still, how can the one who wrote this letter be the right woman for his lordship? She not only confessed to deceiving him in every way possible and accepting a great deal of money to do so, she apparently left him to return to her former life."

"Because she loves him, don't you see?" Albert explained patiently. "Why else would she tell him what she done? She could just as easily have married him, and him none the wiser. It's what a woman as didn't care for nothing but his title and estates would've done—and it's ducks to dumplings that's what that pawky father of hers tried to talk her into.

"But women—good women—is funny that way. She wouldn't want the earl if she had to trick him into marrying her. Because she loves him, don't you see?"

"I suppose that makes a certain sense," Stepford admitted. "I wouldn't know, since I've never known what I considered a 'good woman.'"

Albert grinned. "Well, I have. More'n one, as a matter of fact, so I knows how they think."

"But if, as you say, Miss Maeve Barrington loves his lordship, why would she flee to London and leave him for her sister to marry?"

"Because she probably thought there was no way he could love a woman as had deceived him the way she done," Albert explained. "But she was wrong. A man don't stop loving a woman just because she's made a mistake or two. If you asks me, the lad is still so much in love with her, it's near killing him. Remember how he was that two weeks they was together—always smiling to himself secretlike, or humming a tune, or laughing for no reason anyone could see?"

"I do," Stepford admitted.

"And think how he is now. I swear he looked happier when we was slogging our way from one battlefield to another on the Peninsula than he does nowadays. Lord luv us, if he keeps trying to forget her by working himself to death the way the lad has this past three weeks, you and me will be seeing him into an early grave."

Stepford frowned. "Well, I certainly wouldn't want that. He's as fine a master as any man could want."

"Then maybe you could say something to him as would bring him to his senses," Albert said hopefully. "I would if I could, but I'm better at polishing boots than giving advice."

"Me? Offer advice to his lordship as to how he should conduct his affairs?" A look of horror crossed Stepford's lean face. "Heavens, no. I could never do that. It would be most unseemly."

For a long, silent moment, he studied Albert thoughtfully. "I am not certain your assessment of this business with the two Miss Barringtons is accurate, Mr. Figgins. But since I have little or no knowledge of the female sex, or this confusing thing men call 'love,' I must take your word for the seemingly illogical dilemma in which his lordship finds himself at present."

He paused, drew a deep breath, and continued, "It so happens Mr. Doddsworth put me in possession of certain knowledge about a . . . a close relative of the earl's, whom he assured me was most concerned with his welfare. In fact, he gave me her direction in the Lake District and instructed me to write to her if ever I felt the earl should be in need of her counsel and support. I do believe this may be one of those occasions."

"The Lake District?" Albert shook his head. "That won't do at all, Mr. Stepford. The wedding will be over and done with by the time this relative, whoever she may be, can find a way to give the earl the talking-to he needs."

"On the contrary, I shall write the letter this very minute and instruct one of the grooms to leave at dawn, deliver it posthaste to the lady, and wait for her reply. That way, she'll have ample time to communicate with the earl."

He crossed to the small writing desk in one corner of the room, picked up a pen, and began to write. "If you will be so good as to wait while I compose my letter, Mr. Figgins," he said, glancing up briefly, "I shall read it to you to make certain you concur with my description of the situation."

A good hour later, Stepford completed his letter, laid down his pen, and read aloud:

Dear Miss Natoli:
On advice of Mr. Doddsworth, I am herewith informing you of the rather unusual circumstances surrounding the upcoming wedding of the Earl of Lynley and Miss Margaret Barrington. . . .

Chapter Sixteen

The sun had already dipped beneath the western horizon when Theo rode home from his usual inspection of his properties. The last place he'd visited had been the fenced meadow in which his newly acquired cattle grazed.

He had great hopes for the prosperity the herd would eventually bring to Ravenswood. London markets were crying for beef, and he planned to build a herd from this small beginning to keep them supplied with the prime article. He was lucky in that Ravenswood was one of the few estates in Kent that had vast expanses of grassy meadows—something absolutely necessary for the raising of cattle—and he intended to use every inch of the acreage to the best advantage.

Leaving his stallion in the capable hands of his head groom, he entered the manor house through one of the back entrances and went directly to his suite of rooms by way of the servants' staircase.

Figgins was waiting for him, an expectant look on his ruddy face. "So here you be at last, my lord," he exclaimed. "I've a hot bath waiting for you, and I've laid out your clean clothes."

"As you do every night," Theo said approvingly. "I don't know what I'd do without you, Figs."

Figgins cocked his head thoughtfully. "Mayhap I should have laid out your evening clothes."

"Nonsense. There's no need to go to such bother when I'm dining alone." Looking longingly at the steaming tub in the center of his sitting-room floor, Theo took off his jacket, then sat down on the nearest chair and held out his right leg so his valet could remove his boot.

Figgins caught hold of the boot and tugged it off with an ex-

pertise born of long practice. "But that's the point, my lord," he
declared. "You ain't alone tonight. Mr. Stepford come looking
for you not an hour ago to say you had a visitor waiting in the
gold salon on the second floor."

"A visitor?" Theo groaned and held out his left leg. "Damn
and blast, I'm too tired to entertain a guest. Who the devil is
he?"

Figgins tugged off the second boot with the same ease with
which he'd handled the first. "Happens this particular visitor's
a female, my lord, and a fine-looking one, too, as I noticed
when I passed the open door to the salon a short while ago."

Theo's heart sank. There were only three women he could
think of who might have reason to call at Ravenswood. He sincerely doubted his visitor could be his betrothed or his stepmother. That left only his former mistress, and he'd hoped he'd
seen the last of Sophie when he set her up in business in Wembley.

"What does the lady look like?" he asked warily.

A sly grin spread across Figgins's face. "Hair black as coal
and dark eyes as put me in mind of yours. From what I seen of
her, I'd venture to say she's one of your close relatives come to
view your wedding Saturday next."

Theo instantly shot to his feet and took off running with Figgins close behind, shouting that he was in no condition to greet
a visitor—especially a lady. Theo didn't care. Rosa was here at
Ravenswood and at long last, there was one bright ray of sunshine in the suffocating blackness that had surrounded him this
past month.

She was sitting on a straight-backed chair, calmly reading a
book, when he burst through the doorway. She quickly put the
book aside, stood up, and held out her arms. Theo had never in
his life been so glad to see anyone. For a long, quiet moment
they simply held each other, basking in the warmth and affection one gave to the other.

"You changed your mind. You decided to attend my wedding
after all," he said finally, struck by the irony of the situation.
She'd flatly refused to do so when he'd looked forward to the
ceremony as the beginning of his life with the woman he loved.

Now, when he felt nothing but dread for the day, she'd come to join the celebration.

She stepped back and held him at arm's length. "No, my dear, I am not here to attend your wedding—but to prevent it, if I can."

"Prevent it?" Theo stared at her, dumbfounded.

"My spies seem to think you're marrying the wrong twin."

Theo gasped. "How in the world did you—"

Rosa raised a hand to silence him. "Never mind how I came by the story. Can you honestly tell me the judgment my informant made of the situation was incorrect?"

He couldn't bring himself to lie to her. Not when he was staring into eyes that were mirror images of his own. "If you're asking if I'm in love with the real Meg Barrington, the answer is no."

"Is she in love with you?"

"Lord, no! The very sight of me sends the timid little mouse skittering off in panic. I see little hope of ever consummating the blasted marriage."

Rosa's finely etched black brows drew together in a puzzled frown. "Then why are you condemning yourself to a life of misery not too unlike that which your father suffered? Have you learned nothing by his example?"

"My honor demands it," Theo said stiffly. "I signed the marriage contract and . . ." He hesitated, loath to admit the rest of the sordid story.

"Let me guess. You've already spent some of the heiress's dowry—probably for the impressive herd of cattle I glimpsed from my carriage window when we passed one of the south meadows."

"As a matter of fact, I've spent more than the mere cost of the cattle," Theo said, his voice sharp and bitter. "I had my man-of-affairs withdraw sufficient funds to pension off both Doddsworth and the countess as well. Didn't your informant tell you my father left Ravenswood in financial shambles? With the exception of his diamond stick pin, everything the late earl left me was debt encumbered."

"Doddsworth imparted that bit of information over a year ago. I was waiting to see how you fared on your own before I offered my help." Rosa stepped closer and laid her soft hand against Theo's cheek. "Money is no problem, my dear. I am a very wealthy woman. My inn has been successful since the day I opened it. I haven't needed to spend a cent of the generous quarterly stipend your father sent me for more than thirty years. Like the simple Italian peasant I am, I've kept it in a strongbox for the day I could present it to my son. My dear Claude guards it, as we speak, in a carriage outside your front door. It is yours, to do with as you see fit."

"No!" Theo leaned forward and pressed a kiss to her smooth forehead. "Much as I appreciate your generosity, ma'am, I cannot accept your money. Believe it or not, I do have some pride left."

"Don't be ridiculous. No matter what, it will all belong to you someday. I have named you my only heir in my will." She raked him with a look of exasperation that was painfully reminiscent of another strong-minded woman he knew. "You didn't quibble over the inheritance your father left you. Why should you belittle what I have to offer?"

Theo couldn't help but smile. "You are a difficult woman to say no to, ma'am."

"And you are a man of strong principle—and a son any woman would be proud to claim." Rosa touched his cheek again. "Now take the money that is rightfully yours, settle your account with the squire, and be done with the dreadful man and his arranged marriage—for your reluctant bride's sake as well as your own. Then use the rest to rebuild what your spendthrift father so nearly destroyed."

Theo could see there was no use arguing with her. To be completely honest, he didn't want to. If nothing else, the memory of the terror in Meg Barrington's eyes when her father demanded he set a wedding date was enough to convince him he should end his hated betrothal.

"How can I ever thank you?" he asked, hugging Rosa to him.

She searched his face with her huge, expressive eyes. "Grant me the one wish that will give me complete peace of mind when I return home—as I must do before your amazing resemblance to me begins to raise questions we cannot safely answer."

"Name it, ma'am, and it is done."

She stepped back, still holding his gaze with her own. "I want you to promise you will go to London and seek out the girl I have reason to believe you love."

Theo couldn't believe what he was hearing. "To what purpose, ma'am," he said stiffly. "I have her own word for it that she deliberately deceived me and demanded a handsome payment for her masquerade. All her seeming pleasure in our shared moments, her innocent passion, even her claim that she loved me, were part of that masquerade. Have I not already made a great enough fool of myself over Miss Maeve Barrington? Would you ask me to play the clown yet once more?"

Rosa frowned thoughtfully. "My informant believed she confessed her sins to you because she loves you and couldn't bear to gain your love by trickery."

She shook her head at his automatic protest. "I know, it sounded improbable to me at first, too. But the more I thought of it, the more sense it made. You once told me she was the most honest and forthright person you had ever met."

Theo stared at his mother, his mind reeling with a mixture of hope and incredulity. Could there be some truth in what she said?

I vow I will always believe that the words my beloved spoke came from her heart. Maeve had insisted he say those puzzling words before she declared her love for him. Could that have been her way of telling him that in spite of everything she'd done, she did truly love him? He had made the strange vow with all the passion and sincerity of the moonlit moment, then discounted it as just another of her clever ploys once he read her letter.

"The girl bared her soul to you, Theo," Rosa said. "Both a foolish and a courageous thing to do, you must admit. Now it is up to you to decide if you can love only the perfect woman you thought her to be, or if you're capable of loving her in spite of her flaws."

Her smile had a faraway look, her voice a touch of profound sadness. "That is, after all, the true test of the depth of your feelings, my son."

*   *   *

Once again it was the housekeeper who answered when Theo pounded the door knocker at Barrington Hall. "The squire's out in the kennels," she declared before Theo could state his business. "Go around to the back of the house, and you'll see it soon enough. But best you hurry before he's taken with the sickness. He's had a bad morning, poor love."

Theo found the man he sought, drink in hand, surrounded by his prize hounds. He looked every bit as down in the mouth as the housekeeper had warned. "Well, me lord, it didn't take ye long to come gloat over me misfortune," he said sourly the minute Theo stepped through the open door.

"I'm afraid you have the advantage of me, sir."

"Ye mean ye haven't heard? I thought sure the news would be all over Kent by now." He kicked at a cinnamon-colored hound that was slobbering on his left boot. "Me stupid daughter's run away again, and the wedding not but a se'enight off."

By sheer willpower, Theo managed to keep from laughing out loud. "Back to the Highlands, is she, sir?"

"Don't I wish. No, it's Scotland she's heading for all right, but this time it's to Gretna Green with that sneaky twit of a vicar." He gave the hound another shove, this time off his right boot. "There was no stopping the pair of them; they'd been gone all of ten hours by the time I read Meg's note."

"Richard and Miss Barrington? How extraordinary." So that was what Maeve had meant when she'd said Richard was in love, but not with her.

"Aye, the mealymouthed psalm-singer's been sneaking around behind me back all the time. Fat chance I has of getting a grandchild out of that union. I knows me daughter. First time the vicar drops his breeches, the silly prude will head fer the hills."

"Don't take it too hard, sir," Theo said with a straight face. "Her wedding to me would never have taken place anyway." He withdrew a sheaf of pound notes from his pocket and handed them to the squire. "My purpose in coming here today was to pay back what I've spent of her dowry and cancel our engagement."

"The devil, you say. Well, I guess that tears it twixt you and me then."

"Not entirely." Theo cleared his throat self-consciously. "As a matter of fact, I would like to take you up on the invitation you offered some time ago to go with you when you seek out your daughter Maeve in London."

He had made his mother a promise, and he would keep it, but he suspected he was simply setting himself up for more humiliation and heartbreak. How could Maeve have left him so easily if she did, indeed, love him?

The squire instantly perked up. "What ho! Don't tell me ye're still swatting at that fly! I'll say one thing fer ye, lad—ye're a glutton fer punishment. There's not many men I know who'd take on that razor-tongued witch."

He bent to scratch behind the ears of the cinnamon hound, now sprawled across both of his boots. "Hear that, ye worthless rascal. Things is looking up. It's off to London town I be at first light, and with his high-and-mighty lordship here in tow."

Straightening up, he surveyed Theo with a benevolent look. "I can tell ye right now, yer lordship, I'll be rooting fer ye all the way, on account of it don't matter a horse's hind end to me which of me daughters produces a brat afore she reaches the age of five and twenty."

He rubbed his hands together in obvious glee. "And I'll be willing to wager ye won't have to chase Maeve twice round the bedpost to get her between the sheets."

Maeve had been back in London a full month, and she still hadn't become accustomed to the constant noise and the dirt and the smoke-filled air that sometimes seemed dense enough to chew. How, she wondered, could a mere fortnight in the Kent countryside have spoiled her for the city life she'd once found so satisfying?

So far, she'd managed to survive on the payment she'd received for her cartoon of George Brummell—a surprise, since she'd drawn the exact opposite of what the *Times* editor had requested. When it came down to it, she couldn't rejoice in the downfall of her friend, the Beau, as the other London cartoonists had. She'd betrayed one man in the most abominable way; she couldn't bring herself to betray another.

She'd drawn him standing proud and tall with his back to

Watier's, the men's club he'd help bring into vogue, and surrounded him with seven vicious-looking wolves, six with the recognizable faces of the sycophants who clung to the Prince Regent's coattails and one with the face everyone in London would know belonged to Prinny himself. She'd entitled it simply "The Wolf Pack Closes In."

Luckily, the editor had been on holiday when the cartoon reached his desk, and his assistant had automatically passed on it since it was one solicited by his superior. Like her earlier cartoon of the Duke of Kent, it had raised an uproar heard all the way from the elegant salons of Carlton House to the dingiest whorehouse in Seven Dials. Once again, Marcus Browne was the most controversial, and the most popular, cartoonist in London.

But now her money was running out, and her cupboard was as bare as Mother Hubbard's. Furthermore, the tradesmen Lily had owed were banging on her door again. Unless her father contacted her soon, she, like the Beau, would soon be faced with the necessity of hiding out from her creditors.

It was late one afternoon in the first week of July when Lady Hermione's footman finally knocked at Maeve's door with a note stating that her father awaited her at the Mayfair town house. The pasty-faced fellow wore the same supercilious expression as when he'd made his first call on her. She didn't care. She could have hugged him from sheer relief. Before he could blink his eyes, she'd donned her bonnet, pelisse, and gloves, grabbed up her reticule and climbed into Lady Hermione's elegant green and gold carriage.

The stiff-necked butler who'd greeted her on her last visit showed her into the salon where Lady Hermione and the squire awaited her.

"So, daughter, ye're quick to heed me beck and call when there's money to pass hands," the squire remarked in his usual surly manner. Without further ado, he slapped a bank draft into her hand. "There now, take yer blood money and may ye never have a minute's joy of it."

Lady Hermione laid a hand on his arm. "Behave yourself, Harry," she admonished the red-faced squire, then turned to Maeve with a smile that looked almost genuine. "Let's all sit

down like the civilized people we are and have a cup of tea,"
she said sweetly. "I've instructed my butler to bring the tea tray
at precisely five o'clock."

Maeve felt anything but civilized at the moment. Nor did she
have the slightest wish to share a cup of tea with these two con-
spirators who had turned her life upside down with their wicked
scheming. But she stuffed the bank draft into her reticule, took
the chair Lady Hermione had indicated, and watched the squire
and her hostess settle onto an oversized sofa opposite her.

"Now, Harry, I want to make one thing clear," Lady
Hermione said once they were all properly seated. "The business with Meg and the earl is over and done with, and I'll tolerate no more of your everlasting complaining. You agreed to
the terms Maeve demanded, and from the look of things, you'll
more than get your money's worth."

Maeve felt as if someone had just driven a knife into her
heart. "Meg did go through with the wedding then?"

"She did that," the squire said. "But not the way I'd planned,
in the village church with all me friends looking on. Once she
made up her mind to marry the poor sod, she talked him into
running off to Gretna Green with her, like she was no better
than one of the local farmers' daughters."

The pain in Maeve's heart increased tenfold. Theo certainly
hadn't wasted any time grieving for her once Meg offered him
a little encouragement. "I wish them well," she said, though it
nearly killed her to say it.

"That's generous of ye, daughter, all things considered. But
then, 'twas all yer own doing, wasn't it. If ye hadn't been so
squeamish about hoodwinking the earl, ye could have been a
countess by now."

Maeve took a death grip on her reticule. "I explained why I
had to tell Theo the truth."

The squire rolled his eyes toward the ceiling. "Like I told
you, Hermione, the chit was *in love*. She couldn't bear the
thought of tricking the earl into marrying her—wanted him fair
and square, with no lies between them, or not at all. Now what
do you think of that?"

Lady Hermione's smile had never looked more like Lily's. "I
think it was very noble—much more noble than anything I

would ever do. But not terribly practical. Wouldn't it have been wiser to have had the earl's ring on your finger before you confessed your sins, my dear? Who knows, he might have been willing to forgive you anything once the two of you had tasted the pleasures of the marriage bed. He's no saint himself, you know."

"No!" Maeve's voice came out a hoarse whisper. "I doubt I could ever make someone like you understand. But in the two weeks we spent together, I came to love Theo—truly love him. I simply couldn't lie to him any longer."

Lady Hermione scowled. "You loved him, yet you left him. How odd. I feel certain your mother would never have done anything so preposterous. I know I wouldn't have. You may have acted very foolishly, Maeve. It has been my experience that a man will forgive a woman almost anything if he desires her, and Harry said the earl was besotted with you."

"Theo deserves better than a cheat and liar," Maeve said wearily. She had never before realized how cruel the squire and Lady Hermione were. From the looks on their faces, she could swear the two of them were thoroughly enjoying her misery.

Lady Hermione smiled sweetly. "Oh dear, I do hope I'm mistaken, you silly girl," she said in her soft, whispery voice, "but it sounds very much to me as though you're still in love with the earl. Doesn't it sound that way to you, Harry?"

"Stop it, you two. I've heard enough."

The familiar baritone voice came from behind Maeve's left ear. She shot to her feet and whirled around to face the man who was her sister's husband—the man whom she'd just confessed she loved, thanks to Lady Hermione's clever prodding. Sick with humiliation, she made a dash for the door, but he blocked her way.

She struggled to free herself from his firm grip. "You've had your revenge, my lord. Is the satisfaction of hearing me admit to being a lovesick fool not enough for you? What more do you want of me?"

"A great deal more eventually, Maeve Barrington, but right now just a few minutes of your time. Surely, you'll agree you owe me that much."

Maeve nodded grudgingly, too conscious of the nerve-tingling pressure of Theo's strong fingers to object to his request.

"Leave us," he ordered the squire and Lady Hermione in that autocratic way of his. The pair instantly rose to their feet and filed out the door.

"Be gentle, my lord," Lady Hermione whispered as she passed them. "Patience and reason will prevail with a girl like Maeve."

"Patience and reason, me ass," the squire said close behind her. "Kiss the sassy chit till she's out of her mind, then have yer way with her afore she scratches yer eyes out. 'Tis the only way to tame the green-eyed cat."

"Really, Harry, must you be so vulgar?" Lady Hermione complained, taking the arm he offered. "Even the best of advice should be couched in more delicate terms than that."

Never lessening his grip on Maeve's arms, Theo reached back with his left foot and pushed the door shut behind them. "Are you?" he asked softly.

"Am I what?"

"Are you still in love with me?"

Maeve lifted her chin in what she knew was a pathetic show of defiance. "I refuse to answer that question."

"Then I'll just have to find the truth in my own way," Theo said, and lowering his head, claimed her lips in a deeply passionate kiss. Maeve did her best to keep from responding, but the touch of his lips on hers sent a rush of heat spiraling through her, melting the last bulwark of her feeble defenses. With a hoarse cry she gave herself up to the exquisite, soul-satisfying pleasure of his lips and tongue and hands . . . until she remembered who and what he was.

With her last ounce of strength she pushed him from her. "What kind of man are you?" she gasped. "To marry one sister and make love to the other?"

His dark eyes gleamed wickedly. "I admit to a certain prowess with the ladies. But not even I could manage the feat you accuse me of when one sister is in London, the other in Scotland."

Maeve stared at him, dumbfounded. "What are you doing

here?" she demanded. "Why aren't you in Gretna Green with Meg, as my father claimed."

"Because I doubt even a generous-hearted fellow like Richard would be willing to share his bride with a friend."

Maeve's heart skipped a beat. "Are you saying Richard and Meg have eloped?"

Theo chuckled. "Boggles the mind, doesn't it? But there you have it. Apparently, anything is possible when love is involved, or so my wise Italian mother contends. Which brings us to this match between you and me that your father seems so anxious to promote."

"There is no match between us and never can be."

"I beg to differ with you, my sweet. Not ten minutes ago, I heard you confess to loving me, despite the fact that I'm no saint—and I freely admit to loving you, sins and all. To my way of thinking, our sinful match is every bit as perfect as Richard and Meg's saintly one."

"You know nothing about me, my lord," Maeve said, determined to keep their conversation on a formal basis. "There is no woman in England less qualified to be a countess than I. With all I confessed, I still left out two very important facts."

"Only two?" Theo raised an eyebrow. "I'm disappointed in you, Maeve. At this rate we shall soon be as dull and proper as Meg and Richard."

Maeve frowned. "I am not jesting, my lord."

"I can see you're not," Theo said, sobering instantly. With Lady Hermione's advice in mind, he gently clasped her hands in his. "Very well, if you feel you must, tell me these two shocking facts about you that I should know."

Maeve straightened her shoulders and raised her little pointed chin. "My mother was—"

"The notorious Lily St. Germaine," Theo interjected.

"I see my father has been unusually candid with you," Maeve said stiffly.

"No, rest assured, the squire is the same devious and manip-ulative fellow as ever. He would never reveal anything that might threaten his latest matchmaking scheme. The Duke of Kent was kind enough to send me a note divulging that interesting bit of information once he remembered where he'd first met you."

Theo shrugged nonchalantly. "Between your mother and mine, we may well be the most scandalous couple in the *ton*. The starchiest of matrons will undoubtedly close their doors to us, but that will be no loss. Their parties are always a dead bore."

Maeve clenched her fists in frustration. Was the man lost to all reason? "There is more, my lord," she said. "I, myself, am—"

"That infamous troublemaker, Marcus Browne, who's made his name pointing out the foibles of our leading Tory politicians. That one I figured out by myself when I saw the cartoon on Brummell that set London on its ear. If you'll remember, I had occasion to see your renditions of him in your sketchbook. Your technique is quite unmistakable, my dear."

Theo smiled wryly. "Now there's a fact I feel we definitely should keep to ourselves, unless we plan to spend the Season in Kent raising cattle and babies from now on—which actually sounds rather pleasant, now that I think of it."

Maeve did not appear to find his teasing manner the least bit humorous. She stepped back out of his reach, her eyes narrowed, her jaw firmed into an unmistakably stubborn line. "I am resolute, my lord. I will not marry you. Not now. Not ever. I love you too much."

"That makes no sense whatsoever," Theo declared, feeling his patience rapidly disintegrating. If this was an example of female reason, it escaped him. In truth, he could never remember feeling more exasperated than he did at this moment.

Maeve backed up yet another step. "It makes all the sense in the world. The secret of your parentage is safe; mine is not. Lily was shockingly indiscreet. She was also an inveterate gossip. I have no way of knowing if she revealed my unconventional way of making a living to one of her friends."

Theo gritted his teeth. *So much for patience and reason.* He could see Maeve meant every word she said, but there was such a thing as too much nobility. If he'd wanted to marry a saint, he'd have made a push to marry her twin sister.

Very well, if one tactic didn't work with the aggravating

woman, he'd try another. He could be every bit as stubborn as she—and a great deal more inventive. Without another word, he moved forward, clasped her in a fierce embrace, and kissed her deeply and thoroughly. As always, he felt as if he were drowning in the tide of love and passion that flowed between them.

Moments later, he lifted his head to stare deep into her bemused eyes. "You've *told* me the reasons why we shouldn't marry," he said softly. "Now I'll *show* you the reasons why we should."

"That's not fair. I can't think when you touch me," Maeve said, twisting frantically to free herself from his hold.

He laughed softly, joyously. "That, my love, is the best news I've heard in a long, long time."

Sweeping her up in his arms, he carried her to the sofa, where he sat with her cradled in his lap. "This is highly improper, my lord," she protested. "What if someone should open the door?"

"You would be well and truly compromised, my love, and I would have no choice but to marry you."

"But I have already told you. I will not marry you, my lord."

Theo couldn't believe what he was hearing. *Devil take it*, why was she still fighting the inevitable? Couldn't she see how perfectly they suited each other in every way?

She had already given him her heart; it was her mind that was holding out against him. But how could any man prevail with a woman as strong-minded as Maeve Barrington?

Like a bolt of lightning parting the midnight sky, the answer came to him. Hadn't she just admitted she couldn't think when he touched her? For one brief moment his conscience pricked him at the thought of what he was contemplating, but the feeling soon passed. What was the saying? "All is fair in love and war."

Cupping her face with his hand, he kissed her passionately—plundering her sweet mouth in a deeply sensual way he'd never before dared. White-hot flames licked through his veins—flames that only Maeve could ignite.

He opened his eyes and studied her face. He could see she had been as deeply affected by their kiss as he. Eyes closed, she lay back across his arm. Her cheeks were flushed, her lips softly parted. Her mind was most definitely not in control at the moment.

His fingers slid to the row of buttons marching down the front of her shapeless gray gown. One by one, he released them from their closures, revealing the plain cotton chemise that covered her small, perfect breasts.

"Whatever are you doing, Theo?" she asked in a dreamy voice, but she made no effort to stay his fingers from their task.

"Something I never in my wildest dreams expected I'd stoop to, my little green-eyed cat," he admitted, while surreptitiously loosening the ties of her chemise.

"What is that?" Maeve asked.

Theo chuckled to himself at this latest ironic turn his life had taken.

"After much serious consideration," he said reflectively, "I have decided to follow the only piece of sound advice I have ever heard that unscrupulous scoundrel, the squire, put forth."

And without another word, he proceeded to do just that.